MW01254808

A Note to the Reader

My curiosity about how Black and Indigenous lineages overlap began as an eleven-year-old Caribbean immigrant in the northern town of Sioux Lookout, Ontario, where the population was half Ojibwe. It taught me the first thing I learned about North America: It doesn't like Indigenous people. Soon after, I learned that it also doesn't value Black people. Black enslavement and Indigenous genocide—our continent's two original sins—when intermingled, create passionate affinities and hatreds. These tensions manifest in the Afro-Indigenous life and body of Ophelia Blue Rivers.

To examine this fault line, I placed Ophelia in the imaginary—yet deeply historical—South Carolina towns of Etsi and Stone River. I wanted to explore the tensions of such an entwined yet segregated world through the eyes of its most vulnerable citizen: a young mixed girl figuring out where she belongs—and to whom. What happens when we cast members of our society out because they are different? Do we wound ourselves? And the most urgent question: How do we heal?

If casting out the Ophelias in our communities harms us, we can only heal this harm by bringing them back.

Black Cherokee

A NOVEL

Antonio Michael Downing

Simon & Schuster

NEW YORK   AMSTERDAM/ANTWERP   LONDON
TORONTO   SYDNEY/MELBOURNE   NEW DELHI

Simon & Schuster
1230 Avenue of the Americas
New York, NY 10020

This book is a work of fiction. Any references to historical events, real people,
or real places are used fictitiously. Other names, characters, places, and events
are products of the author's imagination, and any resemblance to actual events or
places or persons, living or dead, is entirely coincidental.

First Simon & Schuster hardcover edition August 2025

SIMON & SCHUSTER and colophon are registered trademarks
of Simon & Schuster, LLC

Simon & Schuster strongly believes in freedom of expression and stands against
censorship in all its forms. For more information, visit BooksBelong.com.

For information about special discounts for bulk purchases, please contact Simon &
Schuster Special Sales at 1-866-506-1949 or business@simonandschuster.com.

The Simon & Schuster Speakers Bureau can bring authors to your live event. For more
information or to book an event, contact the Simon & Schuster Speakers Bureau at
1-866-248-3049 or visit our website at www.simonspeakers.com.

Interior design by Paul Dippolito

Manufactured in the United States of America

1   3   5   7   9   10   8   6   4   2

Library of Congress Cataloging-in-Publication Data is available.

ISBN 978-1-6680-6610-2
ISBN 978-1-6680-6612-6 (ebook)

To the Black Freedmen of all the Nations

Black
Cherokee

That night they made succotash.

It was Ophelia's job to shuck corn, split lima beans, and dice okra. While she got busy with this, Grandma Blue chopped onions, peppers, and celery with the whetstone-sharp knife Ophelia wasn't allowed to touch. *Chop, chop, chop* filled the silence of the cabin. Grandma Blue's fingers danced dangerously. Precise. Mesmerizing. Hurry was called for. The young girl needed to be ready by the time her grandmother was done. Finished, she proudly presented the ingredients. Then it was her turn to chop.

Grandma Blue handed her the heavy knife.

"Child," she warned, which meant *watch yourself, now.*

As the little girl had been shown, she gripped where the handle met the blade and slid the first okra across the cutting board. Knuckles out, rocking the knife back and forth, she crunched right through in one clean stroke. There was no approval when she looked up for it. Nothing impressed the old woman. Head down, Ophelia kept chopping.

Wood crackled in the fire. A lone nightingale crooned its song. *Chop, chop, chop* echoed through the cabin and, as always, the river could be heard rumbling under everything.

"You know where okra come from?"

"Where, Grandma Blue?"

"Africa. The same place Black people come from."

Ophelia's neat stack of okra rings kept growing. She didn't want to cut herself, but she didn't want to miss what her grandmother said, either. "Talkative" Grandma Blue said surprising things.

"You know who Black people are?"

"No, Grandma Blue . . ."

"That's us. Or who we used to be. Blacks, the Cherokee, and the whites is who made this place."

"They made the land?"

"No, child, the land made them. All three of them ate off this same land."

Grandma Blue scooped up her diced okra and left. That was her way—she gave a saying and then a silence.

From the direction of the stove came a sizzling storm; the iron deep-bottom pan was heating up. Only after the old woman had tossed in the vegetables did she speak again. "You is what you eat. The land grows food. The people eat the food. The food is the people. You understand?"

"The land grows food. The people eat the food. The food is the people."

"Repeating ain't understanding."

Grandma Blue's grizzled fingers rained salt into the frothy pan. A spell casting. Sweet smoke took over the kitchen. Mingling flavors filled Ophelia's cheeks and became shapes in the rafters. Green, brown, and yellow. She imagined the shapes were ingredients: okra, beans, and corn. All shucked and diced and ready. All headed to the same place. To the same pot.

"Grandma Blue, if the food is the people, are the people like succotash?"

"How you mean?"

"They're all different ingredients, but in the pot they make one food?"

"Yes, child, that's what I mean."

Ophelia's brow scrunched up between her eyes. "Grandma Blue, can I ask a question?"

There was no answer. She proceeded but measured her words in careful portions.

"If we're all the same people, why can't I go to school with all the other Cherokee kids?"

Ophelia noticed Grandma Blue's breath go shallow. The old woman's insides seemed to convulse. Her brow clenched. A savage tension gripped her proud, dark mouth. For a moment, a window into her wounds flung open. It gaped wide. And then—just as suddenly—it slammed shut.

"It's my job to protect you and that's what I'm gonna do."

"But . . ."

"Child."

Grandma Blue had given her sayings and now she wanted silence.

PART ONE

1993

Chapter One

Grandma Blue was an old Black woman who lived in a cabin by a rustic river that ran through a Cherokee reservation that was no longer a reservation. The river's name was Etsi, which meant "mother," and the old woman's skin was rough as the river after a storm had made its banks burst: choppy, weathered, covered in deep grooves. Yet her arms were fit and firm as though carved out of stone. They seemed as immovable as the will that drove her. Her eyes sat back in her head, tiny beads the color of chocolate. When she got angry, they sank even deeper into her forehead, like two pits of blackness from which no one ever returned.

Her granddaughter Ophelia was born on December 12, 1986, the same night that her husband—Chief Trouthands—died. But she wouldn't know about this coincidence or the birth of her first grandchild for eighteen months. Until the day she was left in her care. The little girl had skin the color of cinnamon, neither the umber of chocolate nor the lightness of tortilla, but lost somewhere in the middle. Her pecan-brown eyes seemed permanently sad. Her wavy hair flourished with curls in the summer humidity. It was 1993—the year she turned seven—and she still didn't know who her parents were or why she lived with her grand-mother.

One night Grandma Blue pulled out the mattress from be-hind the water heater, made the bed in the corner of the cabin, and laid herself down. It was June in South Carolina, so it was muggy inside. She raised up the flap of the blanket, like the open-ing to a tent, and grunted "hmpff" at the little girl, which meant *go on, get in, I don't got all night.* This was as wordy as Grandma Blue got—a grunt, a sigh, a grumble, a whistle—Ophelia had to fill in the rest.

They awoke on the mattress on the floor the next morning, and right away Ophelia inhaled Grandma Blue's warmth. She radiated a heat that made Ophelia want to get closer to her. She wrapped her arms around the old woman's flanks and squeezed. It was the only time her grandmother accepted any kind of soft-ness. At any other time, if Ophelia offered her affection, she'd watch her like a centipede she wanted to squash. Grandma Blue wasn't the cuddly kind.

Ophelia fell back asleep to the rattle of pots and the rush of the river.

By the time Ophelia woke up again, the cabin smelled like her favorite food—fried okras. Seared so they wouldn't be slimy. Fried okras were Grandma Blue's way of saying sorry for being cranky at Ophelia the day before, and the little girl knew exactly what she meant. Grandma Blue never did apologies, or any kind of what she called "long talking." When she had something hard to say, she said it in food.

Their cabin was one big room. In one corner was their kitchen with the gas stove and the coils for burners. In the other corner was the fireplace; that's where they huddled on nights where they were cold and where once a week Ophelia would have a bath in the big enamel basin. Grandma Blue would heat the water on the stove and braid her hair.

Sitting down at the counter on the tall stool, Ophelia wiped sleep from her eye. When her world came into focus, she saw Grandma Blue observing her with a stern eye. From the outside, she seemed as she ever was. Yet the old woman's chest clenched with worry upon seeing the girl. *What a strange little chicken my son has hatched. But she's mine to raise now, isn't she?*

A plate full of fried okra, fresh tomatoes, and boiled eggs landed in front of Ophelia. But she knew that before they could eat, they had to go down to the river to pray.

They left by the back door. The world was still gray and gloomy. A fierce South Carolina rain had fallen the night before. It washed out the world, soaked their crops, and swole the river's banks. This made the Etsi River even more full of chatter. Ophelia knew that there were trees—water oak, river birch, bald cypress—but her eyes saw only blurry outlines. Giant shadows standing guard.

The air was prickly cool. A mourning dove cooed, a thrush tuned up, frogs croaked to the coming day. A symphony of critters waiting for the conductor.

Tucked into Grandma Blue's belt were three eagle feathers. They scraped against her thighs as she walked. In her other hand were a box of matches and a little bundle of tobacco. They arrived at the river just as the sun began to streak through the branches. The water rushed past them, booming and forceful. It smelled of sulfur—"plouff mud," Grandma Blue called it—but to Ophelia it smelled like home.

Flick. Flick. Flick. The matches scratched at the matchbox, but something damp was in the air. "Hmpff . . ." Grandma Blue grunted. *Flick. Flick. Flick.* Grandma Blue's head was dredging up the past that morning. Her "apology" to Ophelia—the fried okras—was the first sign. Something deep in her waters was being stirred. Ophelia felt it, but knew that there was no point in bringing it up.

When the match caught, Grandma Blue took the tobacco from Ophelia and blew gently until it burned strong. The rich, woody smell leaked into the air.

Grandma Blue wasted no time. She pulled out the three eagle feathers from her belt and used the feathers to waft the milky smoke over them. Ophelia's job was to say their prayer. She didn't know it in Cherokee, but her grandmother had taught them to her in English:

"Great Spirit—
Thank you for waking us.
For the land that feeds us.
For the people who keep us.
And thank you for the river, our Mother.
We will mind the river.
Amen."

And everything Ophelia had ever felt, folded into that moment. The morning, the wren, the robin, the redheaded woodpecker, the streams of glistening light, and the chatter of Etsi, crashed in and doused the little girl's senses. Her breath went deep down into her ribs, her head swam with possibilities. Ophelia thought she might float away far over the treetops, off to where the river disappeared into the ocean, but a sandpaper-rough hand gripped her shoulder and shook her back to reality.

"Come, Tsunasdi ..." Grandma Blue grunted—it meant "little crab"—and she started back towards the cabin. Over her shoulder she said the saying that was her motto, her go-to: "Don't work, don't eat."

Their cabin was a hundred feet from the river. And between the cabin and the river was their back patch. It was there that Grandma Blue spent the rest of that morning.

She did so bent at the waist, working with her mouth turned down as if set against the evils of the world. From a sack slung on her shoulders she retrieved sweet potato sprouts and planted each in little pockets of dirt one foot apart. A small, curved paring knife was what she used to harvest the squash, which hung from six-foot-high wooden slats. Then she checked the green-skinned, pregnant bellies of the pumpkins. Ophelia was expected to help and to learn. As they moved through the yard, Grandma Blue quizzed her on the names of plants: blackberry, wild ginger, mint, yarrow. When she didn't remember the name "yellow dock," Grandma Blue's eyes glared, disgusted.

In the late morning, as they sat in the dirt digging holes to plant beets and sweet beans, Ophelia asked her, "Where are my parents, Grandma Blue?"

"Hmpff ..." the old lady answered, which meant *child, don't aggravate me with your questions.*

"I had to come from somewhere, right?"

"You're half-Black, half-Cherokee, and all mixed up," said the old woman, as if that explained everything. Ophelia was still confused.

"But the other little girls all have fathers and mothers."

"Psshh ..." said the old woman, which meant *if they all jumped in the river and drowned, you'd do it too?* Then she got rid of her with a "Go fetch me the shovel."

Ophelia left unsatisfied, but on her way back she wandered down to the water.

In the shade of the beech tree she let the river soak the tips of her toes. It arrived from someplace she could not see, swept past her feet, then disappeared around the bend, towards a world she could not fathom.

She saw her reflection—tiny nose, kinky hair—and declared, "There was a girl named Ophelia Blue Rivers. And this was her face." She noticed again that while the other Etsi children had skin like coffee with dollops of cream, her skin was closer to the color of the coffee beans themselves. And every girl in Etsi had straight, shiny hair that fell down their backs like black water-falls. Not like hers and Grandma Blue's.

"Where did you come from?" she asked her reflection, but the girl in the water had no answers, so Ophelia left to play in the sunflower patch.

"Hello, Brother Sunflower . . ." she said. "Could you reach down so I can kiss your face?"

She bent the stalk and watched the ants and stingers and crawlies and the yellowness. The bright, rough-in-the-center-smooth-on-the-leaves yellowness. If she pressed her thumb into the middle, the pollen trailed up into the breeze and traced that color everywhere. She wanted it on her cheeks, her hands, her eyelids. It smelled pretty, almost rotten, and suddenly her world blacked out.

SMACK!

Ophelia pulled away before Grandma Blue could hit her again with her sandal. But the old woman was already marching

12

back towards the cabin. She said, "Don't put your face where your head can't reach."

They spent that afternoon at the table in the cabin doing long division.

Grandma Blue felt sorry for hitting Ophelia. But she lived in terror that she was too old to properly raise the young girl. As she saw it, her job was to protect Ophelia and prepare her for a heartless world. A world this child's nature couldn't bear. To her mind, Ophelia was a "daydreamer," and daydreamers became "wastrels," and only bad things happened to wastrels.

Ophelia always took advantage of Grandma Blue's sorry feelings because then she could ask otherwise unwelcome questions.

"Grandma Blue? What do you mean when you say, 'don't be like them other children of mine?' Do you mean my daddy Shango? And Auntie Belle and Aiyanna?"

Ophelia had heard their names, but never from her grandmother's lips. Grandma Blue tried to ignore the question by writing on the small blackboard in a haze of chalk. The flesh under her arm shook as she wrote. And her black jelly bean eyes sank deeper into her forehead. She did not like the question, but remorse compelled her to respond.

"What you know about Shango?"

"I remember the singing man."

"The singing man?"

"The man who drove me here the day that I came."

"You don't remember that! What do you remember?"

"I remember the car grumbled like a bad dog, it smelled oily, and it smelled sweet. I remember the steering wheel in his hands, and there was music playing and he was singing along."

Ophelia came close to what Grandma Blue called "being

frivolous," which was a word the little girl liked when it happened in her mouth.

"You too young to understand these things."

"But Ama is younger than me and she knows her parents . . ."

Ophelia sensed the hole inside her grandmother. It was right beneath her chest. Dismal and deep, it seemed to pitch and heave like a skiff in a storm. It was a void. The place where she stored up all the things she wished to never speak about. All her hurt. All her worry. All the things Ophelia wanted to know.

"Little child, stop asking big people's business. One day, when your children abandon you, you'll understand."

That night, while the heat of the day hung about the cabin, they readied for bed.

"Will you tell me a story, Grandma Blue?"

Grandma Blue watched Ophelia with her cocoa eyes and weighed her thoughts carefully, like beans on a scale.

"Yes, Ophelia, which one would you like to hear?"

"Stone Dress! Stone Dress!"

"Fine, don't make no fuss, and I'll tell you the story."

Grandma Blue laid out the mattress on the floor and they got into their nightclothes, faces washed, teeth brushed, and settled into the bed.

"In the Land of the Midday Sun, there was a fast river that cut through a thick wood. There, there lived a shape-shifter named Stone Dress. She could turn into any creature she chose—a buck, a wolf, an eagle—but her normal shape was an old woman. She had skin made of rock. No blade could cut her. No arrow could stab her. This is why the people called her—"

"Stone Dress," Ophelia said. "Stone Dress is the best."

"But they also called her Spear Finger, because she had a long

14

bony finger made of stone on her one hand that she used as a spear. Disguised as a person, she'd enter someone's house and stab their relatives with her long bony finger. Then eat their liver. Ogres love people-liver. Sometimes she masqueraded as a loving grandmother and tricked children by saying, 'Let your sweet granny braid your hair.' After feasting on their organs she would sing, 'The liver of a child is sweet. It's my favorite meat to eat.'"

Ophelia sang this part because it always made her giggle. To her, Stone Dress was a nice old lady whom the people didn't understand. She imagined that Stone Dress had her own family living in the forest with her and that she wanted to protect her children from everyone else. She didn't like being mean, but the hunters were always trying to kill her. They always failed. Stone Dress was invulnerable.

"One day, a little bird, a chickadee, told a warrior that Stone Dress's heart was in the wrist of the hand with her spear finger. If they aimed their arrows there, they could hurt her. They dug a pit along a road they knew she'd take, and when she fell in, they fired their arrows at her wrist for hours. Finally, one arrow pierced where her bony forefinger joined her wrist, the place where her heart was. She fell back into the pit, never to terrorize the people again."

Ophelia had her own end to the story, where Stone Dress and her children moved to another forest, far from the warriors, where they were safe. In her version, the children of Stone Dress always ended up happy.

Chapter Two

Grandma Blue and Ophelia woke in the murkiness before dawn.

Steaming coffee vapors filled the rafters of the cabin. Grandma Blue sipped from her chipped sky-blue mug. "Tiny dollop of cream," Ophelia mouthed sleepily. That was how Grandma Blue took her morning coffee. Ophelia recalled what day it was and yelled, "Etsiiiiiiii." She received a stony look from across the cabin, which meant *Child*—which was short for: *Child, if you don't hush.* Ophelia—chastened—whispered to herself, "We're going to Etsi!"

There were two ways to get to Etsi from the cabin: the road and the river. The road was the long way, and they had to walk. They only took the road if the river was too rough, or if Grandma Blue had something stirring inside her, in that silent, hidden place of hers. Walking gave her time to think. That day they took the river and two straw baskets, so Ophelia knew that they were getting groceries from Moytoy's General Store.

Taking the river to Etsi meant taking the raft. It was flat and made of chestnut boards, but the bottom was dried pitch and deer skin. Dressed in her denim overalls, Grandma Blue pushed them along the riverbank with the cherrywood stick working as an oar. Ophelia sat center raft, facing backwards to watch the sun poke its head between the clouds and turn the river silver.

At first there was nothing but more trees. "In-ah-ge-I ..." Ophelia practiced swishing the new Cherokee word around her mouth. It meant "forest." The cypress were so tall that her neck hurt to twist to see where in the sky they ended. There was nothing but tall trees before the first trailers of Etsi appeared, one by one, on either side of the river.

Jim Silverfish's was first. His—like all the riverside trailers—was covered in green moss and raised up on cinder blocks. It looked, to Ophelia, as if it had sprouted out of the ground. Grandma Blue never spoke to Jim, even if he said hello first. Everywhere he went he took his ax, and the scar along his cheek partitioned his face into two. When she asked her grandmother how he'd gotten it, she gave her that look that asked, *Is that your business?*

As they got closer to Etsi, the trailers started appearing more regularly. Ophelia saw Tanner, a great, lengthy man, his hair in a single braid that wagged about as he moved. He boiled a pot of chicken stew outside that left the air smelling yummy. Next, they passed an old grandmother whose name Ophelia didn't know. She sat picking at a two-stringed guitar. Her arm half waved at them, but the wave didn't reach her face.

Finally they could see Etsi's little dock and Rock Hill Road, the town's only street. Half-paved, it rose up a steep hill from the water like a skinny tree with back-alley branches and fruit made of trailers. As they approached the flimsy dock, which was twisted sideways and bare of any paint, Ophelia could sense a stern spirit descend on the old woman.

"Ahhha..." Grandma Blue said to no one in particular. Ophelia did not know what this meant, but she knew that her grandmother did not like coming to Etsi.

Ophelia's eyes found their destination at the top of the hill: the bloody red roof of Moytoy's General Store, with its pointy attic. Next to that was the big meetinghouse they called "Chief's." Ophelia knew that it was named after the man who built it: Grandma Blue's dead husband Chief Trouthands. Once upon a time, she'd been told, it was the place where powwows were held. Grandma Blue said that powwows were full of dancing, sing-ing, and celebrating the "Old Ways." Ophelia had never seen a powwow. Yet every time she saw Chief's, she tried and failed to imagine what one might be like.

On the dock stood three kids Ophelia recognized: Salila Ganega, whom everyone called "Moose" because she was the big-gest kid their age, and her smaller but older brothers—Chuck and Bryan—who followed her everywhere. Moose stood up, defiant, sticking out her chest at them—like a dare—as they approached. Grandma Blue barked, "Get from there, you three. Can't you see we're trying to come in?" Moose and her brothers scampered from the dock, but when they got to the road they turned. Moose stuck her tongue out at Grandma Blue, who shook her head and said, "Just like a Ganega. Goats don't make sheep."

Once Grandma Blue roped the raft to the dock and dusted herself off, she gave Ophelia a huff of breath: "Pfftt..." Which meant *keep up now*. Then she started up the steep hill with her cherrywood stick leading the way like a third leg. Grandma Blue always walked too fast. Ophelia's tiny legs did not like walking with her up Rock Hill Road. They got heavy and wobbly. Yet Ophelia never complained, because Grandma

Blue called that "bellyaching," and that was the worst thing a person could do.

From the rusty trailer on their right, Auntie Walela waved them over. She was overweight, perched on a stool, knitting her beads and smiling to herself as if still chewing the crumbs of some delicious dessert.

"Osiyo, Grandma Blue!"

"Osiyo, Walela."

Ophelia knew that Grandma Blue hated to be stopped when she had somewhere to go, but she always stopped to talk to Auntie Walela. This puzzled Ophelia, as Auntie Walela was not at all like Grandma Blue: She didn't chop wood or work in the garden; she just sat in her yard beading and talking about people. In fact, she never minded her own business; she minded everything but. Odd friendship aside, Ophelia's legs were happy for the rest.

"I'm surprised you weren't at the meeting last night . . . "

"What meeting? You think I have time to go to meetings?"

Walela pursed her hungry lips and ran her fingers twice along her beads. Chestnut-brown eyes sparkling. Face greedy with gossip.

"They poisoned the river . . . "

"What you mean?"

"That's what the meeting was for. They poisoned the river."

"Who poisoned the river?"

"Beauregard Farms. That cattle farm out west of Stone River?"

"Walela Trouthands, how do they know it's poisoned?"

"Some say a funny smell was coming off the river that side of Etsi. Haven't you smelled nothing? And why didn't they invite you to the meeting? Everybody else was there . . . "

Ophelia could tell that Auntie Walela was excited to see

Grandma Blue. Auntie Walela wanted to be the one that told everyone how the old lady reacted to hearing that she was deliberately not invited to a town meeting. Behind her eyes were careful cameras watching Grandma Blue. Capturing everything. But the old woman did not bite.

"How should I know?" she asked, then turned on her heels and kept climbing.

Ophelia lingered and stared at the way Auntie Walela's lips seemed to be chewing without any food until Grandma Blue called over her shoulder, "Child, stop tending to big people's business."

A thought occurred to Ophelia: *Maybe finding out everyone's business is why Grandma Blue always visited Auntie Walela.*

"Child . . ." came her grandmother's sandpaper voice again. Which meant *hurry up. We ain't got all day.*

Waya Ganega, the uncle of Salila and her brothers, tumbled down the hill in a rush towards them. Broad-backed and tall, he always seemed to be slouched over. Beady eyes that floated over his jowls. A fancy blue shirt, glasses tinted brown, and a hundred-watt smile. His face was flabby and fretful.

"Grandma Blue, we missed you at the council vote last night. We sure could've used your voice in the circle."

She did not slow down to greet him but kept up her hard march upwards. He sped up to match her stride and bend her ear.

"If you wanted me there you would have invited me."

"It was disrespectful not to invite you, Grandma Blue. You're the old Chief's wife after all."

"Etsi has no Chief. Haven't you heard?" She dipped her tone in sarcastic surprise and asked him, "Weren't you the one who proposed the vote for us to stop being a reservation? Weren't you the one who promised everyone that privatizing the band's land would make us all rich?"

"That was a long time ago, Grandma Blue. Can't we let bygones be bygones?"

"Bygones? We should forget all about it and just be friends?"

Impatiently, her stick snapped at the ground. Her legs kept up their powerful pace.

"That ungrateful Chief Trouthands . . ."

Ophelia knew that Grandma Blue was about to compliment her dead husband. She only ever called him "Chief Trouthands," and she never said his name without an insult. If the insult came after his name, she was actually mad at him. If the insult came before his name, then she was about to say something nice.

" . . . he wasn't good for much, but he knew how to care for his people. Who cares for the people now, Waya Ganega?"

"Not everyone's forgotten the Old Ways, Grandma Blue."

This stopped Grandma Blue in her tracks.

"No? You haven't forgotten the Old Ways? Then why did you dissolve the rez as soon as your Chief died? Why did you listen to that Charleston lawyer instead of your own elders? And who did you sell our land to? That same cattle farm that's poisoned the river. Are you gonna clean up the mess ya'll put us in?"

Ophelia recognized the gloom that briefly gripped her grandmother. Her free hand clutched her chest as if there was a hole there. Ophelia pictured this place as a bleak, grape-colored sea that heaved and pitched her grandmother this way and that. It seemed big enough to swallow the whole morning. Waya Ganega stumbled back, amazed. Then, quickly as a cloud, it was gone.

"Get out of my way."

"You're right, Grandma Blue," Waya Ganega admitted. "We didn't invite you because we didn't want you there. We wanted to move things forward. Every time you're there we just rip the scab off old wounds. But now we need you. Our lawyer, Mister Smithers, says that we need a respectable plaintiff. Somebody a jury will have sympathy for. You being the biggest landowner left—not to mention the old Chief's wife—would look perfect in court."

Grandma Blue heard him but she wasn't listening. Waya Ganega gave up and stopped following. Ophelia looked back to see him taking out his handkerchief. He dabbed the sweat pooling on his temples and watched them warily as they continued their climb.

Further up the hill, Miss Sequoia stopped Grandma Blue. Ophelia was glad for this because it gave her a chance to catch up again. Miss Sequoia was a thick-bodied woman with a flat face and a smile that promised mischief. Her hair fell down her back like a black, silky curtain. Ophelia lived in awe of Miss Sequoia because she talked to Grandma Blue as if she wasn't scared of her. And often—for the silliest reason—she would throw back her head and guffaw until her face was full of tears. When Ophelia caught up, Sequoia was leaning close enough to whisper. Closer than Grandma Blue tolerated anyone else to be. Ophelia heard her grandmother say: "Is it serious?"

"They didn't invite you because you're a truth sayer. You told them not to sell and now the people who bought up all our land are the ones they want to sue. They didn't want to hear you tell them 'I told you so.' You're the last real Elder left in Etsi."

"If these old bones is the people's last Elder, we're all in trouble . . ."

She spoke to Auntie Sequoia as if she was mad, but Ophelia

could tell that Grandma Blue was happy to see her. Of course, she wasn't Ophelia's auntie by blood, but every grown lady in Etsi was automatically every child's auntie. Miss Sequoia put her hands on her hips and dared to do what Ophelia couldn't even conceive of: give Grandma Blue attitude.

"You gonna hide out there and grow tomatoes for the rest of your life? Some people don't accept you because you're Black, but they don't speak for all of us. You were born here. Your grandmother and my great-grandmother played together. Right there in that same river. And a lot of people remember how good it was when Chief Trouthands was alive."

"If I'm so wise, then how come I couldn't stop them from selling our land in the first place?"

"That's ancient history, Grandma Blue. I'm worried about now. I got three girls to think about and you got a little one too. What kinda future they got if the river's sick?"

The women looked behind and saw Ophelia—ears cocked— carefully devouring their words. Ophelia pretended that she hadn't heard anything.

"And how is Little Miss Ophelia doing?"

"She always lost in her tiny head full of tall tales."

Ophelia understood that sometimes grown-ups needed to talk about you as if you weren't there. Impatiently she waited for her chance then said: "Auntie Sequoia, can Nola come and play?"

"See? Single-minded. You would think with all the work I give her that she wouldn't have time to play."

"Yes, Ophelia, I'll bring her and the twins tomorrow and you can play while me and your grandmother catch up."

"Now, if you two layabouts are settled on how to disturb my peace, can an old lady see about her business?"

Sequoia threw her head back and let go a howl as if she didn't care who heard.

"Wado, Grandma Blue, I will find out what's happening and come see you tomorrow."

"Wado, Sequoia."

And the old woman went back to her climb.

Chapter Three

By the end of her climb her thighs cramped, her left foot ached, and Grandma Blue was an angry bull.

Ungrateful. Not one year from when we buried him, they voted to undo everything he'd done. That scoundrel Chief Trouthands lived and died for his people. He deserved better. And now they've ruined the river?

Swirling thoughts haunted her. In 1987 the Etsi band disbanded, and most people left. Either west to Tulsa, or—as the last Black Cherokee families did—to Atlanta. The Blue Rivers family and two dozen others had always been there at the bend in the river. For two hundred years they had survived. Andrew Jackson. The Civil War. The Dawes Rolls. Smallpox. Jim Crow. But the vote to disband—sold to them by a Charleston lawyer— taken up by their desperation, had made Etsi unrecognizable to the woman who had once been one of its pillars.

Ain't nothing left for me in Etsi but ghosts.

As she crested the hill, her eyes winced at the sight of Etsi's school. It reminded her of Shango, Aiyanna, and Belle, her children who no longer talked to her. Dead ahead loomed Chief's—

the building her husband had built. She and Chief had bundled into a sleeping bag, the heat of his chest pressed against her, the ice-blue stars above them. This was the first time he told her his dream: "Night has the moon, Day has the sun, Etsi needs a center. A focal point." Big dreams. Big talks. This was his way. But then he built it. And the people he built it for met there to unbuild his legacy. This was why she hated coming to Etsi.

Moytoy's General Store was a sprawling feast.

Grandma Blue let Ophelia rush past when she opened the door. She knew that her grandchild could not help herself. The scents held her captive: redeye and largemouth bass, ripe pears, apples and apricots. *I don't think she's normal.* Grandma Blue knew that the child would "daydream." That's what she called it, but the frightening truth was that she did not know the word for the thing Ophelia did. For the way she acted as though she could see smells. Or would stand listening to music no one else could hear.

She found Moytoy sneaking up on Ophelia with a lollipop.

"Looking for this?"

His head of silver hair was tied into two thick braids. Pasty, light-brown skin spotted with splotches of darker brown.

"For me?!"

"Yes, ma'am!"

There was a spicy, warm smell to him like fresh bread.

He was ancient now, but Grandma Blue remembered when he was light on his feet and couldn't grow a beard. Ophelia took the lollipop and tried and failed to not stare at his dancing eyes, then she felt Grandma Blue's eyes on her also.

"Wado, Moytoy Trouthands."

He grinned at her with his gums.

"Gully ah lee jae ha, Ophelia."

She couldn't pronounce it yet, but Ophelia knew that he meant she was welcome.

"You still here, Moytoy, you old pestilence?"

"Well, if I'm old, what does that make you, Grandma Blue?"

Her husband's brother had been her best friend since before she married Chief.

"It makes me in a rush."

She handed over her grocery list, which she had made Ophelia copy out the day before, to practice her writing.

"In a rush or tired of talking?"

Moytoy's eyes skipped around her. They danced endlessly.

"Did Chief Trouthands, that drunken brother of yours, tell you all my secrets?"

"Who can keep secrets in Etsi?"

Ophelia studied them from the shadows of the shelves. Grandma Blue wondered what the child got from listening to two old people talk. But then she recalled that she had known Moytoy since before she was Ophelia's age. That she had had many friends when she was Ophelia's age. It made her uneasy to think that she was depriving the girl. The only conversations she could overhear were grown-up ones. *It's for her own good*, Grandma Blue thought. Pushing aside her doubt she turned to Moytoy.

"Well, is it true what your niece says? Did Jack Beauregard's farm poison the river?"

Moytoy flapped his lips fast like an engine.

"Seems so . . ."

His eyebrows reached up towards his scalp, an invitation for her to come closer.

"Three weeks ago the river to the west of town started to stink like Clorox. Last week a whole school of trout floated up belly first. People suspected Beauregard Farms' big cattle operation outside Stone River. Now—according to Waya Ganega—it's been confirmed."

Grandma Blue took a long drink of air and waited, and then another tall breath before she investigated Moytoy's restless gaze. *So it's true. This is the last straw. If we lose this, we lose our home.*

"If we were still a reservation, the U.S. Marshals would shut them down."

"Yeah?" Moytoy shrugged. "Too bad we lost that argument."

"Now we have to sue them." The old woman sighed, as if resigning herself to a catastrophe she hadn't seen coming.

"Let me see what I can do about your grocery list."

While he was in the back collecting those items, another man—whom Grandma Blue recognized as Wes Ganega, Waya's youngest brother—came in. He was in his twenties and had long black hair, but his bare chest was smooth under his vest and his young face seemed hardened as if etched in concrete.

"Moytoy man, let me get an Export A, King Size."

Grandma Blue stiffened.

"Aye!" said Moytoy. "Can't you see your Elders here?"

"I don't see no Elders here, just some no-clan Pretendians."

"You know who this is? Show some respect," Moytoy demanded, but Wes Ganega turned around, made a scraping sound with his mouth, and spat a heavy wad of tobacco on the ground in front of Grandma Blue.

The cherrywood stick whacked the floor, and the dust it stirred up hung suspended in the air. Grandma Blue crossed the distance between them and raised her stick to hit him.

Wes Ganega's eyes and nostrils flared wide, two veins streaked up his neck, and his fists balled up to hit her back.

"You get from here," Moytoy shouted. "Don't you have any respect? Grandma Blue helped raise your mother and is a Long-Hair same as you. Who are you to say she ain't one of us?"

Wes Ganega spun towards Moytoy. "Stop lying, old man. No monkey raised my mother."

Moytoy came from behind the counter, but as he did, Wes Ganega turned and left, saying, "This is why all the real Cherokee packed up and left Etsi."

The front door to the General Store banged shut. He was gone.

The walk back down Rock Hill Road was even faster than uphill. Grandma Blue strode to the dock with the determined blindness of someone who wanted to get something over with.

Auntie Kay filed in beside the old woman while Ophelia trailed, struggling to keep up. She was high-waisted, slim and bouncy. Fluffiness was her style: Her flared dress had fuchsia flowers printed on it, and she wore bracelets that twinkled with charms. Auntie Kay struggled to match their pace.

"Can I have a word, Grandma Blue? About Ophelia?"

The old woman neither answered nor slowed down.

"When is she going to come to school? I'm worried that she is missing out ..."

"You sayin' I can't teach her right?"

"I'm not saying that ..." Auntie Kay said, chasing her breath. "Nola says that she's better at math, and Nola is a year older. I'm sure you're doing your best ..."

Grandma Blue checked to see if Auntie Kay knew how condescending that sounded.

"I'm worried that Ophelia is missing out socially."

The march stopped abruptly. Auntie Kay almost tripped over her skirt. When she found her balance, she also found Grandma Blue scowling at her.

"And what kind of society do you have for her there? You want me to send her to your school so some mean kid can send her home crying and hating herself? Like they did to her father? To my daughters? What society you got for a little Black Cherokee girl?"

Auntie Kay had no answer to that. But she summoned a question. A question that planted its hooks firmly into the old lady's chest.

"What is this little girl gonna do when you're gone?"

When the forced march resumed, only Ophelia followed.

Auntie Kay's question had churned up a whole country of pain inside the old woman. It struck her where she was already obsessed: Was she too old to raise a young girl? Didn't she make a mess of raising her own children? Children weren't plants. What did she know about raising a child right? Her face winced. The end of her stick splintered on the ground like tree trunks snapping in the bush. This question stirred her up in a way Wes Ganega's ignorance could not.

At the bottom of the hill, Moose and her brothers waited on the dock again. They took one look at the snapping of her stick and scampered for shelter.

Chapter Four

"Mind the river, you hear me? Don't you go in that river!" is what Grandma Blue told Ophelia the next afternoon as she clattered out the back door.

Ophelia took this to mean that it was okay to splash a little as long as she didn't get caught. So, she rolled her jeans up her shins to avoid the evidence before plunging in toes first. Her nose wriggled at the rotten-egg smell.

"Pollution," she declared, without understanding what that word meant but knowing that it was what had caused the shushed whispers in Etsi and Grandma Blue's grim mood.

"I'm brave," she said, and waded into the stinky water.

After a few minutes she heard voices coming from the front yard.

It was Miss Sequoia and her three girls: Nola, who was a year older than Ophelia, and the twins, Ama and Ayoka, who were three years older than Nola. They all had cascading black hair that streamed down their backs when their mama combed it and got oily and stuck to their necks when she didn't. The twins were slim and wiry. Their arms were so long that they could touch their kneecaps, and they would do it if the younger girls begged them. They spoke to each other in their own language of whispers, side glances, and discreet hand signals. Nola was built more like her mother: short and wide. They all had an air of permanent astonishment that excited Ophelia and was why she adored playing with them.

"Osiyo, Sequoia," Grandma Blue called from her rocking chair on the veranda. This was where she went when she needed time with her thoughts.

"Osiyo!" Sequoia called back.

The children started to buzz about like a nest that had been stirred up.

Grandma Blue liked Sequoia because most others from Etsi would talk to her only to ask her for something—advice, credit, attendance at some event—but Sequoia never forgot to ask how Grandma Blue was doing and could she help with anything. She'd pick up a broom and sweep the deck or bring the girls to help harvest or just sit with her while she rocked in her rocking chair and stared up the alley of oak trees, saying nothing.

"Well, old woman, ready to move into town yet?"

"Now why would I do a damn fool thing like that?"

"Join civilization."

"Is that what you call it?"

"Can't say that I blame you for staying. It's a beautiful piece of land you got here."

The girls were off to the side, keen to listen to "big people's business," but more eager to go play. They knew from all the whispering and the meetings that something momentous was afoot. But they also knew that adults never explained themselves to kids. And yet unsupervised playing trumped grown-up gossip. They managed these competing priorities by pretending to play nearby while they eavesdropped and also inched closer and closer towards the back patch and freedom.

"What them jokers up to now?"

"Them jokers" is what Grandma Blue called the Etsi town council.

"If they're jokers, why are they asking for your help?"

"Beats me. They think I have time for their problems?" Ophelia could tell that Grandma Blue was pretending to not be interested in the town meeting. "I'm an old woman. And crops don't plant themselves."

Ophelia, Nola, Ama, and Ayoka were almost free. They studied the grasshoppers and ran sticks through the short grass to make the critters jump so they could chase them further and further towards the river. But their ears remained perked.

"They sent me to ask you to be the plaintiff in the class action lawsuit. They need you. We need you . . ."

"Who sent you?"

"Who else? The town council. Waya Ganega."

The old lady spat at the dirt.

"Waya Ganega? Can't say that I'm surprised."

Sequoia watched her sideways.

"What is it with the Blue Rivers and the Ganegas anyways? If one said that grass was green, the other would swear it was purple."

Grandma Blue huffed.

"Why don't you ask them? Since you're running their errands now."

"I'm not doing it for them. I'm doing it for my girls. Seriously, why are your families always fighting?"

In the stubborn silence, they both stared out at the walkway between the oak trees that touched at the tops to form an arch towards the road to Etsi. Grandma Blue looked at the woman side-eye. Had she seen it, Ophelia would have known that this look meant *why you asking me my business?*

"Inola Ganega—Waya's mother—wanted to marry Chief Trouthands. Back when he was chief of nothing. Long legs, proud nose, handsome mouth that man had. They all wanted him, but he had eyes for me. Don't skin your face at me, Sequoia. I wasn't always a crotchety old woman."

Sequoia cackled.

"Over a man? That's what started all of this?"

"No, that's not how it started. For that, you have to go back to the roots."

"What you mean 'the roots'?"

"I'll tell you what my daddy told me: The Blues and the Rivers, Trouthands, Ganegas, Walkers, Reeds, all these families have been here—by the river—since before the Civil War. We never went east like those other Cherokee bands. No Trail of Tears for us. We hid out here—the band and their slaves—then we fought for the Confederacy, and after the war we got recognized by Washington as a band. After that, there weren't no slaves. The band agreed to live in peace and give Blacks the same rights as everyone. But that never sat right with everyone. Right up to my time there was a rule: Black families didn't mix with blood Cherokee. That was the deal. That kept the peace. But that wayward husband of mine, Chief Trouthands, had other ideas. He had to marry the one girl he wasn't supposed to marry."

Grandma Blue paused and stared off into the oak treetops as if she was remembering those times. As if the Civil War and all that contentious history was a parade passing before her eyes.

The old lady said, "Hurt don't got no expiry date."

Sequoia noticed the girls and gave them her twisted smile.

"What ya'll still doing here? Go play. Stay away from the river, you hear?"

The four girls darted away in unison like a school of guppies.

Chapter Five

Ama, Ayoka, Nola, and Ophelia went straight for the water. They knew that whenever it was town council business, Sequoia and Grandma Blue would talk longer than normal. Ophelia and Nola tried to race Ama and Ayoka, but the big girls beat them to the shallow part with the flat, smooth pebbles. They splashed each other, their long brown limbs and thin ankles kicking up specks of wet light and giggles. The twins didn't have their mother's twisted grin like Nola did; they looked like their dad: lithe, fast, bright as silverfish. The stinky egg smell of the river was forgotten in the fun.

The twins stood on the landing and watched with the exact same placid gaze as if they knew what each other was thinking. Nola and Ophelia decided to pretend they too were twins, but the elder girls ran away towards the river beech tree to hide. As Ophelia and Nola raced after them, they laced their hands into each other's. She held onto Nola's fingers and squeezed tight.

If she and Nola were like sisters—Ophelia thought—then that meant that she almost had a family too. She almost had a pretty mother, who was fearless and laughed carefree and didn't annoy Grandma Blue. Almost . . .

Nola asked her, "Are you coming to school next September?"

"I don't know . . . Grandma Blue says I get on fine without it."

"I'm going back. School's fun. We have jump rope and big kids and recess."

"What's recess?"

"It's when Auntie Kay rings the bell and everybody yells and rushes out and there's snacks, and playtime, and jungle gyms and hopscotch and big kids playing stickball and sour gummies and everything."

"I want to go to recess."

The way Nola told it, recess sounded like the most fun ever.

"Why don't you come?"

"Grandma Blue says that she can teach me more at home than they can at that school."

"Can not!"

"I can do long division. You can't."

Nola's big eyes scrambled for a comeback. But it was true that Ophelia could read the newspaper and add up how long they'd been playing and even weigh beans and give back the right change.

At last, Nola said triumphantly, "But you don't have recess, do you? I get to play with everybody, but you just play here alone."

"Yeah, well . . ." Ophelia was now the one at a loss for a comeback. "Well . . . you don't have Grandma Blue."

"Nobody needs somebody's Black grandma . . ."

"You take that back."

"I didn't mean nothing by it."

"Then why'd you say it?"

37

"I'm sorry, Ophelia. I like Grandma Blue, but she's not as fun as recess."

Ophelia's face boiled. Her hands balled up into fists. But before she could bubble over, she saw from Nola's sad face that she was sorry, and she decided not to be mad. She decided to think of the most fun thing they could do in the backyard.

"Wanna go catch frogs?"

That evening was Ophelia's bath night. Water steamed from the tub, spiced with eucalyptus. While Grandma Blue braided Ophelia's hair into two great plaits, she pop-quizzed her granddaughter on that day's math tables. Outside, the night had claimed the back patch. Only the wind shaking the trees and the ever-present rush of the Etsi River could be heard.

Stop splashing about is what the swift rap on Ophelia's arm from the comb meant. She winced. "Child, why are you so restless?" Grandma Blue knew that she would regret asking what was eating at her granddaughter, but the trouble with the river had made her worries for Ophelia multiply.

"Grandma Blue, why can't I go to school with all the other Cherokee kids?"

"Hmpff," she answered, but knew that the young girl had a point. "Because I can't protect you there."

"Why do I need protection? Nola can protect me. She'll be there."

"I've sent three children to that school, and none of them came back unharmed."

Ophelia splashed at the water with her palms.

"But does that mean you have to go everywhere I go? To protect me?"

It was Auntie Kay's question. The shift in Grandma Blue happened instantly, though her hands did not stop making parts and braiding. Ophelia could feel the old woman's insides churn. It was worst when she remembered Shango, Aiyanna, and Belle. Ophelia slapped the water gently, to avoid another rake from the comb. *Were Grandma Blue's children ever coming back?*

Hard, resolute hands gripped and shook the little girl's shoulder.

"You're not going to that school. Understand? You have everything you need right here."

Ophelia smacked the water in frustration. This time, when the comb came crashing down on her wrist, she didn't wince.

Chapter Six

Grandma Blue's birth name was Ophelia Blue Rivers.

When she was almost seven years old—the same age as her granddaughter Ophelia, the year the river was poisoned—her daddy, a man with lazy eyes and a slow temper, taught her how to fish on the Etsi with wooden traps and trout minnows for bait. His name was John Blue Rivers, and when he got sentimental, he would stare her down with his runny-egg-yolk eyes, as if she was an apparition. Then he would swoop her up in his right arm, the hand with the pinky and ring fingers missing, and say, "There she goes, looking just like the lady I named her after. Just like my mama . . ."

Then her head would collapse onto his shoulder and her neck would lose all its uprightness and her whole self would tumble into the salty smell of his work shirt.

"Ophelia." His voice was deep as a rumble in a cave. "That was my grandmama's name, Ophelia Blue, just like you, and she was the first free Black baby born in Etsi. She wasn't born no slave."

That wall of a man, whose palms were giant as the leaves of the great sugar maple tree, would chuckle at his odd, quiet daughter and say, "You just like her—always watching, always thinking. Always full of deep feeling. Just like her."

Grandma Blue was thinking about her father on the walk to Etsi, to the meeting to decide what should be done about the poisoned river. John had lost his right pinky and ring finger while working on a Beauregard Farms tractor. He forgave them, but Grandma Blue never did.

She and Ophelia walked down the gravel road past the teeming bush, which sung with the noise of a million cicadas. Grandma Blue wondered if the first Ophelia Blue Rivers—her grandmother—was anything like this little girl beside her, who was forever lost in her own head.

It was not unusual for Grandma Blue to dwell on her dead husband whenever she was forced to go to Chief's. It was, after all, the building he had dreamed up and erected with his own hands. When Chief was young, he had lean limbs, pretty hickory-colored eyes, strong thighs, and could charm a fox out of his pelt. Even the old grandmothers thought he was handsome. This was the problem. He was a little too handsome for Grandma Blue's tastes. She didn't want to be chasing some jackrabbit around like a leaf in the wind. Chief was a whimsical, unpractical man, she thought. Too quick to smile at any fool for any reason. Too many nights down a bourbon bottle. Too many "friends," that weren't really friends. Too many big dreams that would vanish like a wisp of smoke as soon as he had given them his breath.

It was her father John Blue Rivers who had convinced her to break the unwritten rule that said they couldn't marry. He believed that intermarriage was the only way to make sure that Etsi children grew up knowing who they were and where they'd come from. He gave his blessing, saying, "Better than marrying some

Stone River nobody that don't care for our history. Trouthands marrying Blue Rivers? That's as Etsi as Etsi gets."

So, she married Chief before he was Chief. And it seemed to settle him down. He talked less and did more. He listened more carefully. He grew gentler. Until his biggest dream, the building the band would name after him, popped right out of his pillow talk and into the space next to his brother Moytoy's General Store.

It was a tall log building with a packed dirt floor, a circle of benches for the clans, and a roof that, at the very top, lay open to the sky. They loved him for it. Said that he would be another great chief like Yonaguska, for bringing Etsi such a beautiful place to feast on the New Moon and Ripe Corn ceremonies, to hold powwows and make big decisions. It was there, mere months after he had died, that they made the band's biggest decision: to no longer be a band.

Grandma Blue hated it. "That chattering chain saw, Chief Trouthands, is barely dead and all he wanted was for this band to stay together. Now you want to do this?"

Inola Ganega and her sons spoke the strongest for privatizing the land.

"It will bring new business," they said. "We can't live in the past," they said. "Put money in people's pockets instead of waiting on government checks," they said. But Grandma Blue knew that they reasoned so roughly because Inola still hated Chief for what he had done: married a Blue Rivers—a Black girl—instead of marrying her. Supporting the disbanding had been her revenge. Her undoing of Chief's doings.

In Grandma Blue's heart, the bitterness of that day melted down into a broth, and in there she threw her remembrances of and her frustrations with her dead husband and the spirit of her dead father, so that Chief's—for her—was forever haunted by both their spirits.

Chapter Seven

When Ophelia and Grandma Blue arrived at Chief's, the drums were already beating. In one corner in between the benches, Jim Silverfish and Moose's dad Keith Ganega—whom everyone agreed were the two best singers—were sitting at the big elk-skin drum and pounding it in rhythm while they sang. Those voices gripped Ophelia in her chest and wouldn't let her go. The drums vibrated her bones, and their voices filled up the room and wafted up and out the hole in the ceiling that let in the sunlight. She heard voices singing from a dim and distant past. Time itself seemed to dissolve in the song.

This captivated her until her grandmother's voice shook her out of her daydream. "In the old days, everybody would sit in a circle in their clans . . ." Her granddaughter could tell from the sour way she stared at everything that the old woman didn't want to be there, but she knew that she had to.

Waya Ganega—dressed in a blue suit, with a steam-pressed shirt open at the collar—excitedly shook his jowls in their direction and waved at Grandma Blue to take a seat on the front bench. Firmly, she took Ophelia's hand and refused. Then it was Sequoia—sitting in matching sky-blue dresses with her daughters—who was waved away by Grandma Blue when she called for her to come forward. Ophelia waved at Nola, but Nola didn't see her before her grandma's rough hand pulled her towards the back benches. Yet rather than sitting, she stood where she could see but not be fully seen.

Grandma Blue had told her that in the old days they would have a fire at the center of the dirt circle, and when you entered, you had to offer some tobacco to the fire before you did anything. But all the ceremony was gone now that they were a village and not a band. All except for the drums and Jim Silverfish and Keith Ganega's singing and the fact that a Trouthands still started most meetings.

"We all know why we're here," said Moytoy, his voice sounding as vigorous as a much younger man's, his eyes dancing from face to face. He had made his way to the center of the dirt circle around which all the people of Etsi were arrayed on the benches. He extended his arms and brought his palms up and down to ask folks to settle down.

"But because there's been a lot of rumors, let me start by saying what we know as proven fact."

He waited for the murmurs to settle down.

"It's true: The smell in the river isn't natural. We all know this, but yesterday Keith Ganega's daughter Salila—who the children call 'Moose'—and her two brothers had to be taken to the hospital in Stone River after going for a swim. They had stomach cramps, splitting headaches, vomiting, and diarrhea."

There was a sharp intake of air and a collective groan throughout the building. The rumor that had blown up and down Rock Hill Road, all through Etsi, had now been confirmed.

"Waya Ganega sent to get the river tested, and I'll let him tell you all about that."

From where they were standing—at the back, near the door—Ophelia could only see the speakers when she peeked around Grandma Blue's overalls, but she could hear everything. Grandma Blue stood with a stony, emotionless look. Yet Ophelia could feel that she was agitated. The way she always was when they went to Chief's.

Waya Ganega—his blue suit sparkling as he turned this way and that—replaced Moytoy at the center.

"Here comes the mayor," someone said, and a ripple of laughter passed through the crowd.

Waya Ganega said, "Thanks for coming, everyone. This is a very important meeting. A big meeting. We need to make sure everyone has their say. When the river started to smell last month, I asked Rip Smithers, from our lawyers Smithers and Smithers, to have our water tested. We got the results, and they aren't good."

The entire room hushed. Each breath hung on for what Waya would say next. He produced a folded piece of paper from his pocket and read it like a judge passing a sentence.

"Eight times the safe amount of nitrogen."

A gasp erupted from the crowd.

"Ten times the safe amount of phosphorus."

A murmur rose again, and a single, long, high-pitched whistle came from Keith Ganega.

"Seven times the normal amount of ammonia."

"Bastards," Jim Silverfish said with finality, the scar along his face gleaming. The meeting collapsed into dozens of side conversations.

"Where is this coming from?" asked Auntie Kay.

"We know where it's coming from," Miss Sequoia's resigned voice answered.

Waya Ganega tried to get the meeting back under control.

"Please . . . Everyone, listen . . . I would like you to hear the words of our lawyer Rip Smithers."

"You mean your lawyer," said Walela Trouthands, and another nervous laugh passed through Chief's.

Rip Smithers—the third generation of his family to be in the litigation business—stepped to the center of Chief's, to the very spot where his father Don had convinced the band that they should hire him to negotiate their transition from a band to a village. Grandma Blue had brought her cherrywood stick and, seeing the son's heavy head of dirty-blond hair—just like his father's—made her knuckles clutch it tighter. That night that his father had "worked his poison," as she liked to say, she had smashed the side mirrors and headlights of his Mercedes Benz. Rip had attended that night too but was then only a twenty-two-year-old associate. Now he was a named partner in the firm.

"Hmpff . . ." said Grandma Blue, and then so quietly that only Ophelia could make it out, "Look at this pup, come to cash the check his conniving daddy wrote."

The room steadied to hear what he had to say.

"It's true: we know what the source of the pollution is . . ."

He started nervously but settled into the breezy, matter-of-fact speaking voice that he had seen his father perform hundreds of times in court.

"Jack Beauregard and Beauregard Farms—that's the who. We all know that they bought up a lot of the former rez land downriver and expanded their cattle farm operation. And now the river is full of dangerous compounds that are known to come from—you guessed it: cattle farms. The question is what are you going to do about it?"

There was grumbling throughout the room, and Rip Smithers' eyes scanned anxiously to see if his speech had had the desired effect.

Waya Ganega, with his sulking shoulders, stepped back into the circle. "Now, I know we don't want any trouble, but I see this as an opportunity to turn things around in Etsi. The river is our mother. The river is our everything. We can't let this Beauregard man get away with poisoning it, can we? What do we have if we don't have the river?"

To this point in her life, Ophelia had only ever seen one Caucasian person—Rip Smithers—once before. Yet while she was peeking around Grandma Blue's overalls at him, five more walked in the door and stood right beside her.

Two were gruff-faced men with broad waists and close-cropped mustaches who stared down anyone who looked their way. They were followed by a frosty-headed older man with a hooked nose, an eagle-handled cane, and a golden watch chain that dangled from the vest of his suit. Behind them came a man in a black blazer, polo shirt, and slacks, who had a scruffy head of blond hair and melancholy eyes. Next to him was a boy who was his baby twin. They even wore the same outfit, except that the boy's tiny blazer was navy. He seemed to be about Ophelia's age.

As Ophelia turned and looked towards them, the man with the eagle cane and the man with the melancholy eyes both walked towards the center of the circle, and the crowd got restless with shuffling. The boy, who was like a toy version of the grown man, bent his gloomy eyes towards Ophelia. She felt as though he had the look of a drowned fox. Although he was clearly dry, the sorrow in his baby-blue eyes made her feel sorry for him. She smiled. He smiled. Then they each turned back towards the circle. But there was something about his eyes that stayed with her.

The melancholy-looking man was not depressed at all. His energy crackled into the room.

"My name is Jack Beauregard . . ."

A storm of boos rose up so loud at the mention of his name that it drowned him out. The man with the eagle cane—Jack's lawyer, Buck Cronkite—banged it loudly against the end of the cedar bench. When the noise died down, the scruffy-headed man with the sad eyes continued in an easy, unconcerned way, as though he was a friend talking to a friend about their good old times. "Yes, my name is Jack Beauregard, but I'm your neighbor first . . ."

A sarcastic whistle from Sequoia caused more laughter.

"My family, just like your family, has been living here a long time. Your people from Etsi fought in the Civil War right alongside my kin. So I understand: You need the river—clean and unpolluted—and I need the river the same way."

"Like hell you do!" Keith Ganega stood up as if he was ready to charge the man. "My children are in the hospital because of you."

"And we will pay their medical bills. As God is my witness, we will spare no expense. It's children—the future—that's exactly why I'm here. Christopher? Christopher, come here, my boy."

The boy who had exchanged smiles with Ophelia walked towards the center, accompanied by one of the broad, mustached men.

"This is my son Christopher. He is the seventh Beauregard

that was raised right here along this same river. I brought him here today as a sign to you that my family is not your enemy. We've been here a long time and we will be here a long time. We're your neighbors. Can't we all just get along?"

The unhappy eyes of the boy-fox echoed in Ophelia's mind, and this echo built until it pushed her out of her body. The noise of the arguments raging at Chief's that night sounded far away. The smell of lilacs in the night seemed to drift in from the hole in the roof, and her head went up near the rafters also. Among the red cedar posts that made up the roof danced sparkling tiles the color of the boy's fox eyes. Blue, blue, blue. Soft, crystal blue. They twirled and clinked as though they were music. She was lost in these colorful tiles when she heard someone call her name.

"Ophelia Blue Rivers," Rip Smithers repeated. "Is she here?" he asked again. "Ophelia Blue Rivers?"

"I am here," she heard her grandmother say. Ophelia's neck snapped upwards to Grandma Blue as if asking, *That's my name. Not your name. How can that be your name too?*

The crowd at Chief's hushed to hear what Grandma Blue would say. This was why they had asked her to come. She was the oldest Elder left, a riverside landowner, and the former Chief's wife. If she wasn't Black, no one in Etsi would have more authority than Grandma Blue. But she was Black. And everyone in Etsi knew that she had only been invited because her age, her land, and her status had suddenly become useful. Yet would she support the lawsuit? Or speak against it simply because the Ganegas wanted it? As Ophelia had heard the old woman say many times, *Hurt don't got no expiry date.*

All of Chief's eyeballed the spectacle of the old Black Cherokee, holding her grandchild's hand, leaning on a stubborn cherrywood stick, to see what she would do. They did not move from their place by the door. Yet to Ophelia, it felt as if something inside Grandma Blue stiffened. The little girl felt this so clearly that she too straightened her spine, to match the change in her grandmother that only she could sense.

Grandma Blue's voice spoke gruff as ever. "Waya Ganega is right. The river is our mother. The river is our provider. The river is our home. What will our ancestors say if we let this man corrupt it and buy us off? I will stand for this class action. I will represent the band . . . I mean . . ." Grandma Blue stopped, sighed, and corrected herself: "I will represent the town."

The whole room screamed and stomped their approval. Etsi wanted a fight. Even those who didn't like a Black lady claiming a place among them hollered their approval. They had found their champion.

Jack Beauregard simply turned and left, but his lawyer Buck Cronkite banged his eagle cane on the ground and yelled back, "If it's a fight you want, it's a fight you'll get."

No headlights were broken that night. Rip Smithers—elated that the long process to begin the lawsuit could go forward, and already counting his billable hours—offered the old woman and Ophelia a ride home as a peace offering. But she would never forgive him and his father for convincing the band to disband. She walked back the way she came: her hand in her granddaughter's hand, and her head conversing with the ghosts of her husband and her father.

That night, as they settled down under the blankets, Ophelia's eyes were still filled with those soft baby-blue tiles she had seen twinkling in the rafters of Chief's and the unhappy eyes of the boy-fox. Grandma Blue was remembering the day she and Chief

Trouthands had dug the holes for the corner posts of Chief's: how much her hands had blistered and how proud she had been of her man.

"That lout," she mumbled out loud.

Hearing that her grandmother was still awake, Ophelia resisted asking her question for as long as she could—which was not very long—then she said, "Grandma Blue? Why is my name the same as yours?"

Chapter Eight

The next day, while scampering in the river, Ophelia felt the first butterfly's feet on her face.

It was a single butterfly. Canary yellow. It landed on the bridge of her nose before she could react. She didn't shriek or run. She stood scarecrow still. A great gust of brightness forced her to snap her eyes shut. When she opened them again, two more butterflies had arrived on her cheeks. The flapping velvet wings tickled her. *Teehee! Don't!* She heard someone giggling—in her voice—but it couldn't be her, because this person sounded far, far away.

Then another butterfly landed on her elbow. Then, all at once, so many came to her neck, her collarbone, and her forehead that she lost count. The glare stitched her eyes shut again. She could feel the sun's heat showering her arms. Butterflies kept landing. Through the rough cotton of her dress, she could feel them. They spoke to each other in a soft hum, and Ophelia felt as though she could talk their butterfly language. *Hello, butterflies, where did you come from?* Instead of panic or swatting at them, her breath became tranquil, and her body grew languid and still.

Again she scraped her eyes open, butterflies were all over her face. *Tens? Dozens? Hundreds?* Her mouth wanted to open, but she was afraid that they might fly in there too.

Looking down, she tried to find her feet. She extended her knee, but instead there was a congregation of wings that opened and closed like little mouths. A soft, feathery second skin. Puffs of sticky dust from their legs went down her throat with each breath. Ophelia felt a weightlessness that made her imagine that she too could fly. That she had been made a citizen of their canary-yellow country, and this was her welcome ceremony. She closed her eyes again and leaned into this buoyancy. It felt as though they had lifted her above the river completely.

But this feeling made her panic.

"Ahhhhh!"

Her shriek broke the spell: her butterfly coat scattered. It sent every single wing fluttering away from her. When she looked down, her feet were still planted in the river's mud and there was no sign that they had ever moved, much less levitated.

She remained rooted in the water, sad that her canary-lemon life was over. "I was flying?" she asked herself, wanting to believe it. "I was flying?" she asked again, needing it to be true. Then she looked downriver just in time to see a fluttering throb of yellow wings turn the bend and vanish to wherever the river always went. She decided to find faith in this wonder. "I was flying!"

Ophelia flew back to the cabin, cutting through the tomato vines, her thoughts outracing her legs.

"Grandma Blue! Grandma Blue!"

"Quiet, alright now?"

Ophelia's breath stopped when she recognized her grandmother's mood. There was no winning when she was in this kind of grouch. The old lady could bite her as quickly as a copperhead snake could. So Ophelia bit her bottom lip and kept her thoughts churning inside. Just barely. Which felt as though she really needed to pee and couldn't. She desperately wanted someone other than her to know.

There was the smell of fat frying. The deep, heavy pan was popping oil on the stove. A pile of fresh collard greens was on the counter.

Under the hard gaze of Grandma Blue, Ophelia washed her hands in the enamel basin and started peeling the spines off the leafy greens by squeezing them through her fingers.

Ophelia tried to concentrate on not crunching her fingers with the big knife, but her mind was full of yellow butterfly wings. The scene kept playing back in her head: her muddy toes, the first tiny feet landing, the blinding sunlight, her face covered, her legs thick with wings like little mouths, the ground being way too far down.

Grandma Blue dropped a sachet of peppercorns, allspice, and bay leaf—*that's the one for pork shank*, Ophelia remembered—into the pan of caramelized onions. The cabin smelled of scrumptious smoke. Then she closed the oven door.

"Why your dress soaked like that?"

Grandma Blue watched her, side-eye, and the story erupted out of Ophelia.

"Grandma Blue, I ran down by the river and butterflies landed all over me and covered me and when I opened my eyes, I was wearing them. They were all over my arms and knees, and my feet, and then . . . they lifted me off the ground. I was flying!"

SMACK.

It rung like a hammer on a bell and vibrated from her cheek bones right through her core and echoed on into eternity.

"Look here," the furious woman said. "In this house, we don't talk crazy. Understand?"

"But . . ."

Ophelia's head was a jumble of hurt, amazement, and yellow wings. More miraculous than being surrounded by pretty wings was seeing her grandmother weep. A huff of air came out of Grandma Blue's face, followed by a ripple of shaking that started in her belly and trembled all the way up her torso. The tears that rose in her sunken eyes never fell. Which, to the little girl, seemed sadder than if they had.

"How am I going to protect you, Ophelia, if you're always lost in your head?"

Ophelia had no answer for this. She wanted to say, *But Grandma Blue, it really happened* . . . and . . . *Grandma Blue, didn't you say that butterflies were messengers from the spirit world?* but she knew better. Besides, had it all really happened the way she wanted to tell it?

She sensed that space inside her grandmother boiling mightily. All the things Ophelia couldn't say bubbled up into tears that also did not fall. She wrapped her arms around her grandmother's spicy, sagging flesh and tried to hold all of her inside that hug. They stayed there for a long minute until the old lady pushed her away.

"Child," she said, sounding like herself again, "I'm burning my pork shank . . ."

Chapter Nine

Two weeks later Miss Sequoia visited Grandma Blue with news, but only Nola came this time. Miss Sequoia brought a worried energy, Ophelia thought. She walked brisk and direct and skipped straight to her point. "Unfortunately," she said with sarcasm, "those three Ganega kids are fine. They're back on Rock Hill Road terrorizing the trailers. I can't wait until school starts back next month."

"So, what's in the river isn't that bad?"

"Oh, it's bad. They don't know what the side effects will be, and you better start boiling your water."

"Go on, you two, go play while grown folks talk. Stay where we can see you, okay?"

When Ophelia and Nola slipped off to the back patch, school was the topic there also.

"School starts in three weeks. Are you coming?" asked Nola.

Ophelia could only respond with a dejected shrug and long-lipped pout. It was late summer, and her hair was thick with curls and her skin a smooth, tanned cocoa.

"Why you look so different?" asked Nola.

"Everybody looks different in the summer."

Ophelia had grown miserable about not going to school.

"I wish I had curly hair like yours. Can I touch it?"

"No, why would you want to do that?"

"I just want to see what it's like."

"Okay, you can touch it."

"Cool."

Nola gave Ophelia's hair a squeeze and toss but then seemed disappointed.

"You wanna feel mine?"

"Okay . . ."

Ophelia swept her palm down Nola's pristine black hair.

"So soft . . ." she said, but just then Miss Sequoia's voice hollered from around the front of the cabin, and they knew it was time for Nola to go. Watching them leave, Ophelia turned her dejected face to find Grandma Blue closely observing her.

"Why you wearing that soggy-bread face? Not happy to see your friend?"

Ophelia didn't answer. She had one thought galloping across her mind: *recess.*

The morning following Nola's visit—two weeks after the meeting at Chief's—Ophelia woke even before the bullfrogs had stopped croaking. She had a plan: She knew that to win Grandma Blue over, she had to speak the only language the old lady accepted: toil. Before Grandma Blue even stirred from their little blanket tent on the floor, Ophelia was up and had the floor swept, coffee made—tiny dollop of cream, just the way her grandmother liked it—and poured into the powder-blue enamel mug she preferred. Two bushels of corn were picked and shucked by noon, and not a peep about Ophelia talking to her or dragging her feet on chores or complaining when it got to be suppertime and they were still back bent and hoeing in the yard. Knowing she was up to something, Grandma Blue watched, her brows raised.

Day two came. Coffee made again, black and bitter with a tiny blob of cream, powder-blue enamel mug, and this time her favorite breakfast: biscuits heated up, sausage gravy and fresh sliced tomatoes, picked two days early but still juicy and sweet. Ophelia then spent all day tending to customers coming to buy produce. This happened once or twice a summer. Three of them were Moose and her two brothers, who had recovered from their pollution sickness enough to return to being the terrors of the town. She and her brothers came by the cabin, not to buy anything but because they were bored of every side street, tree fort, and rock pile in Etsi. Moose asked Ophelia in her mocking sing-song voice, the same question that Nola had asked three days before, "You coming to school next month?"

"Sure am."

"Yeah? I think you're scared. Doesn't she look scared?"

Her brothers showed teeth and nodded. But this was their reaction to everything Moose said.

"Yeah? Well, I think you're stupid."

Moose screwed up her cheeks and stuck out her tongue. "We'll see who's stupid," she promised, and they shuffled off, looking for someone else to harass.

In those two days Ophelia uttered not a single complaint, not a whine or a solitary word about wanting to go to school either.

When on the third morning the cabin filled with that roasted coffee fragrance and the glare of the sun spread itself across their floorboards, Grandma Blue awoke, shocked to discover that she'd slept in. Ophelia presented the steaming powder-blue enamel mug, and her grandmother breathed it up like a draft sucking the mist off the river. Grandma Blue's tough, crusty knuckles grazed the little girl's cheek and neck, and she smiled a wicked smile.

"Okay, Ophelia Blue Rivers, you can go to school."

On the inside Ophelia detonated, but on the outside, she bit into her lip, scared that if she said the wrong thing or showed too much excitement, her grandmother might change her mind. After a breathless pause, with all the composure she could muster, she said, "Oh . . . that sounds like a nice idea."

The old woman watched her from her dark bean eyes, sunken in their sockets, and her mouth creased together slightly. It was almost invisible, but Ophelia understood that the old lady was laughing at her.

The next day Ophelia realized that Grandma Blue had tricked her. That was the day that—for the first time ever—Auntie Kay came to the cabin. Her tiny brown mouth was set to a people-pleasing array of teeth, her poofy dress was printed with Texas bluebonnet blossoms, and her wide eyes wore a look of surprised satisfaction as she bounded up the walkway between the oak trees.

"Thank you for inviting me, Grandma Blue," she gushed as they sat down on the porch and she took out her forms to register Ophelia for school.

The little girl's head was dizzy with questions. *Inviting me? What does she mean "inviting me"? When did Grandma Blue have time to invite anyone? Much less Auntie Kay, who she doesn't like, who she said, "Know the book, but don't know the page."* Burning with curiosity, Ophelia focused on sweeping a corner of the floor that was close enough for her to overhear what was said.

Her grandmother watched her cooly and dropped her left

eyelash too fast to be resting, yet too slow to be blinking. The old lady had winked at her. And suddenly it occurred to Ophelia what had happened: she had asked Miss Sequoia to ask Auntie Kay to come visit because she had intended to let Ophelia go to school all along.

Auntie Kay blushed for no reason and continued to ask the questions on her registration forms. "Who shall I list as parents?"

"I'm her parents."

"Do you have any legal paperwork listing you as her guardian?"

"Nope."

"Yes, but ... ummm ... I need to list a father or mother or both." Auntie Kay's tone got serious.

"Well, she doesn't have any. All she's got is me."

Grandma Blue could out-serious anybody. There was a long, uneasy moment where the two women locked into a test of wills: the elder lady was hard-faced but pleasant, the younger one bubbly in her eyes but tense around her jaw.

Auntie Kay's little brown mouth then suddenly blossomed into a smile. She leaned in as if conspiring and said, "I think we can just list you as the sole guardian and keep this between us."

"You're too kind."

"Now, in her first week we will focus on testing what level she is on, but I'd like to check some boxes on what you have taught already. If that's okay with you?"

"That sounds fine."

In the end, Auntie Kay skipped her way back down the walk between the oaks, towards the road, and on the wind they could hear her giggling. It was not often anyone could say that they got the better of the old Chief's wife. Yet the old lady folded her arms as if she was very satisfied with losing the test of wills.

There was still a kernel of worry underneath Grandma Blue's lightness that day, but on the surface she seemed content. Ophelia folded her arms and tried her best to stare down Grandma Blue. Her grandmother pretended to not notice for a minute, then she turned suddenly, declaring, "What? You thought I'd let you play in that poisoned river all September?"

Chapter Ten

Salila never liked the nickname "Moose."

Wes, her uncle, gave it to her because she liked to watch a cartoon with a talking moose. "Plus," he added, "you big as a moose, soooo . . ." He said this because, even though she was ten, she was a head taller than her two brothers—Chuck and Bryan—who were two and three years older than her, respectively. Chuck and Bryan had gotten their father Keith's build and temperament: slim, tranquil, sleepy-eyed, easily convinced to do mischief. Salila, however, had the broad-backed, heavyset build of their Uncle Waya and the vengeful spirit of their famous grandfather, Wanei Ganega. The three siblings slept in the same bed, shared the clothes in their dresser drawer, and would collectively decide where they were going, because splitting up was not an option. Track pants and baggy hand-me-down T-shirts were their uniforms. Around Etsi, Salila and her brothers had a reputation for dunking kids in the river, breaking windows, and generally being a nuisance.

The Ganegas prided themselves on being shrewd dealmakers and one of the founding families of Etsi. So, after the disbanding, their mother Inola Ganega sold the family land to the east of the village and set herself up on a ranch just outside Tulsa, Oklahoma. She did this because, as she said, "I'm sick and tired of this place. Now that we got some money, I wanna be around some real Cherokee." The brothers—Waya, Keith, and Wes— and Keith's three children were all that remained of the Ganegas in Etsi, and of those six, Salila was the only girl.

The night before the first day of school, the Ganega brothers started a fire in the pit behind their trailer and were drinking beers from the cooler and shooting the breeze.

"Moose, go get me another beer, but make sure it's a lager this time, alright, dummy?"

Wes Ganega stood facing the river, trying to skip rocks across the surface. Salila's shoulders slumped, and she went off towards the fire to fetch the beer, while Bryan and Chuck took turns skipping flat brown stones, imitating their uncle. Beyond the trees and the river the light was dying.

Moose's father didn't like her nickname. "I already told you, stop calling her that. What kinda girl are we raising? She already looks like a boy."

Keith also didn't like fighting with Wes.

"We? We aren't raising nobody. You're gone most of the time to Charlotte with Waya. I'm the one looking after them. Who do you think they listen to when you're not here?"

Keith tried to keep his voice monotone, nonchalant, uninterested.

"We're working our asses off in Charlotte to pay for your new jeans and fancy sneakers. And nice job you're doing. Where were you when they were swimming in the river? I never saw you in the hospital last month."

Wes got feverish. "When do I get to leave this place?"

"This place? You should be proud to be from Etsi. Be proud of your roots. We survived Andrew Jackson, the Civil War, and two world wars right here. We're the only band of Cherokee this far east."

Wes flicked at his lighter aggressively—*flick, flick, flick*—then laughed at his brother. "I don't know if you got the news, but we're not a band anymore; we're a town."

Keith, who was sprawled out on a lawn chair, couldn't hide the grating annoyance in his voice. He drained his bottle of beer. His Adam's apple bulged as he swallowed. This was his preparation for the argument he felt was coming. Wes, spitting out the words, said:

"Whatever it was when you two were growing up here, it isn't that anymore. Niggers run Etsi now."

Waya Ganega's cheeks shook as he responded, "Grandma Blue's family been part of our band since it started."

He too was splayed out in his own lawn chair wading deep in his own thoughts.

Wes continued. "But they ain't Cherokee. They ain't got none of our blood. I don't care what the federal government says. I don't care that she's put her name on the lawsuit for the river. She's using it to pretend like she's leading us. But she ain't got our blood. Sure, them Negroes lived here forever, but it can't change the fact that they ain't Cherokee."

Keith spoke out of the side of his face. "Stop talking about what you don't know, Wes. Stop talking and listen for once." Keith avoided eye contact. He knew what he would see if he looked over at his youngest brother: neck veins throbbing, face purple, spraying spit as he raised his voice.

"Why should these white settlers in DC who stole our land,

who raped and murdered us for hundreds of years, be able to decide who is one of us?" Waya Ganega stood up after squeezing his bulky backside out of the lawn chair, but when he pulled himself up to his full height, he stood six inches over his little brother. He said, "Show some respect."

Wes shivered but didn't back down.

Waya was built like their father Wanai, who disciplined his boys with his fists closed. Waya was not like their father, but he knew how to use their resemblance to make his brothers fall in line. His bulk cast a shade over his little brother. Without knowing that he had, Wes clenched his neck and ground his back molars as if he expected to be punched. But Waya, knowing that he had Wes' attention, tried to reason with him.

"That old lady nursed Mom when they were children. Without her, you wouldn't be here. We don't agree with them, I know, but they're Cherokee just like us. Not because some court in Washington, DC, said so, but because that was the deal we made: they fought with us, bled with us, ate with us, starved with us, built this place up to what it is. And we agreed to give every freedman full membership in the band."

Salila had returned with the beer and had pushed her way between her two uncles. "It's a lager, just like you wanted, Uncle Wes." It was risky to get between them, but she didn't like it when they fought. "I got you one too, Uncle Waya."

Wes flashed a cruel look at her, but it passed quickly. Her intervention had worked—for the moment.

Waya lowered himself back down into his lawn chair and his thoughts. But Wes held Salila there by the shoulder.

"Moose, if you get your hands on one of those niggers, you teach them a fucking lesson, okay? Show them how we fight."

"Well there's only two of them. You want me to fight the old lady?"

"I want you to do what I tell you to do. What about the little one?"

"The little quiet one? She's weird, but she alright."

Wes' right hand coiled and uncoiled so fast that Salila had no chance to avoid it. The left side of her face went blind from the punch. Keith made to get up. Some part of him knew that he should defend his daughter, but after glancing at Waya, he sat back down and drained his second beer in peace.

Through her bulging right eye Salila could see Wes spit as he yelled. "Is she worth getting your ass beat?"

Her eye throbbed. Salila turned away from the fire and towards the river. The half-light had claimed it and left only shadows and the steady sound of it gurgling along. Keith appeared next to Salila and pressed the cold glass of a bottle of beer against her throbbing face. Salila shrugged off his comfort, and the brown bottle smashed at her feet with a POP.

Rage boiled in her guts, although she did not know at what or whom. It roamed about her body. A headless fury seeking something to devour.

"Don't do what he says," her father's gentle voice pleaded. "You don't wanna be like him, do you?"

Chapter Eleven

"Stop fussing," Grandma Blue said to Ophelia the morning of her first day of school. Except—Ophelia noted—it was Grandma Blue who was "fussing." She had checked the shoulder straps of Ophelia's overalls three times to make sure that they were not too long. The space between her brows had tension chiseled into their lumpiness. It seemed to Ophelia that her grandmother had said three words to the world since Auntie Kay had left that day, and all of them sounded like "hmpff . . ."

It was not like Grandma Blue to fidget, but Ophelia had no other word to describe how she packed and unpacked her lunch. Her haggard head tilted, her jelly-bean eyes buried in concentration as if willing her fingers to focus.

"Hmpff . . ." she said. Then Ophelia left her on the porch, with her chipped sky-blue coffee mug and her heavy thoughts.

Upon Ophelia's appearance at the top of the school bus steps, Nola waved, stomped a dance of joy, then did a twirl.

"You're heeeere!"

"I told you I'd come."

Unconsciously their hands found each other's, and the familiarity of this made Ophelia feel that she would not be alone.

"Auntie Kay sent me to meet you and show you around."

"Okay."

"But we have to hurry, we only have fifteen minutes before school starts."

Fifteen minutes was more than enough for them to tour the school grounds. The school sat in a dip across the road from Chief's and was a simple square building with a playground and playing field beside it that ran all the way to the edge of the bush. Behind this was a hill that descended sharply to the river.

"Don't play down there or you might tumble all the way down and get lost forever," warned Nola, who was a thorough but hurried tour guide.

Ama and Ayoka, Nola's older sisters, waved at them from the jungle gym. Their arms calling her over to say hello.

"No time to play, we'll do that at recess," said Nola, rushing Ophelia along.

But Ophelia stopped to watch the playground fill up from a distance. Children played jump rope, hide-and-seek, and hopscotch as the younger kids swung on the swings and screeched as they chased each other. Older students stood by the edges of the field. Clumps of boys pushed and leaned on each other as they caught up and paid no mind to the girls they were all aware were watching them. The girls stood in nonchalant lines pretending not to care about anything, especially those dirty, loud-mouthed boys.

Nola eventually got her moving again.

Inside, the school was one big square room. Three of the walls were blackboards and one was a long window facing the playground. Rows of desks faced each blackboard so that the classroom was divided by which blackboard you were looking at.

"This is where we sit with the ones, twos, and threes. Grades six, seven, and eight face over there, and grades four and five there. Got it?"

There were thirty-six desks in total, which to Ophelia felt like a thousand.

"Got it," she said, as she noticed Moose and her brothers pointing at her, smirking. She waved an animated hello, but Moose stuck her tongue out at her. A Moose Ganega welcome. A purple bruise bulged over her right eye.

There were bookshelves under the blackboards and pencil sharpeners with the little crank handles attached to the walls on either side of the bookshelves. The room smelled of the plastic of new Kmart sneakers, mildew, and chalk dust, but the tingly sense of everything-about-to-happen was palpable.

"That's where Auntie Kay's office is." Nola pointed to a side room with a barely cracked door. "You only go there if you're in trouble . . ." Nola smiled a preoccupied smile as she replayed all the places on her list for the tour and counted them off on her fingers and thumbs. Then she gave a satisfied nod and led Ophelia to Auntie Kay's office.

"Don't worry, you're not in trouble. You're just new."

When they arrived at the door and pushed it open, Auntie Kay sat in a low chair checking off her lesson plan on a piece of lined paper with a pencil. She rose and said, bubbly as ever, "Osiyo, Ophelia! I'm happy to see you. Nola hasn't stopped talking about you all morning."

"Osiyo, Auntie Kay."

"How is your grandmother?" Ophelia heard this as: *How was your grandmother's temper this morning?*

"She's a little sad but she's weeding in the yard today. She's strong."

"Oh ... well, that is something we agree about."

And it struck Ophelia that Auntie Kay was a lot nicer than she had been prepared for her to be.

"Let me show you to your desk."

True to her brand, Auntie Kay wore a bright white cherry-tinted dress that flared out past her hips and underneath had soft, pillowy layers like cake icing. Bunches of cherries climbed up the print and her famous charm bracelet hung from her wrist. She was too young to be an old lady, but old enough that her two sons—who were in grades one and three—both attended Etsi District School as well.

"You'll be sitting right here." She pointed Ophelia to a laminated desk that opened at the top so she had a place for her books, and a folding chair of wooden slats sat there also.

"Nola, I've put you right next to Ophelia so that you can help her if she needs it."

Nola reached down, grabbed Ophelia's hand, and squeezed it again.

"Yes, Auntie Kay. I'll make sure nothing bad happens to her."

Ophelia's first recess was everything Nola had promised: jump rope, hopscotch, jungle gym, meeting the other four kids in her grade. There were also sour keys and fruit berry candies—which melted on her tongue, stuck to the ridges of her mouth, and made her head spin.

After recess, when the grade sevens couldn't do their word problem, Ophelia stuck her hand up because she'd finished her math early. Maybe it was Grandma Blue in her head saying, "Don't work, don't eat," but Ophelia started on the grade seven math problem without being told to. It was one of those "if two trains leave at different speeds" ones, and she solved it before anyone else had. Auntie Kay couldn't hide her shock, so she called her up while Salila was at their blackboard struggling with the problem. Ophelia wrote the answer out and the whole school cheered. Embarrassed, Salila punched the top of her desk before she sat back down. Everyone around her stopped cheering.

When the short hand of the clock got to one and the long hand went to six, Auntie Kay's watch started to beep. She looked down, huffed, and said, "Where does the day go?" Then she pushed a button on her watch, walked to her desk, and rang the bronze bell. It cut through the room; every grade dropped what they were doing to run outside. "It's second recess," Nola declared to Ophelia's puzzled look.

As they were walking towards the teeter-totter, Salila, surrounded by five other grade sevens, said, "What are you doing here anyways, nigger?"

Ophelia had no idea what this word meant.

"I'm going to jump rope."

"Not out here. You're not one of us. Look at you."

Ophelia was confused. *Is she mad because I did the math question?*

Salila got so close to Ophelia's face that droplets of spit sprayed her when she talked. "My uncle says that you and your Black grandma are just pretend Cherokee ..."

"Yeah? Well, my grandma says that we're both."

"Are. Not."

Salila two-hand pushed Ophelia and she stumbled backwards. She found her feet and yelled back: "Why doesn't your uncle say it to her face? Last time he tried, he nearly got her stick cracked over his head."

"I'll beat you with a stick, you little nigger."

Salila's fist blinded Ophelia. When the punch came, she heard it before she felt it. There was a crunch. Ophelia's body twisted around violently and she landed face down with a mouthful of grass.

Chapter Twelve

It took Grandma Blue a few seconds to see that something had happened at school. And another handful of moments to find out what.

"Child . . ." she said. Which Ophelia understood to mean *tell me what happened, or else . . .*

Two rivulets of tears ran down Ophelia's bruised cheekbones.

"Moose punched me and called me a nigger and a pretend Cherokee. On recess. On recess."

To Ophelia, this was the worst part. Recess was sacred. It was a desecration.

"Show me where you're hurt."

There were lines scraped into her palms where she had braced the fall. There was a swollen patch of tender flesh growing around the right side of her face. Grandma Blue restrained herself with effort. The last thing she needed to do was overreact.

"Child, you've got to fight your own fights. That's what school is for."

Ophelia set her face in defiance. She felt as if she had failed.

All I had to do was have a good day at school. Be nice to Auntie

Kay. Have fun with Nola. And show Grandma Blue that I learned something. Now she'll never let me go back.

Grandma Blue lit the flame under the steel kettle and brought back tea tree oil and rubbing alcohol from the closet. Ophelia couldn't stop the trickles.

"And what did that teacher of yours say?"

"Auntie Kay said that it was true, but that Moose shouldn't have hit me."

"She. Said. What?"

"Auntie Kay said, 'Well, Ophelia, you're obviously not Cherokee, but no one should make you feel unwelcome for that.'"

Auntie Kay had said this so loud that the whole school had heard. Ophelia felt flattened. She had lost the fight and lost the argument. *Moose was right. Auntie Kay said it: I'm not Cherokee.*

That day Ophelia thought: *None of this is mine? It doesn't belong to me?* It was as if she'd stolen it. *Had Grandma Blue stolen it too?* she wondered, and *If Grandma Blue was wrong about that, what else could she be wrong about?*

The next morning, Ophelia and Grandma Blue walked—no raft or school bus—they walked into town. Grandma Blue was in her overalls, her three eagle feathers on her waist, her cherrywood stick whacking at the ground.

In a hush they walked the two miles in twenty minutes. Not only was Grandma Blue thinking about the bruise above the little girl's eye. There was something about how Ophelia's dejected face fought to stay calm. She remembered her father John and how he had said, *That was my Grandmama's name, Ophelia Blue, just like you, and she was the first free Black baby born in Etsi.* And she was thinking of the many scrapes her son Shango had come home with when she'd told him "fight your own fights," until he hated Etsi and her and everything she'd taught him to love. Her walk was so vengeful that Ophelia only caught up with her when they both stood on the lawn of the school.

Grandma Blue didn't bother going inside. She stood on the lawn and yelled:

"I'm Grandma Blue, wife to that slip-talker Chief Trouthands. We built this schoolhouse. Pillar and post. You hear me? You're walking on my sweat when you climb these steps."

Her words echoed in every corner of the town.

"This is my grandchild, Ophelia Blue Rivers. Who here says she don't belong? Who here says she ain't Cherokee?"

To Ophelia, her grandmother grew taller than the school-house. Higher than the tree line. Longer than the Etsi River. Nothing in Ophelia's memory would ever be so enormous.

Grandma Blue stood there. That cherrywood stick tapped the pavement impatiently. Those jelly-bean eyes sank deeper into their sockets. Under her arms her flab shook and trembled. Mouth clenched. Nostrils flared. She waited. She dared anyone to move or breathe or say anything.

Etsi held its breath for a lifetime that morning. Not a soul spoke.

At last, Grandma Blue turned and stomped back the way she had come.

Ophelia didn't know if she should go to school or not. Then the old woman yelled, "Child, move from there; you're coming home."

Chapter Thirteen

Long, leisurely, singing a soul song, Shango Trouthands returned to the place that had birthed him.

Grandma Blue's yard had been his playground, his fiefdom, and he knew the notches in the barks of the beech trees, the whine of the patio floorboards when someone heavy stepped on them, and he knew the smell of the river in September and that it wasn't supposed to reek of rotten eggs.

A portrait of ease in blue denim, jet-black hair, long to his shoulders. Caramel complexion. Grand, epic mouth. Soft eyes set in a flat face. Eyes that reflected creation without commentary.

He saw the little girl scurry into the yard from somewhere, take note of him, then retreat behind the cabin. It was as though she had seen a bizarre being from another world.

Shango was tall enough to reach up and graze the bottom branches of the oak trees that lined the path. Pausing, he threw his arms wide, inhaled with satisfaction, and spread his purple lips into a smile. He inhaled his past: Uncle Moytoy lifting him from his cradle on the deck; breaking his leg climbing the big oak; forever planting corn in the spongy dirt; the day that he left there and his promise never to come back. He breathed in his history, written in the landscape like the pull of the blunt smoke he had gotten used to. Crooning Bobby Brown's "My Prerogative," like a slow jam, he sent its notes whispering through the trees.

"Osiyo, Chief's wife."

Grandma Blue was unmoved. She sat, squat in her rocking chair, on the veranda observing his lanky frame. Unimpressed.

"Etsi has no Chief. Don't they have news where you come from?"

He answered sweetly despite her spite. "Well, you know what they say: once a Chief's wife, always the Chief's wife."

Grandma Blue's feet dragged restless circles on the floorboards. "Still laughing at your own jokes? Too slick for your own good. Just like him . . ."

Her chiding didn't shake his mood. Shuffle, shuffle said her feet.

"I'm surprised you came. Five years. Five years? I was starting to forget I had children."

They both straightened up like coiled rattlesnakes.

"How is the little one?"

Her voice got whispery and conspiratorial. "She fine, always in a daydream, talks to frogs and imaginary friends, always pestering me about feelings, not much good in the yard but she can do figures though. Not a half-bad cook neither."

"And how is she doing at school?"

"That didn't go so good."

"I heard."

"You got spies looking in on me?"

"I got friends who call me when you cuss out the entire town."

"They lucky a cussing is all they got."

They stared each other down: Grandma Blue frowning, Shango wary.

"And the whole lawsuit thing?"

Her brow raised at how much he knew about Etsi despite being gone.

"I left; I didn't die. I still talk to people."

"But you don't talk to me ..."

He pounced up the stairs in one stride and Grandma Blue's body leaned into him for a kiss. A gesture that stunned Ophelia. Then she pulled back gruffly.

"The child has a right to know what happened to her mother. It's not right you keeping her in the dark. And it's not my business to say." He stood above her looking towards the back patch. Noticing how much it had changed. Noticing how little his mother had changed.

"She don't stop asking ..."

"I'll tell her when she's old enough to handle it."

Shango leaned in and wrapped his long man arms around his mother. Into her temples his lips pressed a kiss. He wrapped her up and she reached over and held him. Those indifferent eyes disappeared behind his eyelids, his denim arms enfolded her in its coils, picked up her pieces, reassembled her parts and tucked them in where they belonged.

As he raised his head, he looked directly at Ophelia, who was still hiding around the side of the cabin, close enough to drink in the sight of him. Then, as easy as pie, he winked hello.

For a slow pour of molasses, the little girl seemed stunned, rooted, peeled open. Shango smiled. Simultaneously, he looked right at her and right through her. Then it was over. Time resumed.

Ophelia turned towards the river and ran for her life.

Chapter Fourteen

"This is my son Shango," Grandma Blue said to Ophelia when the little girl had found the courage to come back to the house and found the man and her standing in the kitchen.

Ophelia stood dumbstruck. The Singing Man was real, standing in their cabin, and had a name. Of course, she had scraped together whispers and rumors of Shango already and stored them away in a place only she could open. Only when she wanted. But now he stood before her—present in a way she couldn't control.

She sat across the table from him staring. Those saucer-sized eyes that let in nothing, sitting low and wide in his face, made her squirm. But this time she wasn't going to run away. His mother rummaged in the kitchen doing the most—and pretending not to listen.

"Hello," Ophelia heard herself say.

"We've met before, but I don't suppose you'd remember that?"

"Child, you wanted to know where you came from. Well, here he is."

Ophelia knew that Shango was her father. Father. What did that mean? Her head spun. Her ventricles kicked at her ribs.

Grandma Blue buzzed like a silver fish in the creek, from kitchen to table. Pans clattered as if they had been thrown down the stairs. She had been cooking since he arrived, it seemed, and her feast fizzed, popped, and smoked the whole cabin with the smell of trout roasting. Just as the old lady was putting a steaming pot down, Ophelia found her voice. "What happened to my mother?"

"I'm sorry I've been gone so long, Ophelia. One day this will all make sense."

His voice still sounded like singing.

"But where is she? Can I meet her?"

"I can't tell you about her right now."

"But why?"

Shango glanced at his mother, begging for her intervention. Grandma Blue got great satisfaction from watching him squirm.

"Mother, can you help, please?"

"Help? Nearly seven years raising her, you don't think that's help enough?"

"She's not ready to know this. Help me protect her."

"What am I not ready to know?"

"I can't protect her forever." Grandma Blue's tone was more fearful than her words. "Sooner or later, she's gonna have to fight her own battles."

Shango shook his head, cornered, wishing for a way out.

"And you're gonna have to be a father."

"What battles, Grandma Blue?"

Shango decided that he had no choice. He inhaled as if plunging under water.

"Your mother is dead, Ophelia," he said, swallowing. "She died the day you were born."

Ophelia would remember this answer. It would ripple out

in her waters for the rest of her life. She did not know how to mourn a mother that had had her but whom she'd never had. So she tucked her mother's death away and charged on. Being Grandma Blue's grandchild had taught her to be greedy when grown-ups were giving answers. Who knew when the trickle of truths might dry up?

"Are you leaving again?" she asked him.

"I was born right over there." He pointed his chin at the corner by the fireplace as if he hadn't heard her. "Wasn't I, Grandma Blue?"

"Why don't you just say what you came to say?" his mother answered.

She put a honey-brown loaf of warm cornbread on the table with a crack.

"Can we not fight today?" he pleaded. A plea that sounded like a challenge. When Grandma Blue refused to respond, he continued, as if answering her nonexistent reply. "I know you want to make me feel bad for leaving, but I don't. So get over it. I don't regret not seeing this place."

An iron pot arrived steaming. Grandma Blue stayed frosty.

"It's not me you have to justify yourself to."

Shango understood this. He spoke to his mother but never took his eyes off his daughter. Though they looked at her and right through her, Ophelia stood up to their gaze. *Don't run. Whatever you do, don't run.*

"She likes to daydream?" he asked.

A gust of savory flavor rushed through the room as the old woman opened the oven. She arrived again with the cast-iron pan with two trout piled high with carrots, roasted potatoes, and onions. Then she accepted his change of subject—his peace offering. "Would chat up frogs all day if I didn't shake her out of it. Reminds me of your father."

Grandma Blue made one last trip for an orange pot of glazed string beans and found a place on the table. Riveted by the spectacle of his lanky, sweet-cologned, epic-mouthed presence, Ophelia heard their talk as if from afar. Her father and grandmother spoke as though having a conversation they had been having all their lives and had just picked up where they last left off.

When they finally sat down to eat, Grandma Blue was done with peace offerings:

"Are you gonna tell her? Or is that my job too?"

They both stared at Ophelia, the only one not in on the secret.

"Tell me what?" she asked. Her voice calmer than she felt.

"Ophelia." Grandma Blue sighed, then said, "tonight is your last night here. You're going to live in Stone River."

So, this was it? She's sending me away. But I've done everything she asked. I haven't been bellyaching or lollygagging. I learned my lessons. I know which moon is for planting and which is for harvesting which crops. She even said that my cornbread gravy was better than hers. What did I do?

"What did I do? Why are you sending me away?"

"This is your father's plan, Ophelia."

Shango tried to entice her. "Don't you wanna see Stone River? You were born there, you know?"

"What did I do?"

"Child, stop whining."

"You want to meet your Auntie Aiyanna, don't you?"

"Will you be there?" she asked him, curious.

"Go on, Son, tell her the rest of your master plan."

Shango took a shallow breath.

"No, I won't be there, Ophelia, but I'll always be close, even if you can't see me."

His wide lips beamed at her; his broad eyes invited her in.

"Do you really want me to leave, Grandma Blue?"

"No, child. You're a nuisance, but you're my nuisance."

From across the table, Ophelia felt the quarrel raging within Grandma Blue. It was said that all Cherokee had two wolves inside them fighting for supremacy. One was fiery and ferocious. One was cold and calculating. Savage versus Serene. The hot-blooded one spoke first. "I can't protect you from the river. If it's poisoning kids, how long before something happens to you? I can't protect you here. There's no future for you with an old woman in a cabin by a polluted river."

"But I don't want to go . . ."

Grandma Blue got on her done-talking voice. Her calculating wolf always won.

"Child, sometimes the way is hard and all you can do is be harder."

To confirm the finality of her words, Grandma Blue pushed a plate of trout and cornbread under Ophelia's nose. And she was ambushed—all at once—by the hunger she'd built up that day. As she ate, her mind wandered to how Grandma Blue had taught her to make this dish: the speckled trout skin had to be seared and then sweetened with cane sugar.

Ophelia scrutinized the old lady, with her sunken, black, cheerless eyes. Grandma Blue wouldn't send her anywhere she didn't need to go. Would she? She knew the old woman would miss their cuddles. She knew that her grandma didn't like to talk but liked being asked to talk. It made her less sad when someone just asked. *Who was gonna ask her to talk now? Or help her shuck corn? Who was going to know what she was saying when she huffed like a cagey old bear?*

Exhausted, Ophelia stuffed her craw and curled up on the bench and yawned and stretched like a sleepy kitten. The last thing she saw before sleep was the old lady and her son huddled at the table and packing pipes. After her eyelids fell shut her brain still fumbled to stay awake. To not miss anything. Eyes closed, but still listening, she heard an eruption of laughter and fell asleep to the sound of: "Your father, that poacher, Chief Trouthands . . ."

The next morning, Ophelia said goodbye to Grandma Blue. Her grandmother handed her the army-green duffel bag stuffed with her overalls, two pairs of pants, and her Pro-Keds sneakers. Ophelia could hear the river rushing. It had rained in the night. The whole air had that bluish-silver look and that rotten smell.

She felt numb. A zombie. Undead.

While Shango waited by the car, Grandma Blue gave her a gruff hug that ended quickly. Ophelia could sense that hole in her grandmother's chest stirring, but not a single tear fell. Her dark eyes retreated deeper into her brows, and from the porch, she watched the little girl walk away.

The river thundered loudly. It rushed forward into some unknown future. Its torrent turned the riverbed inside out.

"Good day for catching frogs," Ophelia whispered absent-mindedly.

Who knew if there were frogs to catch where she was going?

PART TWO

1998

Chapter Fifteen

After noticing the ratchet state of her nails, Aiyanna Trouthands next observed that she was bored. At her apartment's kitchen table, she sat like a six-foot-tall toddler: grand, grumpy, and though her house was poor, her attitude was opulent. Flesh poured out of her halter top. Her nail file stabbed at her cuticles with malice. Aiyanna hated boredom above all things. She despised doing dishes, because under those soapy suds lay thoughts she kept busy to avoid. Groceries exposed memories. There were ghosts in those long aisles and behind all that cart pushing. Mostly she hated cooking because that was what her mother had spent her whole life doing, and more than anything she wanted to avoid being her mother.

It was March 15, 1998—nearly 168 years since President Andrew Jackson's Indian Removal Act—but Aiyanna was not interested in history. "The dead already had their turn," she would say to shut down any conversation about past generations. She lived in a two-bedroom on the sixth floor of a six-floor apartment building in Stone River, South Carolina. Just down from her on Whyte Street sat the Whyte House, one of the town's defining landmarks. It was a jalopy that was broad and flimsy, its paint flaked and falling, but it sat at the highest point of Stone River on a plot of land that used to be a cotton plantation. The commemorative plaque in front of it read: DURING THE WAR OF 1861–1865, NEEDY CONFEDERATE SOLDIERS WERE CARED FOR HERE. In 1961, at the Greyhound terminal, segregationists had beaten Freedom Riders until they were bloody, including congressman-to-be John Lewis. Since then, it was a town locked in a comfortable Southern stalemate: Black and white neighborhoods, Black and white churches, Black and white schools, Black and white lives. No one recalled that all the land it stood on was once Cherokee land or that if you followed the river that ran through the town eastward, you would end up at a bend surrounded by trailers at the once-reservation called Etsi.

Aiyanna had chosen her side. Most people that knew her assumed she was a Black woman with milky-cinnamon skin and deep-set almond eyes. Her hair was wavy—but often cut and box-dyed blond. She never mentioned Etsi, and if asked by someone, "Where did you come from?" she'd suck her left gold tooth with scorn and declare, "How's that your business?" Which wasn't really a question. "Something about a flower" is what she would say her name meant, although she knew that in Cherokee it meant "forever flowering." Legally she was still Aiyanna, but whenever she spelled it she wrote "Ayanna," because it sounded more African, or—more accurately—because it sounded less Cherokee.

Usually, doing her nails was not boring, because then she was likely going to a party. A party was anywhere there was alcohol (*good tequila, preferably*), eligible men (*boys need not apply*), a dance floor (*new jack swing, please*), and anywhere her children were not. The oldest, Kevin, looked too much like his father, and she never wanted to see that face again. The middle one, Kurt, gave good back rubs, so she could tolerate him. The youngest, Kaevon, was always yelling, *rawr rawr rawr*, disturbing her peace. He also looked too much like his father. They were twelve, eleven, and ten, respectively, and when they weren't fighting, breaking her things, and eating everything in the fridge, they slept on a bunk bed and a cot in one bedroom. On the sofa in the living room was where her niece Ophelia slept. Shango's bizarre little grown-up daughter who did weird things like homework and enjoyed reading books. Her sons took after Aiyanna as a student—the Brothers K would rather rip out the pages. Also, Ophelia cooked like a chef, cleaned like a butler, didn't make much noise, but—annoyingly, and this was her only fault—reminded Aiyanna of her mother. As she flicked at the jagged ends of her nails, she thought, *No twelve-year-old should sound like an old lady.*

On the first anniversary of her father's death, ten and a half years ago, she had heard the news: Shango had a baby. From where? With whom? He wouldn't say. And how'd he kept this child alive for eighteen months in that house full of hoodlums and heat scores? But Shango's daughter was an Etsi problem, not an Aiyanna problem. Until they poisoned the river. Family only mattered in catastrophes: weddings, deaths, sickness, and environmental contaminations. The rest of the time they were a plague. But Aiyanna had to admit that the little girl had made life easy for her in the almost five years since Shango had dropped her off at her door.

"That's it, it looks like rum o'clock to me."

She poured some club soda, half a glass of dark rum, and squeezed a lime into it. For Aiyanna, the party never started soon enough.

Chapter Sixteen

After almost five years of living with Auntie Aiyanna at apartment 66, Ophelia was used to climbing up to the sixth floor. It was not unusual for her to daydream about the first time she had walked down that hallway.

On that day in 1993 when Shango drove her to Stone River, they piled into his old man muscle car, a Pontiac Pegasus. Ophelia felt a dizziness of nostalgia. *This is it!* she thought. *This is what I remembered. This is the car, this is the seat, the rumbly engine, the oily smell, the steering wheel slipping through his hands.* Absorbed by the South Carolina bush, Shango had nothing to say. Marvin Gaye's "Distant Lover" played. The shriek of the ladies in the crowd washed over her and Shango softly hummed along: *Distant Lovaaaaaaaah.* The bush became the freeway, the road crowded with cars—a river of rubber and fumes. Her head buzzed with that never-been-this-far-from-home excitement.

After they had driven through downtown Stone River—the biggest town she'd ever seen—they pulled up by the redbrick apartment. On the sixth floor he knocked on door number 66, where the second 6 was dangling from the nail so that it looked like a 9. Loud music throbbed, and a spicy smell leaked from under the door. When the door opened, they were hit by a blast of heat: the hot breath of a room full of people, food being cooked, and the thermostat set to "furnace."

A jovial Black woman came out of the door. Her face popped out at Ophelia, and her huge eyes got even wider when they saw the little girl.

"Aiyanna, this is Ophelia," Shango said.

"Hel-lo" was all Ophelia could muster.

Waves of pleasure broke over Aiyanna's face. Ophelia looked at Shango questioningly. She would later understand that this was her "fun" auntie in full party mode. But that day Shango simply smiled and she could see the bright line of his perfect teeth behind his great mouth. Shango's heavy hand gently brushed the thickness of her curls from her eyes. When she looked up and saw herself reflected in those eyes, he whispered, for her ears only, as if it explained everything, "A Queen has come."

Those epic lips pressed to her forehead, and then he was off. Her eyes followed him longingly down the hall. It was hard for her to turn from her father, the Singing Man, striding away from her.

Five years later, her walk down that hall was no longer a mysterious entry into an unknown world; it was just the last leg of her journey home from school every day. Before she pushed the door open she could hear the R&B group Jodeci crooning, with Aiyanna yelling the lyrics over it. This meant that Auntie Aiyanna was already drunk—most likely from a succession of Captain Morgan's rum mixed with RC Cola and lime. Aiyanna had one volume: loud. "Ophelia? Girl, I'm in the kitchen. Come make a rum cocktail for me?"

Ophelia dropped her backpack and took off her shoes in the front foyer. She walked into a living room with too many chairs and a tan love seat that faced the television and the boys' Sega Saturn game console. There was a tall wooden dinner table with a clear plastic tablecloth on it. The room felt cramped and overfull. There were cabinets stuffed with knickknacks—Aiyanna loved Black children's dolls—and her "nice" dishes, which they never used. To the back, past the balcony door, were the bedrooms. Ophelia could smell that Auntie Aiyanna had been cooking the food Ophelia had prepared for dinner.

Aiyanna came out of the cramped kitchen bubbling. Hips rolling. Mouth open. Eyes closed. Arms spread out like Jesus on the cross. Glass full of rum and cola. Feeling herself. *"Every freaking night and every freaking day. I wanna freak you baby, in every freaking way."*

Ophelia, determined to squash the party, turned the music off.

"My dough? Why did you cook it? People are coming over tonight and you asked me to make food, so why are you messing with my dough?"

"Excuse me, Chef. I didn't realize I couldn't cook the food I paid for."

Ophelia gave Auntie Aiyanna her best impression of a Grandma Blue death stare. This prompted a pout from her aunt. "I'm sorry. Okay? You happy? I only made one. I needed something to soak up the booze. Forgive me?"

Aiyanna made a kissy face at Ophelia. *Not the kissy face.* Ophelia couldn't resist the kissy face. It made her feel that Aiyanna was a giant child that needed caring for. It felt nice to feel needed. Ophelia rolled her eyes at her in mock annoyance, but she had already decided that there was no point in holding a grudge. She inhaled a great breath, took in the glorious mess that was her aunt, and let it go.

"Okay, but there better be enough for everyone tonight."

Aiyanna sucked her gold cap teeth and smacked her lips in mock thirst.

"Now mix your auntie a rum cocktail? Mine never taste as good as yours."

She was already on her way to the kitchen but took one last shot at Aiyanna. "For a person that drinks so much, why are you so useless at making them?"

"I'm good at drinking drinks, okay?"

Ophelia checked the fish she had put to marinate. When she rolled back the plastic wrap on the bowl, a gust of garlic, fresh tilapia, and cilantro hit the room.

"Why is tonight so special anyways?" Ophelia asked her aunt. "Who's coming?"

"Miss Destiny and her niece. And your Auntie Belle." This last name seemed to sour the taste in Aiyanna's mouth.

"You don't like her, do you?" Ophelia asked.

Unlike Grandma Blue, Auntie Aiyanna loved to talk, and the more gossip the better. Generally, it brought out her playfulness, except for three subjects: Grandma Blue, Shango, and her younger sister Belle. When she spoke of them, she would screw up her face in disgust.

"I don't have to like her. I just have to take her money."

"Why does she bring you money?"

Aiyanna's copious lips twisted with wicked thoughts as she weighed whether to tell the truth.

"For you."

"For me?"

"That's right, Miss Ophelia. For you. How's that drink coming?"

For me? Ophelia nodded and concentrated on the cocktail: first rim the glass with salt, then measure and pour the rum, one lime wedge to squeeze, another to garnish, just a dash of peach juice. She handed it over, knowing that it would be delicious.

Her aunt's eyes danced circles.

"At least she's coming tonight," Aiyanna sighed, and licked salt off the glass' rim. "I wouldn't want her here when we're having a real party!"

Chapter Seventeen

Two hours later, Ophelia, Auntie Aiyanna and her three sons, and two guests sat down to dinner at the table in the linoleum-floored living room.

Aiyanna's sons were apartment 66's resident evils.

"Kevin, behave," she said wearily, as he flicked Kurt's ear while Kurt pretended to cry.

"Kurt, do you want something to cry about?"

Kaevon, feeling left out, not-too-subtly kicked Kevin under the table. The terror of Aiyanna's wrath was the only thing that kept them in line.

"Do that again, Kaevon, do that one more time and see what happens . . ."

They kept up this steady stream of low-grade agitation just below their mother's annoyance as everyone sat down to dinner.

The guests, Miss Destiny, a Black woman about Aiyanna's age, ignored the boys' rambunctiousness and tipped cognac into her mouth from a flask she stored in her bra. Lucy, her niece—a year older than Ophelia—watched the boys as if they were zoo animals she might have to fend off. Lucy had tiny doll features.

Neatly starched and tucked, she had the exact motions of a petite android.

Miss Destiny watched Ophelia side-eye and wrinkled her nose at her as if she were a nasty odor.

"This ugly niece of yours knows how to cook, Aiyanna?"

"Ophelia? She can cook better than Chef Boyardee."

Unconvinced, Miss Destiny licked her top lip to get the last drop of cognac and didn't let her gaze leave Ophelia. She said, "What is it about you that I don't like?" Ophelia froze and couldn't think of what to say, so she stared back at Miss Destiny, whose face grew even more rotten.

"This cinnamon skin? This good, fine hair?" Then, as if she had finished calculating a sum, she said, "I think this little bitch feels she better than us."

Miss Destiny had made it known before that "I don't like Indian people." Since her husband had left her for a Creek woman, she had collected and repeated every awful thing she could remember about them. This vendetta was relentless. Aiyanna had told her that Ophelia grew up in Etsi, and this was enough for Destiny to point her malevolence at Ophelia.

The two older women took an uncomfortable glance at each other. Ophelia recognized their arrangement even if they didn't. Miss Destiny hated "Indians" but ignored that Aiyanna might be one. Aiyanna hated her attitude but was proud that she made an exception for her. It meant that she was "passing" for Black. This unspoken arrangement, Ophelia was often reminded, did not extend to her.

"Do you? Do you feel like you're special, bitch?"

It was phrased as a question but delivered like a fact. Miss Destiny smacked her lips together as if she didn't like the way something tasted.

"Ophelia," Aiyanna interrupted. "It smells like your food is ready, no?"

Destiny's mouth hushed, but her face kept speaking spite. Thankful for the chance to escape, Ophelia went to check on her pans.

When the food was tabled, the feeling in the room changed. They reached lustfully for Ophelia's fry bread and stuffed it with battered, deep-fried tilapia, lettuce, cucumber, a pepper sauce that made eyes water, and her homemade garlic sauce. The boys finally settled down, mesmerized, googly eyes glued to their steaming-hot sandwiches. There was more R&B music playing—112 and SWV—and the table tucked into her cooking. This settled her nerves. Ophelia watched with a glow of pride as even Miss Destiny shut up to enjoy her food.

Ophelia was entranced by Lucy's behavior.

Lucy fussed over which lettuce slice, turning them all over with the wooden serving tongs until she found one that met her specifications. She moved her fork a quarter inch from her plate, eyed it suspiciously, then moved her knife the same distance on the other side. With another knife she chopped the already cut slices, *crunch-crunch-crunch*. Knife returned, she checked her fork-to-plate distance, satisfied.

When she thought she had it right, she turned away from everyone and leaned over towards Ophelia and said with a stiff doll face, "I like you, but why are you serving them alcohol?" Ophelia had to look twice to see if she had really spoken. "Pastor Hamilton says, 'Wine is a mocker and whosoever is deceived by it is a fool.'" Without waiting to see if Ophelia understood—she didn't—Lucy continued, "You need to come to church with me or you will go to hell with them."

"My drinks are going to send them to hell?"

Lucy's android lips tensed. "No. Their drinking and mocking God will send them to hell," she added assuredly. Ophelia nodded as if she knew what Lucy was talking about.

While the boys continued to annoy each other, Destiny and Aiyanna leaned in and whispered loudly about a man who "looked better from the back than the front."

"It's gross how they talk, isn't it?" said Lucy, as she moved closer to Ophelia. "Fornicators!" she continued, as if they had a disgusting disease. "You should come to church with me this Sunday and every Sunday if you don't want to end up like them."

There was a knock on the door. No one rose to answer it. After thirty awkward seconds of knocking, Kurt got up and answered it out of curiosity.

It was Belle. She was flagpole-thin in a lacy white hat and a milky-white dress that clung tightly to her slimness. Her bones were tiny as a bird's. Her face was light-skinned—coffee with two tiny creams. Around her neck were chains she wore like a collar. Ten of them glittered in different lengths down the front of her.

"Bonsoir, Aiyanna. You want me to knock all night?"

"Welcome, Your Highness. That was you knocking?"

Belle glided over the floor like a snake. And when she spoke, it was in a French accent and with a hiss that also reminded Ophelia of a snake.

"Is this what you're feeding les petit enfants?"

"Judging me already." Aiyanna sighed with resignation.

"Don't make excuses for your sloppy life."

"You know, you don't have to come here; you can just mail me that check?"

"Pfft. Pfft. Pfft," she said, then stared down the table. Emerald

98

eyes. Sharp as daggers. A mouth that sniffed at everything disapprovingly.

Madame Belle did not even look at Ophelia—she never did. Which only made Ophelia more curious about her. Before that day, she had no idea why for five years she dropped in from time to time, dressed immaculately, hissed like a serpent, and left Auntie Aiyanna with a big check. Ophelia knew it was big because Aiyanna would give a nod of satisfaction when she read it.

"And leave you to do whatever you want with my money? You will spend it in a fortnight on rum and greasy men in tracksuits. Mai non. I will see what I'm paying for, oui?"

She opened her checkbook and wrote with a silver pen from her sequined clutch. As she wrote she scoffed. "If the old lady wants this, then fine." She peeled the check out of her checkbook and leaned over to watch Aiyanna's face. A draft of her perfume took over the table. "But after this?"

She clipped the check under a plate of fried fish.

"After this, you'll not get another dollar out of moi," she hissed, and slithered towards the door. After the door closed behind her, her money and her perfume lingered as if she was still there.

Chapter Eighteen

Waking up before everyone else did was how Ophelia avoided them.

At apartment 66, the bathroom light was spooky in the morning. There were two bulbs on either side of the mirror, and one was broken. Staring into the dimness she tried to see what it was in her color that made her math teacher call her "redbone" and always favor her with an encouraging smile. Or what it was that drew comments about her "good hair," which meant that it wasn't as tightly curled—as nappy—as the other students' who were all Black. She knew which of her features people found exotic, but she had no idea why that was so important. In the murky light she caught sight of her own little caramel nose, the stubborn way her hair curved close to her scalp but then straightened out the longer it got. She said out loud to her reflection, "There was a girl named Ophelia Blue Rivers, and this is her face."

These words were involuntary relics from her childhood by the river. She still hung her days around phrases like these. "Don't work, don't eat," or "Stop lollygagging," or "Don't mind big people's business." But whenever they appeared in her head she would immediately feel ashamed. Ophelia had become— like her Aunt Aiyanna—a Grandma Blue contrarian. The "Old Ways" became "superstition," her grandmother not talking became "abuse," Etsi became code for "country" and "backwards." But, more than anything, it meant "Cherokee." A thing Ophelia no longer wished to be. She wanted to fit in.

Riverwalk Elementary & Middle School was two blocks towards downtown. It sat on a hill and on a small plateau.

As she always did, she went to the library first. Ten minutes later, Durell came. He was wearing golf shorts and a golf shirt that was too tight and, of course, his extra-thick glasses that made his eyes appear to bulge out of his head. They sat face-to-face on two opposing benches and talked excitedly so that their knees touched occasionally. His carefulness made her laugh. But they kept their voices bubbling with a low simmer of excitement as they tumbled into the topics they reserved only for each other: marks, mean kids, and fantasy novels.

"Is *Lasher* better than the last Anne Rice novel you read?"

"Well, I like it better than the vampire ones because witches are smarter than vampires."

He shook his head as if this had never occurred to him. Then he began to rub his thumb and pointy finger together. She knew that this meant he was nervous but she had no idea why. They had been friends since Durell arrived at Riverwalk the year after her. They both enjoyed reading and homework, which made them odd. For Ophelia, applying herself to her studies was her natural habit after living with Grandma Blue, who expected complete commitment and punished anything but.

Durell's parents were both graduates of proud Southern

Black colleges. "You don't have to be the best," they had told him in unison, "but you do have to be better than the others." This Durell understood was the exact wording his parents had agreed upon—to motivate but not pressure him. Excellence was their expectation. A destiny decided. And they assumed that their scion would one day soon outgrow his timidness, his sensitivity, his shrinking bookishness.

"You're right," he decided in answer to her question. "Witches are better than vampires. Witches know spells and chants and runes and how to tame familiars. Vampires are basically just hungry all the time." It was a sensible Durell answer, but his fingers still rubbed together nervously. Without waiting he added, "Will you have lunch with me?"

Both stopped what they were doing and stared at each other for a moment. His fingers rubbed together even faster. To ask to have lunch together was to ask someone to go on a date, which was to ask someone to be your girlfriend. When she had heard girls giggle about boys, she thought they were silly, but she always listened. Boyfriends were for other girls; Ophelia liked books.

"I mean, it's okay if you don't want to . . ."

"Yes. I want to." Ophelia was surprised to hear herself answer with so much certainty.

"Really?" Durell lit up.

"Yes," she reassured herself more than him. "Yes, I want to . . ."

The two cackled their sudden euphoria. Harsh and loud. Bulging pupils. All teeth. Then they settled down before the librarian could come to shush them.

Faintly, something inside of Ophelia wanted to glow. It began in her belly and beamed up through her chest and into her face and she started to smile until her cheeks felt like flashlights. Until they hurt from smiling. It was a grin she did not know that she was waiting for.

Durell looked at her, fixed his glasses with a knuckle, and grinned back. Ophelia reached over, gently lined his glasses up for him, then placed her hand in his. Him shy, her hopeful, their palms ran hot one inside the other.

"Is that your boyfriend, Cake Face?" said a voice from behind them. They turned to find Tejah, who stuck her tongue out at them. "Did I st-st-stutter? Is that your boyfriend, Pocahontas?"

Tejah looked perfect and Ophelia hated it. She smelled like cherry lollipops and wore a checkered miniskirt. Brown sugar skin. Pink eyelash glitter playing against her complexion. Mocha eyes that always seemed to be putting the world in its place. Ophelia wished her eyes weren't so pretty—it would've made it easier to fight back when she picked on Ophelia. But there was a part of Ophelia that still wished they could be friends. That day, Tejah's hair was in a high black ponytail with two strands that fell and framed her face. Her rose-pink T-shirt read: THAT'S THE WAY LOVE GOES.

"Pocahontas is not my name, Tejah."

"Oh? You stop claiming that you're a Black Indian?"

"That's who I am."

"You can't be both. Stupid. That's two totally different things."

Tejah looked Durell up and down and made a smoochy face. "So you two nerds gonna make some nerd babies?"

Ophelia's conflicted feelings for Tejah matched Tejah's own for her. She was obsessed. Perhaps Tejah thought she was pretty enough to be her rival. Why else did she spend so much time trying to tear her down?

"What will you name your nerd baby? 'Humperdinck'?"

Ophelia loaded her voice with sarcasm. "I like your shirt, Tejah, too bad Janet is played out."

This made Tejah decide that Durell was the weak link. "Come on, Poindexter, what will you and your girlfriend name it?"

"She's not my girlfriend!"

"Then why you over here holding hands?"

"We're just friends, okay?"

He got up, hyperventilating.

"Leave him alone, Tejah. Why can't you just mind your business?"

"Nerd Regulation is my business."

Tejah could taste the blood in the water.

"Durell?"

Ophelia reached for his hand, but Durell pulled away and rushed towards the door. Briefly, he blinked apologies at Ophelia. And then he escaped.

Tejah put on a satisfied grin.

"Sorry, Pocahontas, looks like you're still a loser."

Ophelia wasn't mad at Durell. They both knew that he was a coward. Tejah was the problem. Tejah had mocked her since her first week at Riverwalk School. If it wasn't her hair, her bad makeup, her pimpled skin, or being good at her schoolwork, she would find something. Ophelia had gotten used to the abuse and knew that she could take it. But that day was different. Tejah had stepped all over something that mattered. Almost as soon as it was born she desecrated it. It was a fragile thing: the sliver of hope that she could be special to someone.

On her walk home Ophelia sensed a heaviness collecting in her belly where the light previously was. It felt impervious. She dragged it down the street and hefted it up the stairs and pulled it along the gray hallway. That weight became the only thing she was aware of. It burrowed into her womb. It howled in her bones. By the time she arrived at the door of apartment 66, Ophelia had decided that she was done being bullied.

And she would start by teaching Tejah a lesson.

Chapter Nineteen

Quite early the next Sunday morning, Lucy knocked on the door of apartment 66. As with everything she did, the knock was measured and precise. "Are you ready, Sister Ophelia? We need to hurry; service is starting."

Lucy's hair was pinned in a perfect bun and beamed with a Vaseline halo. She wore a peach-colored dress that was bright enough to be fluorescent. There was a tremor inside Ophelia when she saw how Lucy looked. If she was a doll before, just then she looked like a doll freshly unwrapped and smelling of new plastic. Ophelia's brain said, *Is this what church did to you? It made you clean and shiny?* She felt like a ten-watt bulb next to Lucy's one hundred watts of holiness.

"I'm ready, Sister Lucy," Ophelia answered. Lucy purred like a satisfied cat as she experienced a throb of hope that her new mini-me was going to be a fast learner.

As they started out from apartment 66, Lucy's tiny, needly voice was full of instructions. "You must call everyone 'brother' or 'sister,' depending on if they are a boy or a girl. Except if they are a deacon. You'll know the deacons because they are older men and they wear black suits and red ties."

"Umm, Lucy," Ophelia dared to interrupt, "do all deacons everywhere wear black suits and red ties?"

"How would I know? At Ebenezer, they do." Lucy squished her mouth together and raised her brows high at Ophelia as if to say, *Pay attention and stop interrupting*, then she continued, "Because you're a heathen, you'll need to follow me when they ask us to turn to a Bible verse or hymn. There's a lot of them, but you will learn eventually."

"Why doesn't Miss Destiny come to church?"

Lucy gave her that look again and took a sharp breath in before she answered. "Because she is a devil worshipper and is going to hell. And she likes it when I'm not there. Ebenezer is my real family, my church family, and one day it can be yours too. If you listen."

They walked down Acacia Avenue, which was wide and lined with trees of the same name. Its houses were close enough to not feel far, but far enough to be back from the road. There were Dodge Caravans and Ford pickups, and every now and then Ophelia saw a Jeep Cherokee. She hated those. *How could they call their car "Cherokee"? They just stole our name.* Only when Ophelia heard her people insulted would she claim kinship. Then some sleeping pride awakened. Then—if only in her head—it became "our name."

Curious about what to expect, Ophelia asked Lucy, "Is God the Father anything like our Cherokee Great Spirit?"

"Blasphemy," hissed Lucy. "Please don't say things like that at church."

"But it's everywhere, all the time, and could do anything. That sounds a lot like God the Father, doesn't it?"

Lucy stopped and held Ophelia by the shoulders so she would hear her clearly. "That's devil worship. All of that is heathen nonsense. Don't ever say that again."

They walked in silence for a block until Ophelia asked, "What am I allowed to say, then?"

Lucy was unequivocal. "Nothing. Don't speak unless I do first. Don't bring any attention to yourself. Understand?"

So bossy, Ophelia thought. But she tucked this away and answered meekly, "Okay."

It was early summer, and a strong breeze came blowing up the hill at Good Shepherd Way, and with the breeze came the lights. Bright lights draped across the sky, shimmering. They sprayed up-up-up into a kaleidoscope, as if the sky was a canvas painted in shimmering colors. They trembled in the trees with the wind. A tall curtain of radiance. When Ophelia looked over, slack-jawed at Lucy, she only smiled. *Was she seeing it too? Was this what Jehovah looked like?*

"Hallelujah," Lucy exhaled. "It's really pretty, isn't it?"

"They're the prettiest colors I've ever seen!"

Lucy looked at her as if she was a dum-dum.

"What colors? I mean the music."

Ophelia realized that Lucy wasn't seeing the colors; she was hearing the sounds that caused the colors. It had been so long since her senses got mixed up that she had forgotten that other people didn't see sounds too.

Ebenezer Baptist Church was shaking the trees. There was a stomping of feet on the floorboards, a drum that rang and boomed, a bass guitar that tumbled down the scale, a voice that shook the branches. Down the hill, the doors and windows of the tabernacle were flung open, and many throats lifted up towards the heavens in one enormous voice. That voice weighed heavy on the air. Both mournful and yet overflowing with jubilation. Both sorrowful and sweet. That voice was the whole choir, the whole congregation singing, and it covered Ophelia's horizon with miraculous light.

Lucy started walking faster. Android-style fast, but still precise. Ophelia could feel her tightening up in anticipation of what was to come. There was a mighty tide coming. There was a thunderous wave headed for her shores, tall as creation, wide as eternity, and its name was Ebenezer Baptist Church.

They floated down the hill of Good Shepherd Way, to the tabernacle, right up the stairs, and into the sanctuary. Every pew was stuffed, every tongue was raised. An elevated altar, with bright red carpet and tall-backed chairs, was thick with deacons. Black suits and bloodred ties. Grand arches of stained glass let in the light and let out their music. Sunlight streaked in from on high. The smell of perfume, cologne, lotion, baby oil, and body sweat. Every kind of euphoria. So many ways to dance for Jesus: the body jerk, the happy feet, the stomp and bounce, the hair flip, the turn-turn-turn, the chasing down a bus, the wave yourself like a handkerchief. The spirit moved the worshippers into joyful contortions. Their hearts raised, calling out, eyes towards the heavens, begging salvation, singing hallelujah, hosanna in the highest, testify, testify, testify.

Ophelia floated to the front. She soared. She levitated. She arrived at the pulpit where Pastor Ronelle Hamilton in his stark-white robes preached in call-and-response with the congregation.

"The scripture says, thou shalt have—praise God—thou shalt have . . ."

WELL.

" . . . no other gods before me."

AMEN.

"No boyfriend. No girlfriend . . ."

PREACH.

"No father. No mother."

HAVE MERCY JESUS.

"No boss. No job. No paycheck."

HALLELUJAH.

"No house. No car."

WELL.

"NOOOOOOOO!"

He shrieked so high that his voice distorted, bleeding its last strength.

"NO GODS BEFORE ME."

Ophelia climbed the steps towards Pastor Ronelle Hamilton, who looked down on her, and the whites of his eyes caught fire. "Oh hallelujah! Oh glory hallelujah! Come unto me, young lady." He beamed. "Suffer the little children."

He spread his arms wide into an embrace big enough to hold all of glory.

"You see? The spirit is talking to us right now. Unless you become as little children, as this helpless babe right here, ye shall not enter the kingdom of heaven. Oh glory!"

LAAAAAAAAAAAAAAAAAWD!

Pastor Hamilton bawled some unpronounceable ecstasy. Ophelia closed her eyes and hugged his leg. She embraced the light of his robes. It felt as though she had arrived at some place she did not know that she was traveling to. Her spirit was sanctified by the unblemished white of his gown. And she became that whiteness. It incinerated her longings, her fear, her doubt. The pastor cried, "Oh glory to God. A miracle is happening this morning!"

Lucy watched in horror as a weeping Ophelia became the center of a spectacle.

Chapter Twenty

After the service that Sunday, Lucy was consumed with embarrassment at what Ophelia had done. "This is exactly what I told you not to do," she scolded outside the chapel. Ophelia's tears had dried, but her heart was still pounding from the experience. Lucy's chastising made her think, *I've ruined everything.*

But two awestruck ushers changed their mood. They recognized Ophelia and said, "God bless you, little sister." This was followed by an elderly woman in a great satin hat who also recognized her from the pulpit. She told her, "So young, such spirit. I'll be praying for you."

Lucy's embarrassment shifted into amazement.

"You're famous."

The wonder in how she said it made Ophelia realize that Lucy didn't know everything about Ebenezer Baptist Church.

By the time the youth pastor enthusiastically shook Ophelia's hand and implored her, "Come to Young Saints this week. Ebenezer needs your testimony!" Lucy had started to downplay Ophelia's budding celebrity. "They're just happy you've turned from your heathen ways."

They were walking to the dining room. It was in the basement with a gray linoleum floor. The congregation piled into this room after the service. Milling about, they talked and hugged and laughed and did what they called "fellowship with the saints." Everyone that was part of the church was a "saint," and Ophelia didn't know what fellowship was, but she knew by how they talked about it that it was important.

Despite the positive reaction to Ophelia being blessed in front of the whole church, Lucy reasserted her dominance by reminding Ophelia of her golden rule, "Don't say anything unless someone says it to you first."

"Really?"

"Yes, really. We want to be the best church sisters and never offend anyone. That way they will always welcome us."

"But they all seem so friendly."

"You got lucky that your little stunt didn't end in disaster. Don't gloat. Count your blessings and follow my lead."

Ophelia could see that Lucy was a little jealous, but she didn't mind. Her luck at having found such a marvelous place and the service had filled her with a euphoric glow.

"Blessed Sunday, ladies," said a friendly pair of women.

"Blessed Sunday, Sister Jenkins," said Lucy, and smiled her holy smile, which to Ophelia seemed very controlled, as if she had spent a long time in the mirror practicing it. The women continued past them. As she squeezed Ophelia's hand, she whispered, "See? Whatever I say, you say."

Ophelia enjoyed how welcoming everyone was.

"Well, aren't you two as cute as peaches?" said a woman in a round hat laced with pearls. Lucy smiled and curtsied. Ophelia tried to do the same but could only manage an uncoordinated stumble. She felt her face flush, but the woman gushed, "So precious. God bless you, little angels."

"God bless you," they said in unison, and Lucy added, "Sister Leteisha."

The tables of food at the back of the room were where they were headed. They were laden with fried chicken, collard greens, candied yams, peach cobbler, macaroni pie, and many more dishes Ophelia could not identify. Her mouth got sloppy wet, her little bell-pepper nose started to twitch, and her eyes started to swivel from this plate to that. As they filled their plates and found a table to sit at, Lucy fielded Ophelia's excited questions.

"Lucy! How do you know so many people?"

"I know everyone in my church family."

"But how? There are so many!"

"I'll teach you. First, you have to volunteer."

"Volunteer?"

"Yes, volunteer to help at church events. They always need help. So we attend the ones that are open invitations, and we volunteer at the ones that aren't. And then you can see everyone all the time."

"Every Sunday?"

"Don't be silly, Ophelia. It's not just Sunday. There's Monday Bible study, Wednesday prayer meeting, Friday Young Saints youth meeting, Saturday choir practice. Some need volunteers to help hand out hymnals, move chairs, carry messages. I volunteer for everything."

"Can I volunteer too?"

"Of course. This is your family now, Ophelia."

"Family" was a word Ophelia had learned to appreciate since coming to Stone River. It always made her ears perk up. She noticed that folks said it so casually, as if it was like breathing: *My family is doing this; my family is going there.* Or often they would say something mean but with love: *I hate my family; my family is so weird; he family, but I don't like him.* What did she have? A grandma she was ashamed of. A drunken auntie who wasn't interested in raising her. Another auntie who had no interest in her. A dad she didn't know. A dead mother. People who never spoke to each other. Never visited. Being in places like Ebenezer Baptist Church, where families arrived and sat together, made her long for something more than what she had.

Lucy had planted a new idea. The idea that all the benefits of a "real" family could be hers. That word "family" pealed inside her like a giant bell had been struck. It pulsed out from her core and made her look longingly at the joyful Black faces that smiled and grinned and chattered and hugged and loved each other over paper plates piled with scrumptious food.

"Family," she whispered Lucy's refrain to herself. "This is my new family."

At Wednesday prayer meeting, she said her first prayer. The sister leading the prayer asked everyone to close their eyes, and the choir director sang "Amazing Grace" in the background. The leader called for everyone to get into groups. In those groups, they stood in a circle and held hands as people prayed to Jesus.

This wasn't like Cherokee prayers, which were outside, by the river, and you always burned tobacco and called on the Great Spirit. *What would Grandma Blue think of this?* Ophelia quickly pushed the thought back down. It all seemed naïve and simple compared to Ebenezer's massive chapel, hundreds of worshippers, Bible, hymnals, and "fellowship." Ophelia felt ashamed that she once believed in the Great Spirit. Lucy had—in the days since Sunday service—reinforced this shame with single-word sermons about Cherokees: "heathens"; "pagans"; "heretics." So at the prayer meeting, Ophelia did her best to not think about the "prayers" she grew up saying.

She listened to the voices of the petitioners. They rose up loud, trembling and full of sadness. Some of the saints "lifted up" other people who were sick, or in trouble, or needed money; others just wanted to "praise you, Lord." Lucy never told her what to do. All she said was for Ophelia to shut her eyes when the saints prayed. "But how will you know when it's your turn?" she tried to ask, but Lucy shushed her.

When the lady next to her had finished her prayer, she needed to blow her nose because she had started to sob. It was then that Ophelia said her first prayer.

"Heavenly Father," she started, because that's how everyone else started, and Lucy pinched her side and squeezed. It hurt terribly, but Ophelia knew that everyone was listening. She didn't know she wasn't supposed to pray. She had to keep going. Her blood started to thump in her ear, and a little dab of perspiration beaded on her forehead.

"Heavenly Father," she said again, trying to mimic what others had said. "I want to lift up my Grandma Blue, who is all alone and a heathen and doesn't like people."

Lucy's pinch dug deeper, and she decided that that was enough.

"Amen."

Lucy let go of her, but it felt like she still held on, pinching her side.

After the prayer meeting, one of the church ladies, Sister Amelia, came up to them. Ophelia thought she was in trouble for saying her prayer. Sister Amelia said, "What is your name, little girl?"

"Ophelia."

"Don't be nervous, I won't bite."

"And this is my friend Lucy."

She had broken Lucy's cardinal rule, say only what's said to you, but she could see that Lucy liked that a church sister was speaking to them. She gave Sister Amelia her practiced holy smile and curtsy.

"That was a very touching prayer you did Ophelia, about your grandmother."

"Thank you."

"I have a grandmother that's just like that too—old, alone, and not too friendly. How often do you see her?"

"I haven't seen her since she visited a year ago."

"You must miss her, don't you?"

"Sometimes. But she doesn't believe in God."

"Awww . . . young sister, that's alright. If you pray for her like you did today, one day she will surely believe. It moved me to hear a young sister so concerned for her elder folks. I'll watch for you in Sunday school."

On their way home, Lucy kept up a steady stream of lectures on how to behave at church to avoid embarrassment. Listening intently, Ophelia decided that—despite being a heretic—she would pray every day to Jesus to help her to be loved by her new family.

Chapter Twenty-One

Two months later, on the last day of sixth grade, Ophelia prayed, "Heavenly Father, please forgive me for what I'm about to do. I know that pride cometh before the fall, but please don't let me fall today. I promise that, starting tomorrow, I'll love everyone, no matter how mean they are to me. Amen."

Although church made Ophelia pray for forgiveness for hating Tejah, it did not stop her from wanting revenge. Her resentment for Tejah had already solidified into calculations served cold.

Everything had to be just right. The night before, she had waited until apartment 66 was deathly still to make them. The popsicles were easy, but the creamsicles were her special recipe: she mixed the water and Jello powder, which she'd whipped up for a minute before adding orange juice and three scoops of vanilla ice cream. It was already midnight, but she didn't want them to overfreeze and lose all their flavor in the first few bites. Her creamsicles had to be immediately scrumptious. To this mix she added zests of oranges and lime, vanilla extract, and after adding her final touches, she poured them into the popsicle molds and went to bed, certain that they would be as perfect as Tejah's mascara.

Ophelia left early with Auntie Aiyanna's cooler bag. It was blue and red with white streaks, and it was filled with creamsicles she had made for her classmates. Preening with satisfaction as she always did when she served something delicious, Ophelia with treats was, for one day, the most popular girl in her class. She had done it last summer on the last day of school because she'd hoped that the kids in her class would call her to hang out. But this year she didn't need to impress anyone. This made the creamsicles perfect for what she had in mind.

On the walk to school, the tacky cooler bag unbalanced her steps, while the thrill of what she had planned unbalanced her head.

What would Jesus do? she asked herself on her walk. Would he turn the other cheek? Would he kick the peddlers from the temple? The stories of Jesus she had heard at Ebenezer were contradictory sometimes. She hoped that Jesus would forgive her.

Ophelia daydreamed about being in that class and being the popular girl who had grown breasts early, who boys fought to sit next to, who seemed unconcerned with anything but being the center of things. She daydreamed about being Tejah. "Idolatry" is what Lucy had called this. Raising the ways of man above those of God. Ophelia prayed that she would overcome this sin one day.

Durell met her by the door of Riverwalk as he always did.

"Did you bring it?"

"What you think I got this cooler for?"

He tried to help her carry it, but she wouldn't let him.

"I got it," she said, trying to sound normal. They had to take it to the fridge in the cooking room. Durell sat with her at lunch every day now. They had decided that they could eat together and talk about books, and they didn't have to be in love.

Besides, Durell's mom and dad were atheists, and Sister Edith said that atheists were "proud idolaters," which meant that they worshipped idols. So he couldn't be her boyfriend anyways.

"What flavors did you make?"

"I made cherry Kool-Aid popsicles for us and orange cream-sicles."

"Yummy! Who are the creamsicles for?"

"Oh, they're for everyone else."

Ophelia gripped the straps of the cooler bag and tried to smile as if everything was normal.

"Did you have time to read the new Vampire Chronicles?"

"Sister Edith says that vampires are from the devil and that I shouldn't be reading those kinds of books."

This disappointed him. They had argued about church the last time she'd brought it up, because his parents had told him that Black people needed to stop letting preachers talk them into being slaves again. They said that church was the same as doing drugs: an escape from real life. After that, Durell and Ophelia didn't talk about God. It made her feel sad, because she wanted him to be saved, but Pastor Hamilton said that when the rapture came, a lot of loved ones would be left behind.

"You know, C. S. Lewis isn't so bad . . ."

C. S. Lewis was a Christian, and she figured if she could get him to read it for the magic wardrobe that led to Narnia, maybe he would see that his mom and dad were wrong.

"Hey," said Durell, puzzled, "why aren't we going this way? We need to take the cooler to the fridge, right?"

"Oh," Ophelia responded blithely, "I just want to see who's around."

Still puzzled, Durell kept following.

"Shouldn't we make sure the popsicles and creamsicles don't melt?"

When they turned the corner, Tejah's crew stood in a circle around her while she showed them how to Crip Walk. Her hair was all teased out and her nails were long with sparkles. Multicolor gloss on her lips. As she talked, she clasped her hands together in that way that made her nails click. Her whole crew cracked up. Although they acted differently when Tejah was around, Ophelia had quietly gotten her crew to tolerate her. She'd helped Shauna with her homework and gotten a tampon for Kelly the day she got her period and bled on her mini shorts. But still, when Tejah was around, Shauna and Kelly pretended to hate her too.

Upon seeing them, Durell and Ophelia stopped as if paralyzed; it was too late to turn around. There was no way to avoid Tejah; she was in their way. It was Tejah, so her eyes were as pretty as sunflowers, but her face was never sunny.

"What's this? Nerdy lovers on a mission? What you got there?"

Ophelia pretended to protect the cooler bag full of treats, and Tejah took the bait: she snatched the bag off O's shoulder for the simple reason that she knew Ophelia didn't want her to have it. Durell grabbed a corner of the strap, and for a few seconds there was a tug-of-war.

"Let go, Steve Urkel."

"It's not yours!" Durell was trying to impress Ophelia.

"Oooo, you wanna fight today, huh?"

This is exactly what Ophelia had expected would happen. Tejah would take the treats she had stayed up until midnight to make. Once again, she would try to take something important from her. This is why she had made two batches.

"Let her have it, Durell." She touched his arm. "It's alright."

"Exactly," Tejah mocked in a nerdy voice. "Let me have it, Durell."

Durell let go of the cooler. Ophelia watched as Tejah unzipped it. Tejah's eyes widened when she saw the creamsicles at the top, and immediately—because she had to show who was boss—took a creamsicle out and started slurping it. Mock moans of pleasure came from her mouth as she stared Ophelia down, daring her to do something. When Ophelia did nothing, she handed two each to Shauna and Kelly.

"And one for you, and one for you, and another one for me . . . double up, baybee!"

She spared no extravagance as she handed out Ophelia's treats. Ophelia stood, hands on hips, and tried her best to pretend as though this was a tragedy. Inside her, that stone in her stomach stayed steady. The calculating wolf emanated calm. Ophelia watched, greedy to lap up every sip of Tejah's face. Tejah watched, hungry to sample the suffering on Ophelia's face. This stare-down continued. And the more Ophelia was unmoved, the more extravagant Tejah's arms were, the more she faked orgasmic groans as she and her girls double fisted the creamsicles.

Eat up, you greedy brats.

Ophelia felt foolish for ever wanting to be one of them, and knowing that there was no going back made her feel in control. *Eat up, you greedy bitches*, she thought. Shauna, Kelly, and Tejah obliged.

". . . yuuumm . . ."

". . . these are so gooood . . ."

". . . so delicious!"

After about a minute, the dull red in the center of the treats was starting to show—Ophelia's secret ingredient.

All at once, Tejah, Shauna, and Kelly began to gag and cough and yak and hack as if trying to cough up their insides. As though they had swallowed gunpowder and needed to get it out. Kaevon had played this trick on Ophelia before: he had poured Auntie Aiyanna's hot sauce—Skee's Hell-On-Wheels—into the popsicles as a prank. But now the joke was on Tejah.

Shauna clutched her belly and keeled over and retched. Kelly knocked her forehead into a locker in an attempt to shut out the shock. Scraping at her tongue, she tried to spit the taste out of her mouth. A long thread of drool trailed from her lips, ran down the face of the locker, and pooled on the floor. Tejah screamed, grabbed her throat awkwardly, and started to run. She blasted right past Ophelia and Durell, towards the water fountain up the hall. Ophelia's creamsicles lay on the ground, abandoned and melting, the cooler bag ditched on the hallway floor.

Satisfaction and horror fought for Ophelia's face. A dry cackle won.

Thank you, Kaevon, she said to herself. *They deserved this.* But another glance at how contorted with pain the girls were, made her wonder if she had gone too far.

"Lord Jesus, I'm sorry . . ." she whispered.

A hand grabbed hers. It was Durell's, and he didn't hide the grin on his face either, wide enough to match Ophelia's now. "Let's get out of here!" He pulled her arm. After she'd picked up Auntie Aiyanna's cooler, they ran and ran and ran.

Frantically she played back Tejah's retching face—so twisted, so uncomposed, so hideous—and it made her holler with delight.

For those few minutes, she had stolen the thing her bully most valued: her beauty. She had made Tejah ugly.

When they had stopped running, braying like donkeys, Ophelia took a breath, wrapped her forearms across her belly and held that firm, implacable stone. *So, this is what power feels like.*

Chapter Twenty-Two

Grandma Blue hated Stone River.

All that pickup truck carbon monoxide, shopping mall fluo-rescence, plaques to the gallant South, mint julep dresses, that rusty factory that squatted on the river, Jackson Street dive bars, Whyte Street strip malls, Charleston Heights where she was too poor to go, Bedford Terrace where she wasn't poor enough to be. She recalled Hampton University where she once worked mopping the classrooms at the culinary school that she could never attend. There she had dragged her mop and bucket, sullen as a child at a carnival full of cotton candy she could never taste. Grandma Blue despised it all and visited only in an emergency. Her granddaughter becoming a Bible-carrying Christian was one such emergency.

As was her style, she gave her middle child the same-day no-tice of her arrival. She wanted her to clean up, but not enough to hide how she normally lived. Once, she had arrived with no notice to find her daughter reeking of tequila and marijuana at ten a.m. This way, Aiyanna could tidy up, but not enough to hide the state of her life.

When Grandma Blue arrived in a plain brown dress and beaded porcupine quill earrings, the black holes of her eyes picked Aiyanna apart. In a purple and teal tracksuit, her hair arranged in a pile of big round curls—crisp as biscuits—she sat. She couldn't resist the urge to chew her nails. Grandma Blue recognized this bad habit from her youth but did not comment—she had bigger fish to fry. Aiyanna was always a disappointment. But at least she was consistent. Her mother pictured her in Stone River talking out of the side of her mouth the things she would only say to Shango: *That lady's abusive . . .* and *she don't run me . . .* But wherever Grandma Blue arrived, Etsi arrived with her, and her mother enjoyed bringing her this dose of "remember where you come from."

The old woman sat at the table—in the same chair she had sat in on her last visit, the year before—and spoke in her gruff way, "You've made off like a bandit since Ophelia's been here, haven't you?" Aiyanna did not mistake this for a question. "And all I asked from you—for all that money—is that you take care of that child."

Grandma Blue paused to put her full scorn on her secondborn.

"And now this?"

"I do take care of her. I feed her. She has a roof over her head—"

"That we pay for. Between the money the boys' father sends you and what your brother, sister, and I give you, you don't even have to get out of bed before noon, do you?"

"I get out of bed." With futility, Aiyanna tried to generate some outrage. "I clean and I cook for her."

Her mother raised her brows skeptically.

125

The old woman gave her a look of disappointment mingled with a lack of surprise. "Hmpff . . ." she said. Which meant *what else did I expect from you?*

This was the cheat sheet of their relationship. Instantly she time traveled and remembered scolding Aiyanna with that look for almost burning down the cabin when she tried to bake a cake, for stealing ten dollars for Jolly Ranchers and soda, for getting caught with her panties around her ankles in a circle of boys behind the school. She recalled her daughter's excuses as well: *The cake was for Shango's birthday . . . I shared the candy with everyone . . . It was only two boys . . .* Facts, explanations, and her intentions never mattered. Most of their conversations ended here, not with anger but with that galled look Aiyanna loathed most. That look that excluded all respect. Disappointed pity. Eagerly, she tried to change the subject.

"What's going on with the river?"

Grandma Blue raised her brow to say, *I see what you're doing.* Aiyanna watched her mother with a look of genuine concern.

"I've never seen you look so tired, Ma."

"If you're so worried about how I look, try visiting sometime."

Aiyanna seemed uncomfortable with Grandma Blue's vulnerability.

"Child, that Beauregard is an evil man." For a second her mother shook her head vehemently as if leaning in to smash Jack's headlights with her stick.

"But I thought we won the lawsuit."

"Won? It's just beginning. It took us this long to negotiate a measly five thousand dollars per house per acre of riverfront. We voted to negotiate to avoid a trial. But it was all games to wear us down. Last week they said, 'Sign and take this settlement or you'll never live to see that judgment money.' His little son Christopher will have grandchildren before we see that money."

"But isn't that illegal?"

"Illegal? You got big but you didn't get sense. Who do you think makes the laws?"

Into this awkwardness came unsuspecting Ophelia. Backpack slung, singing "Go Tell It on the Mountain." She entered oblivious to the ambush waiting at the dining room table. Upon seeing her grandmother a cold douse of terror trickled down her spine. She was—suddenly—alert as a soldier in enemy territory.

Noticing her, Grandma Blue smoothed her dress and got straight to her point.

"So, you want to pray to the dead white man on the cross?"

"Grandma Blue, I can explain—"

"You don't have to explain yourself to me. I know what this town does to my children."

She rolled her eyes at Aiyanna, who squirmed. Ophelia scrambled to remember the justification she had rehearsed for this moment, which she knew would come. "But Grandma Blue, God is just like the Great Spirit—"

"Unetlanvhi . . ."

Ophelia nodded recognition of the name. She assumed an attentive posture as though she had been teleported back to the cabin by the river to learn yet another lesson.

"Unetlanvhi. You remember this name?"

"Yes, Grandma Blue."

"You don't have to explain yourself to me, little crab. You can pray to whichever god you want. Just know this, the people who murdered and enslaved your people served that same blue-eyed Jesus. Understand?"

Grandma Blue had unleashed the chilly calm of her calculating wolf on Ophelia. The girl drove the palms of her hands into the chair and rocked her butt from side to side anxiously. The bottomless caverns of her grandmother's eyes rested their judgment on her. Grandma Blue remembered that you had to pay attention to this one's tendency to daydream. It seemed to her that Ophelia was watching her mouth as if her words were visible. The girl's eyes trailed up slowly to the roof as if she was watching a light show. There she was, thought Grandma Blue. *She's grown, but that head of hers is still full of fancies.*

"Ophelia," she tried to bring her back down to earth, "you and me are connected, by blood and by name, to the first Ophelia Blue Rivers. The first Black baby born free in Etsi. Maybe in the whole of South Carolina. Maybe in the whole of Dixie . . ." She paused, filled her lungs, and let her shoulder sag. "That's no easy seat to sit in."

Ophelia stopped the nervous side to side of her butt. Her breath got shallow and fierce. Her eyes still traced a path upwards from Grandma Blue's lips.

"Mind the river. You hear me? Mind it good."

Ophelia all at once snapped to attention.

"What about me?"

"What?"

"Who minds me while I'm minding the river?"

"Child, lower your tone."

"No."

"No?"

"No." Repeating it with more steel.

"You've lost your mind too, huh?"

"I'm not crazy. I just don't want your name or your god or

any of this dead-people noise in my head." She stood up. Double fisted. Eyes fierce. "I just want to be normal. An everyday girl with a real family," she shrieked. "Why can't I just have that?!"

The frigid beast inside Grandma Blue did not stir. It calmly accepted the child's onslaught. Aiyanna's mouth caught flies.

"It's all your fault." Ophelia bared her teeth and stepped aggressively towards her grandmother. "Etsi, my stupid childhood, you!" She stuck a thumb out at the old woman. "My drunk auntie I live with, the other aunt who won't even talk to me, being Cherokee or not being Cherokee, or whatever I am. It's. All. Your. Fault."

Blindsided by the acid in her granddaughter's words, Grandma Blue observed the child's savage wolf awakened. Ophelia's nose ran. Her pupils constricted into needles. Her voice shredded like shattering glass.

"I look weird. I'm a nerd. Nobody likes me. My skin's too dark, then it's not dark enough. My hair is too curly, then it's too straight. You did this!"

Grandma Blue was struck mute. The sting of the child's words and the toll of the day had made her bones heavy. Ophelia, power drunk, showed no mercy. "I'll go to church if I want to. Ebenezer Baptist is the only place I feel like myself. They're my real family."

This bit the deepest.

Grandma Blue could recall the day Shango had dropped off the wet, feeble baby. While lost in a pit of mourning for Chief and for Etsi's future, her son had dropped the baby off without a name or a diaper or a crib and hopped right back into his car. *What heartless children I've raised*, she reflected. And that night a dream was born. That night she saw her own salvation. Unetlanvhi had answered her prayers. She had failed with her children, but this baby was blood of her blood. This was the hope not just of her family, but of Etsi, a new generation brought up right—in the Old Ways.

Ophelia's savage wolf bit the heart right out of the old lady's dream.

Chapter Twenty-Three

Grandma Blue returned to the cabin by the river to a relentless night of worry.

That summer, the summer of 1998, the lawsuit of *Blue Rivers v. Beauregard Farms, Inc.* stretched into its fifth year. Grandma Blue had become the lead plaintiff on behalf of the complaint, and the entire village of Etsi opted into the suit. But that afternoon when she returned home to the cabin, the burden of lawyers, motions, and prospective settlements had been replaced by the rage of Ophelia.

"Prettiest flowers have the wickedest thorns," she repeated her father John's saying. Her granddaughter had stabbed her where it hurt the most: her shattered family. Despite her tireless trying, her family felt finished. Chief was almost twelve years dead, Shango had vanished, Aiyanna scorned her, and Belle despised her upbringing so thoroughly that she pretended to be from France. None ever came by or called. And now, her last hope—the grandchild she gave her own name to, whose backside she'd wiped since she was a tot—had turned her back on her. This bitter cup was hers in her old age.

"... the wickedest thorns ..."

Grandma Blue woke the next morning and wondered, *Why do these fools trust me with their lawsuit when I can't even keep my own house in order?* It had been comforting for her to think that if she couldn't save what she'd spent her life building, she could, at least, try to save Chief's dream. Saving Etsi was no match for her emptiness, but it was the best she could do. Ophelia's words blew that ruse apart. They both knew that she was just avoiding the ever-present absence that stirred in her chest.

She distracted herself by kneeling in her garden until late afternoon. The pink azaleas had bloomed early by the river. They blossomed like she'd not seen them since before she was a teen. Their ruddy freshness almost covered the rotten-egg smell of the water. When she closed her leathery eyelids she could see her daddy John there pulling weeds, but never the pink azaleas. "The mother in the river sent us these," he would say of the perfumed azaleas. "Don't ever disrespect what your mother gave you."

It was unlike her to brood. Or regret. Or look back. But the older she got the more the past, future, and now got ladled in together like batter in her head.

Late afternoon, as she was rocking in her chair on the deck, Jack Beauregard's lawyer—Buck Cronkite—paid her a visit. They had both gotten noticeably slower in their step since that meeting at Chief's where Jack Beauregard, his son, and Buck had tried to slip-talk their way out of the lawsuit. Grandma Blue was not amused. "Why you come here to disturb my peace?"

"Miss Rivers, thank you for seeing me."

His voice had a slow charm.

"Let me save you some time. I've got nothing to say to you."

"Well, as much as I love talking to Rip Smithers, I think two folks of our vintage can appreciate that the young are a bit hasty."

"So you've come here to see if you can buy me off?"

He chuckled. "Can I? It would save a lot of trouble."

Grandma Blue kept her frown.

Buck took the opportunity to sit down in the chair next to her. He tapped his cane on the floorboards and let his hand slide up the obsidian handle to the eagle perched on top. It was late afternoon, so there was still plenty of heat in the day. He offered her his flask, then, when she refused, he offered her a fake smile and took a sip himself.

"How can you do what you do? They poison poor people's water, then call you to protect them. How can you work for those people?"

"Your daddy worked for the Beauregards when we were kids, didn't he? Oh, don't deny it. I've pulled the farm's past records: John Blue Rivers. We paid him for those two fingers if I recall correctly: two hundred dollars."

Grandma Blue coiled up like a rattlesnake at the mention of her father. John was always there with her. Buck bringing him up felt as though he might be able to see him too. It unnerved her.

"That was a fair offer. Two hundred dollars in 1927?"

"You might have some papers with a name and some numbers, but you don't know my father."

"I didn't mean no offense. I just wanted to point out that he was a reasonable man. He didn't make a fuss. He took a fair offer."

His implications didn't take long to settle on her. She went back to rocking in her chair. "Jack Beauregard is offering Etsi five thousand dollars per acre on the riverfront to drop this whole thing. That's a fair offer."

Buck tapped the cane on the deck as he had been doing occasionally. He felt relaxed and sure. Grandma Blue's chair kept grinding back and forth but she locked him and his cane in her sights.

"First: don't mix John Blue Rivers' name up in your schemes. Shame on you! Next: you and me both know that money won't be enough to help people with anything. Their livelihoods? Feeding their families? I'm speaking against this 'fair deal.' As the lead plaintiff, I'm going to say we should stop this negotiation you've dragged on for years. We'll see Jack Beauregard in court."

The cane didn't tap. All chair rocking ceased.

"Is this about your father's fingers? Because we could come to a separate arrangement for that—"

"This is about respect. Our history is your history, but nobody ever remembers our sacrifice. If we're your neighbors, as you keep saying, then make us an offer that shows us some respect."

Buck sighed and stood up. Grandma Blue didn't want him towering over her, so she stood up too. The breeze cut the failing heat, and the azaleas' fragrance rose up around them. He extended his well-manicured hand. She took it, although hers were still dirty with the garden's black soil.

"Been nice catching up with you," he said as if they were old school friends.

"Don't come back here."

Grandma Blue reflected that she and Buck were the same age. Born the same year, not ten miles apart. But, watching him walk back towards the road, she didn't feel one jot of solidarity with him. Right then, she wanted to smack his skull with that cane and hear him plead for mercy. *You smug water snake.* She felt that at last she had met her true enemy: not Jack Beauregard's money but the filthy hands it enabled.

Chapter Twenty-Four

In July of that year, that greedy boy who never tucked his shirt had eaten his belly full of the Wednesday prayer meeting meal. He licked his fingers clean and stared at the crumbs as if it was all the food he would ever eat for the rest of his life. He said to Ophelia, "Sister Marshala make the best cornbread gravy in the whole world, don't she?"

In her head Ophelia thought, *No, she don't! Sister Marshala leaves the heat on too high, and her cream evaporates and gets all thin. Cream needs to be creamy.*

What she was thinking must have showed up on her face because the greedy boy said, "You think you can do better, Ophelia?"

Ophelia was never a boaster: she only spoke of things she had seen herself or knew exactly how to do. And so, matter-of-factly, she prescribed the solution to the problem. "She just need to turn the stove down when she deglazes the pan."

Having not understood what Ophelia meant, he stared at her, unsure, and dabbed his wet fingers in the crumbs, savoring them one by one. That was the last of it—or so she thought.

The next week, after prayer meeting, Sister Marshala pulled

her collar. "Come with me," she said roughly. She was an old spinster who wore foundation that was too light for her face and a wig of wispy tangles that brushed down her cheeks in an unruly way. Her voice was high and condescending. But what made the children afraid of her were the three angry moles along her chin and jaw. They were too big to ignore, but if she caught you staring at them, she could tell your parents, who would spank you or worse: embarrass you in front of the church.

Not having parents to protect her, Ophelia dreaded Sister Marshala and her angry trinity of moles even more. Sister Marshala was part of the Senior Sisters, the group of wives and women who (not so) secretly ran Ebenezer. To have her furiously demand that Ophelia "come with me," set off an avalanche of ideas of what she might have done wrong. Each idea ended badly. Ophelia's armpits began to sweat with nerves. This was a disaster.

"After all we've done for you, you ungrateful wretch," Sister Marshala screeched, then fell silent. A flustered Ophelia followed her through the church halls as if to her execution. She led her towards the back corner of the church, down two flights of stairs, into the basement and the wide, fragrant kitchen.

There they discovered another three of the Senior Sisters preparing a meal. Ophelia scanned their unimpressed faces quickly then looked away. She noted Sister Jenkins, Sister Carter, and most terrifying of all, Sister Edith Hamilton, wife of Pastor Ronelle Hamilton—the leader of the Senior Sisters. A Mount Rushmore of Ebenezer Baptist Church women. Ophelia felt the uncomfortable deluge in her armpits soak through her blouse. Sister Marshala announced, "This is the one."

"One of those little no-family girls, isn't it?" remarked Sister Jenkins.

"So young and so ungrateful," added Sister Carter.

While avoiding their eyes, she spotted rows of plucked quail, diced vegetables, and stacks of cornbread. Countertops arrayed with ingredients and spices. Pans bubbled. Sister Marshala's tone was, as usual, needly and thin.

"This here young'un is apparently gifted by the Grace of God and would like to help us poor meddlers improve our cornbread gravy."

It was then that Ophelia realized what this was all about. She wanted to poke that messy boy in his untucked kidneys. The other sisters turned fully around and now they too were eyeing her like vermin that ran across their kitchen floor. Her trap set, she egged Ophelia on smugly, "Well, go on, show us how you do . . ."

Cornered, Ophelia didn't know what Sister Marshala was expecting, maybe for her to cry and hang her head and garble out some apology, but Ophelia wouldn't have said it if she couldn't do it. This was one of the first things Grandma Blue had taught her how to make. It wasn't difficult. But she saw the trap: if she made it and it was bad, then she'd be humiliated. If she made it and it was good, she would make an enemy out of Sister Marshala. What could she do?

"Pride cometh before the fall," Sister Marshala huffed as they watched the dilemma pass over Ophelia's face. Ophelia thought, *But I was right. Cream needs to be creamy.* She decided to show them what she could do. From somewhere she found the courage to look the Senior Sisters in the eye, took a deep breath, and got to work.

Fine and close, Ophelia chopped the carrots, onions, and celery. Knuckles out, hand where the handle meets the blade, rocking back and forth, just like Grandma Blue had taught her. Then she heated the pan and tossed in the vegetables with that satisfying sizzle. By the time she had finished this step, her sweaty pits had dried and her nerves gave way to the familiar rhythm of the kitchen. The whole vibe of the room shifted. She caught it when Sister Edith, in her grass-green apron, moved closer to get a better view. The lanky Sister Carter tilted her eyebrows up, impressed.

"Can I have some chicken stock, please?"

It appeared after a few cupboards were rattled. When the vegetables got some color, she poured in the chicken stock. This brought a gasp from somewhere. Ophelia guessed that they didn't know how to deglaze with chicken stock. When she poured in the cream, she eyed Sister Marshala. Those three moles looked ready to jump into the pan. She eyed her deliberately and turned down the heat as if to say, *Just like so.*

Ophelia broke up some cornbread, the oldest cornbread she could find, smushing it up in between her fingers, getting lost in the crumbs, as she always did—this was her favorite part. Then she mixed in the jus and larded the baking pan and set it to bake.

They watched her as if she were a biblical being who had just appeared in front of them and they couldn't decide if she was sent from God or Satan. A dazed quietude prevailed. Sister Marshala tapped her foot impatiently. Sister Carter stirred a whisk of batter. Sister Edith's mouth had a small turned-up smirk at the corner of one side. By the time the oven door shut, all they had were questions.

"Where did you learn all of this?" asked Sister Jenkins. "Chicken stock to deglaze, who taught you to do that?" asked Sister Carter, and her favorite question of the night, "Why did you turn down the heat under the cream like that? Was that important?" And with every question they asked, Sister Marshala shrunk in the room and her three angry moles grew bigger.

What really won them over was that Ophelia had the good sense not to gloat when she explained what she'd done. "It's not mine, Sisters, it's my Grandma Blue's recipe. She taught me how to make it since I was young."

"We all know about your unsaved pagan grandmother by the river; we didn't know that she could cook like this though."

Sister Edith Hamilton shook her head. "Worshipping birds and trees like godless heathens."

The Senior Sisters chuckled.

"She not godless; she just have different gods," she said meekly. Yet Ophelia could hear the verse the pastor had preached just a few months ago: "Thou shalt have no other gods before me." They all huffed, and Sister Edith clutched the cross around her neck tightly. Then she held Ophelia's face in her clammy hands and told her, "Young lady, there's only one God, and I'm thankful he revealed himself to us in you tonight."

"You're welcome down here in the kitchens anytime," said Sister Carter.

"Amen," Sister Jenkins agreed.

Even Sister Marshala managed to grudgingly whisper, "The Lord moves in mysterious ways." Glowing with pride, it occurred to Ophelia that perhaps not everything she had learned in Etsi was an abomination.

The following Wednesday Sister Edith, round and elegant, dressed in a skirt and jacket a demure shade of teal, met Ophelia at the church door. Her eyes sparkled with a kind of omniscience. She handed the young girl a neat light-brown shopping bag with the logo of a store on it. It said, "Buckhead Boutique." She had never heard of it.

When Ophelia got home she found in the gaudy wrapping two brand-new dresses in her size. One was red like the blood of Jesus, with a sharp collar and buttons on the short sleeves. The other was black with a high neck. Both were more beautiful than anything she had ever owned. She put them on, and she wept.

"Sister Edith gave you that?" Lucy asked with disbelief. "All because you cooked some gravy?" Lucy's face was a mash-up of envy and awe. Her holy robot act gave way to a look that said, *This should be happening to me, not you.* Ophelia held the black, high-necked one up to the light as if it were evidence of a miracle.

"I've never even heard of this happening before," said Lucy.

"Isn't it pretty?"

"It's . . . it's . . . it's the hand of the Lord." Lucy looked on in wonder.

Lucy's reactions were not lost on Ophelia. Lucy had wanted a mini-her. But, unlike her, the church family liked Ophelia instantly. This was why Lucy always reminded her of her faults. That she was born a heathen. That she did not know anything about Jesus. That her family was full of idolaters. If these things were true, Ophelia could be kept in her place. But her new status changed everything. Ophelia was no longer in Lucy's shadow. The tables had turned.

Chapter Twenty-Five

That Sunday morning, when—for the first time—Ophelia stepped into the church in her new clothes, she felt born again.

Her ears and eyes twinkled from the colors of that big ole voice—yes, THAT voice, the one that turned the sky into a light show—it had never stopped singing to her, but she knew better than to say, "I see music in a kaleidoscope of colors." Her grandmother's SMACK, when she told her that butterflies had made her fly, was still ringing in her ears. Did it mean she was crazy? What did "crazy" really mean? The saints in the Bible talked to angels, built boats in the desert, heard voices in burning bushes, had babies without sex. Were they crazy too? Or maybe, like the prophets, she was blessed by God. Maybe seeing sounds and hearing colors was a "gift of the spirit."

Her new dress was cracking. That first day she chose the high-collared one—modest is hottest, as the Senior Sisters usually said. From the looks of approval she got from the pews, she knew nothing would be the same.

Lucy couldn't hide her envy. She could not help but stare down Ophelia's new look, counting the ways her own outfit was better. They arrived together and took their regular seats towards the back. But as soon as they'd settled, an usher with a juicy smile tapped Ophelia. "God bless you, little sister, but Sister Edith asked for you to sit up front with the pastor's family"—and he nodded to acknowledge her ascension—"in the front pew."

And so, she spent the service right between Ruth and Jeremiah—the pastor's teenage daughter and son. They made room for her with their glowing angelic faces like those little cherubs on Italian buildings, except Blacker. Jeremiah whispered solemnly, "We're so happy to meet you," as if he hadn't seen her there for months and ignored her because she was poor. Ruth simply reached her satin-gloved hand over and squeezed hers discreetly. Ophelia was confounded. Her little head felt like it might burst like a dropped watermelon all over the pulpit. If she'd known that all it took to go from outcast to front pew was cornbread gravy, she'd have cooked the hell out of those pans a long time before that.

Since that day she levitated into Ebenezer Baptist Church and Pastor Hamilton had reached down his hand towards her and said, "Suffer the little children," he had become the center of her universe. And yet, they had never spoken. He had a stern face but kind eyes and wore a buzz cut with a goatee always. A slim but muscular man, from Fayetteville, North Carolina, who used to be a U.S. Army Captain. For this reason, they gave him the nickname "Army Ron," and called him "Track Meet," because he always walked with a purpose and never stopped to gossip. But any real pastor was judged by the quality of their preaching, and this is where Pastor Ronelle Hamilton shone, and why she waited eagerly for his message every Sunday, because it transported her back to that first Sunday—her anointing.

Pastor Hamilton was mid-sermon. The church bursting with praise. The deacons mopped his brow. Men and women hopped up and down the aisle. Constant cries of "Hallelujah," "Praise God," "Preach," as the sun rained its majesty down.

"I thank God for the love of a good woman." He looked at Sister Edith, but Ophelia imagined that he meant her. She wanted it to be her. She knew this part of the sermon. He did it every Sunday, and it was something the congregation waited for and swooned at every time. "I said, I thank God for the love of a good woman, and the blessings that she brings." He nodded to Sister Edith and then Ruth and Jeremiah with her sat right between them. An intimate moment between a husband and his family, performed to perfection for the entire congregation. And Ophelia was there, sat right between the Prince and Princess of Ebenezer Baptist. The hand of God had lifted her up to heights she had never dreamed of.

After service, the same usher said to her, "You are invited to the Front Room for the Young Saints meeting." Only the children of the important got invited to the Front Room. Other church kids gossiped about the "Young Saints" meetings and longed to be invited. "You're just not Front Room material," they'd say, putting each other down in that serious kind of joking way kids do when they can't have something they want and all they can do is mock it. Ophelia was invited into the inner sanctum.

Jeremiah, Ruth, and twelve other deacon's or minister's kids around their age joined her. She knew their names but did not know them. Before that Sunday, the Front Room kids had nothing to gain from being her friend. The girls were Mavis, Cleotha, Yvonne, Clarise, Denise, Dorinda, and Mattie. They wore exclusively flared and frilly dresses. The boys wore suits of navy,

143

teal, and burgundy with vests over their shirts. They were Clark, Leon, Frank, Doug, and Melvin. It was called the "Front Room" because the meetings took place in a room on the second floor of the church building facing the front of the church. White walls. Half a dozen tables with chairs. Gigantic windows. A constant stream of brightness.

All the "Young Saints" were young enough to still require adult supervision but old enough to be left alone while their parents tended to church business. A pair of elder ladies chaperoned but not especially closely. Ruth and Jeremiah were the ones who chaired the proceedings. Giddy and bug-eyed with blessedness, Ruth turned to her, and in a gesture of inclusion asked, "Ophelia, tell us your favorite Bible verse."

"Tell us, tell us!" the group encouraged warmly.

Ophelia lit up. Not only was she invited but they made space to make her feel like one of them. Determined not to mess this up, she wondered which verse to pick. Deuteronomy 31? Psalm 27? Isaiah 40? She settled on Isaiah. "But they that wait upon the Lord shall renew their strength, they shall mount up with wings as eagles, they shall run and not be weary, and they shall walk and not faint."

The whole room politely clapped their admiration and surrounded Ophelia in a chorus of warmth and welcome. Which was so overwhelming that she fell to speechless blubbering. No matter how she tried to express gratitude her mouth would not work. "Don't worry," Jeremiah comforted her. "You'll get used to it." As he said this, she noticed his eyes slide towards the back of the room, where their two wife-chaperones watched with contented smiles. "God's little angels," one said and they turned and left the room so that the children could continue their blessed time together.

"That was beautiful," Jeremiah said to her, but his eyes tracked the sisters until the door shut behind them. Then he stiffened his left leg, flapped his arms like little chicken wings, and dragged himself across the room mocking her in a low dopey voice, "They that wait upon the Lord, shall bl-blah bl-blah bl-blah."

They all fell out rolling on the ground. The laughter was muffled but they were all in on the joke.

Ruth watched Ophelia slyly. "Okay, Miss Holy Roller, now tell us some dirt." They all quieted down to listen. "Dirt?" Ophelia said, still reeling from the mocking. "Dirt?" Jeremiah repeated in his dopey Ophelia voice. Ruth insisted. "Yeah, you ain't kissed nobody yet? Got your bunkie squeezed? Felt up?"

Her mouth got dry.

Ruth poked her with a vicious finger. "Listen, you might impress my mom with cooking gravy, I mean—first of all, gross!—but you gotta impress us. Tell us your dirty little secrets."

Jeremiah, who had taken off his suit jacket, chimed in, "That's how we know you won't tell on us."

"I . . . I'm not sure what you want . . . I don't have any secrets . . ."

Ruth's nose crinkled, as if she was smelling something foul. "You been playing stinky finger with that creepy little friend you're always with, haven't you?"

To the accusation that she and Lucy were sinners she managed a wimpy, whiny, "Noooo . . ."

She was saved by the door cracking open.

As if some switch had been flipped, the pack of praise posers became instantly sanctified. Ruth sweetened and said, without dropping a beat, "CeCe Winan's *Alone in His Presence* is my favorite gospel album, but Jeremiah's old-school. He likes the Staple Singers. What's your favorite?"

The door clicked shut. The adults had left again. Instantly they switched back from Team Young Saints to Team Young Satan. Ruth, suddenly sour and threatening, accused her of stalling. "You wanna make this tough, huh?"

"No, I-I don't," Ophelia stuttered.

"Then give up the goods, poor girl."

Her brain scrambled. Words stuck in her gullet before she could pronounce them.

"Umm ... one time ... Lucy watched me change ... we were in a hurry ... so ... then she changed, and I watched her ..."

"Ooooooooooooh!" They all chimed together, but it was mock shame and then real laughter at her bewilderment.

"You can stay in the Front Room—for now—but if you tell, we'll all say you're a liar and then you have to go in the closet with my brother."

Jeremiah grinned ominously.

The girls started talking about who was hotter: D'Angelo or Maxwell. *Clearly D'Angelo*, Ophelia thought, trying her best to keep up a scandalized face. The kids broke out into one of D'Angelo's songs, "Sh*t, Damn, Motherf*cker ..." and cracked up looking at each other ecstatically accentuating the "Muh. Dah. Fuck. Ahhh ..." while they snapped and swayed like they were in a music video. The easy, comfortable way the church kids talked about things they shouldn't be talking about left Ophelia dumbfounded. Lucy called D'Angelo a "fornicator," but Auntie Aiyanna loved his songs. The Front Room was the last place she expected to hear a D'Angelo song.

They stood in a circle to shield what they were up to while Clark guarded the door. He was nominated because he was tall and broad shouldered and made the hardest obstacle to see around. Dorinda, wide-eyed and giggling, entered the circle to take her turn being "hugged" by one of the boys. First it was Melvin and then Frank and then Leon. But the "hugs" lasted a little too long before the next girl, Denise, entered the circle. Frank's hands wandered down to squeeze her soft, budding bits. Then Mavis entered and Doug's hands strayed upwards, fondling her breasts over her clothes. Ophelia stood horrified yet mesmerized. She had no words for what they were doing but she knew that it was sinful. To her, the worst part was that those not in the circle all watched the show greedily. The excitement built with each forbidden line they crossed. Legs crossed. Then uncrossed. The horny titillating the holy.

"Your turn," Jeremiah announced to Ophelia.

Into the circle she went before she could protest and he pressed her up into him so tightly that it knocked the breath out of her. He smelled of man cologne. His mauve dress shirt untucked. His chin pressed against her forehead, and she felt his hands reach down to her bum and lift each cheek as if hefting two sacks of milk.

Ophelia pushed Jeremiah away. "Stop!"

The whole room giggled, then she said out loud what was ringing in her head, "We'll all go to hell!" This went off like a gunshot. They all roared with laughter again. Ophelia felt tears swell up in her eyes and she turned to run from the Front Room. The place she'd always wanted to be.

Before she got to the door she heard a voice say, "She won't tell on us." It was Ruth, cool and certain. "She don't got nobody to tell."

Chapter Twenty-Six

"Modest is hottest," Sister Edith and the Senior Sisters would remind the girls Ophelia's age—preteenagers about to enter what the Sisters called their "curious phase," when the devil would tempt them to sin.

She would say it in her high, bubbly voice as if to educate them, but they knew that it was also a warning. Necklines and hiked-up skirts and the arrival of breasts and the consequences they would have on the boys—and the men—around them. They heard how the Church ladies *hmmm*-ed and *haaah*-ed and clutched pearls and fanned themselves vigorously when a skirt got too mid-shinbone for their liking. Hemlines started at ankles, then crept up to knees, then dancing would follow, then nakedness, then fornication, then shame, shame, shame.

Take, for example, Beula White, whose poor mother and father had to move to Durham, a whole other state away, when her pregnant belly started showing. Or Drumonte Green, who church elders would point out, stinking, greasy drunk, sleeping on the street, to their children as a warning of the dangers of not doing exactly what they said, when they said it. Or Lola

Washington, who took a half a bottle of aspirin rather than tell her poor mother—mothers were always poor in these stories—that she had a baby brewing.

Shame. Shame. Shame.

Lucy refused to speak of it, but Ophelia understood that shame sat like a cloud over the congregation. Her keen observations revealed that shame lurked behind the slips of flesh that their pious blouses, shirts, and choir robes suggested. It crept out of their privates, down their silky thighs, to their kneecaps, when they snuck in secret dances to D'Angelo or Monica or TLC, in the Front Room. It leaked out from between the broad shoulders, hips, and chests that rolled down the aisle on their way to Sunday School. It could leap out at you at any time like a mugger. *The Devil cometh like a thief in the night. No man knoweth the time nor the hour.* No woman, either. Certainly no poor, no-family girl would know the time nor the hour. Only eternal vigilance could prevent the whiff of impropriety from becoming the rot of sin. So why take chances? Modest is hottest.

One Thursday, in early July, they held their church youth meeting at Cherry Park, right in front of the big dogwood tree. Ophelia wondered why they would need to host it there when they had a newly renovated sanctuary with all the trimmings just down the road. Sister Edith had an answer. She explained why they were in the park loudly enough for the whole assembled group to hear, as she spoke before blessing the food. "The devil's tools are really God's tools perverted. If he can catch your eye and lead you astray, then God can catch your eye and lead you home. Today, we are fishers of men!"

A little later, Ophelia spotted a lost soul. The girl wore a halter top, bootie shorts—hot pink—with nails done long but the polish chipped. The young girl hovered sheepishly around the table with the peach cobbler and the bread pudding. She hovered but didn't eat anything. Just pretended to be interested, and every now and then snuck a glance at the cluster of kids from the church. Ophelia recognized the signs: this girl wanted to talk.

"Cobbler or pudding?"

"Umm, pudding . . ."

"Okay . . . just let me serve you up some, then."

Ophelia gave the girl her friendliest smile. Juicy seemed older than her age, but at the same time younger. Ophelia noticed that her bottom lip trembled as though she was cold, but the day was sticky warm.

"Here you go."

"Thanks," said Juicy, and gave her a wounded look as if she had troubles that only old people should have.

"My name's Ophelia, what's yours?"

"Juicy."

"Juicy?" Ophelia tried not to sound judgy.

"That's what they call me on Beauregard Ave, but my real name's Shevaun."

"That's where you live?"

"That's where I . . . umm"—a panicked breath—"that's where I work. I mean . . . I'm a working girl, you know?"

"What you mean 'a working girl'?"

"I mean, I turn tricks . . ."

Ophelia's eyes widened in recognition. She felt horrified that she had asked. How could she be so slow?

Juicy's bottom lip shivered. Ophelia said, "Sorry."

"Why you sorry? I ain't ashamed. But I ain't no church girl. I just didn't want to take your food under no false pretenses."

"You don't have to talk about it . . ."

A thick lump gathered in Ophelia's throat.

"Besides, you're not really eating that bread pudding are you? Do you even like pudding?"

"Real talk? I don't like anything sweet. I hate dessert. I prefer salty, but I didn't wanna be rude."

And they both broke out laughing. They couldn't stop until the whole meeting started to look their way. Juicy laughed as if it had been a long time since she'd been silly. She seemed to Ophelia fragile enough to drop and shatter into a thousand pieces.

"Does your family know? About your . . . your job?"

"Nah, nobody knows, but that's 'cause I don't got nobody."

"What do you mean?"

It started with a trickle of a teardrop from her left eye, then three more tears fell from her right eye, then the whole scaffolding of her composure tumbled down.

"I'm sorry to be such a weepy bitch. It's just that . . . you seem so nice . . . girls aren't always nice . . . they always stealing my shit, and they hit me if I complain. It's been a long time since anybody was nice to me."

"You really nice too. Pretty girls usually don't like me."

Juicy took a forkful of bread pudding, but Ophelia could tell she didn't like it.

"You know, I don't really have parents either."

"For real?"

"For real, for real."

"But you with these churchy people. They let orphans up in there?"

"Sure they do. My Grandma Blue raised me out of town,

151

country as a chicken coop. I got my auntie though. She crazy but she look out for me."

"You wanna be friends?" Juicy asked, and her eyes blinked back tears.

"Yeah, we cool. Us orphans gotta rock together, right?"

Ophelia passed her a napkin to dab the streams of eyeliner that trailed down her cheeks.

"Thanks. You can call me Shevaun if you want, but Juicy is fine too . . ."

"Would you come to church with me?"

"They don't like people like me there. Would they really let me come?"

"Of course they will. I don't have a momma or daddy, and I go to church four times a week." Then she remembered what Lucy had said to her. "This can be your new family."

Shevaun's face bubbled with relief.

"Thank you."

When Shevaun showed up to Ebenezer Baptist the next Sunday, Ophelia met her at the door like her own personal usher.

"Blessed Sunday, Sister Shevaun," she said, and she understood Lucy's pride on Ophelia's first day in church because she felt something similar welcoming Shevaun. Lucy agreed to meet them at the door when Ophelia told her that she'd be late because she was "bringing a special friend to Jesus."

Lucy was scandalized. "This? Is your friend? What is she wearing?" Then she pulled Ophelia off to the side and continued, "You can't walk around church with her. She has got to go. If you sit next to her, her shame will be your shame." Lucy marched off wanting nothing to do with what happened next.

Shevaun had worn all her fragile hope and not much else. Ophelia was embarrassed but she didn't want to embarrass Shevaun. *Maybe that skintight tube dress was her best dress? Maybe those hooker pumps were all she had?* Ophelia remembered that she only had one pair of shoes when she first walked through those same doors. She hugged Shevaun and squeezed, and it felt like she was hugging that version of herself. She gave Shevaun the hug no one had given her.

Sister Shevaun's reception was anything but juicy: eye rolls, jaws dropped, stares, mutterers fanning themselves, and finally Sister Marshala cornered them by the vestibule inside the doors and said, "Do you have to dress like a whore in the Lord's house? My husband needs to keep his mind on Jesus. Why is this . . . thing . . . trying to distract him with her nakedness?"

Ophelia felt that hard place in her guts keenly.

"Jesus was friends with Mary Magdalene! Who are you to judge her?"

Sister Marshala's face convulsed.

"You? You! YOU. You filthy heathen wretch. What do you know about Jesus? You don't belong here. Go back to that dung heap reservation where they found you."

A crowd had gathered to watch. They formed a gawking semicircle that pressed Ophelia and Shevaun against the entrance. Sister Marshala continued to pass sentence, "Take this whore and get thee behind me, Jezebel." Her trinity of moles flared up like parasites trying to eat her face. Then, to emphasize her point, she pushed Shevaun in her chest with both hands. Then again and again, she pushed her in the direction of the front door. Shevaun got the message and turned to go. *It's okay, it's not your fault* her dejected eyes seemed to say to Ophelia.

Though Ophelia scanned the faces of those watching for sup-

153

port, no one took her side. Between her and a Senior Sister her defeat was not only expected, it was entertainment. Jeremiah couldn't stop giggling. Ruth's eyes gobbled it up. Most observers folded their arms in disgust. Their lips already repeating the most delicious details. Lucy's last look at Ophelia said without saying, *I told you so*. And then she too turned her back and left Ophelia standing by the doors Shevaun had just walked through.

Shame. Shame. Shame.

Chapter Twenty-Seven

Three days later at Wednesday prayer meeting, Lucy wanted nothing to do with Ophelia. Her huffy attitude was back, and she sniffed her android nose at Ophelia when she motioned for Lucy to sit with her.

Before she could ask again, Deacon Jenkins came up behind her and waved Lucy further down the pew. The deacon was a walrus of a man. Big sausage-roll fingers, a great wide girth. Whiskers shot out over a wide mouth. A voice that boomed when he laughed. He rolled his great bulk into the pew next to her. The smell of seasoned fish meshed with his sugary cologne. His voice rumbled.

"Young Sister, I saw that you had a bit of trouble last Sunday."

Everyone knows! Ophelia looked at her shoes. He came close to her ear, and the fishy smell nearly made her gag.

"It hurt me to hear how you and that young sister were treated the other day."

Ophelia wasn't sure why he was talking nicely to someone covered in shame.

"So much so, that I prayed on it, these few nights gone by."

For all the time she had been at Ebenezer, no deacon, including Deacon Jenkins, had ever taken any interest in her. She had heard him preach and he gave her and Lucy a ride home once, but that was just what the deacons did. She would have been surprised if he knew her name. Now he was in her ear—reeking but friendly. To distract herself she tried to name the spices in his fish breath as he spoke. Parsley, chives, paprika—smoked (she thought)—ginger . . .

"Ophelia, you seem like a wise young lady."

She started to nod but then stopped because it might be immodest.

"I'm sure you've noticed that some Christians don't always act Christlike."

It sounded like he was getting somewhere, but she had no idea where.

"So much have I prayed on your situation that the Lord has moved me to take a personal involvement in you and all our high school–aged congregation. You start high school this year, isn't that right?"

"Next year, Deacon Jenkins."

A small glow started to build inside her. It warmed her insides that someone in the church family hadn't condemned her. If Deacon Jenkins took an interest in her, then that meant that she wasn't totally shamed. There was hope that everything would be alright.

"You'd like me to look out for you with the congregation, wouldn't you, Ophelia?"

To her meek yes he said, "Come to the deacon's room on Saturday after youth choir. Let's begin your special instruction in the Lord's Grace."

———

That Saturday around five in the afternoon when youth choir was wrapped up, Ophelia tried to make up with Lucy. She cornered her as she came up the Sunday school stairs.

"Lucy, please don't be mad at me," she pleaded, but Lucy sniffed and kept her precise steps moving away from her.

Ophelia tried again. "Deacon Jenkins wants to meet with me. He doesn't think I did anything wrong." Lucy's polished black shoes with the silver buckle snapped like a whip as she kept focused on leaving.

"You should come with me to the deacon's room."

Lucy's mouth tightened into a proud little pocket. Lucy wasn't trying to hear her; she had gotten the upper hand in her battle to keep Ophelia in her place, and she wasn't going to give it up easily. She left Ophelia standing there still pleading.

After choir, when the chapel was quiet and everyone had headed home for early supper, Ophelia waited at the back for Lucy. Still hoping to win her over. Deacon Jenkins' special instruction was the carrot she'd hoped to tempt her with. *She won't resist making friends with a deacon, will she?*

But after the meeting, Lucy was nowhere to be found.

Having failed to find Lucy, Ophelia made her way down to the deacon's room, which was in the same corner as the kitchen.

Deacon Jenkins knelt in prayer there. The great bulk of his backside was low down as he knelt facing the podium. In one corner the communion silverware was laid out, ready for the Sunday sacrament. She didn't want to disturb him, so she waited outside and watched through the window in the door.

After about five minutes, she decided that she should at least walk in, so that he knew she was there. As soon as the door opened, he looked back and stroked his whiskers and laughed his deep rumble of a laugh. It felt like his chest was a barrel that churned and rattled about when he laughed like that.

"Come, Ophelia, let us pray."

And he folded his hands and leaned his elbows on the table in front of him. As she approached, she saw that he was kneeling on a low prayer bench, and she took a spot next to him and closed her eyes to pray.

Before even a minute had passed, three things happened: (1) She felt his great, padded hand squeeze her bum cheeks together; (2) Her whole body went stiff, her nose could smell nothing, her skin rose up into goose bumps, her ears started to ring, and all she could hear was the *thump-thump-thump* of her heart in her ear; and (3) He pressed his lips between her collarbone and her neck, and a thick slurp of drool rolled out of his mouth, down her neck, and into her armpit.

In that moment she thought she heard Grandma Blue say, *Child, move from there, you're coming home.* And her legs picked her up and moved her across the room away from the deacon's bulk.

There was a ringing in her ears. A high-pitched tingle like cicadas singing. Her feet hit the ground in a luminescent echo that sounded very far away. She was hovering over her head, watching her shoes touch the floor. She was a puppet attached to strings, and she was picking up and putting down her feet in this tender, uncertain way that felt like she might crumble. As though, at any second, she could collapse into a puddle of shoes, and Bible, and girl.

What had she done? How had she seduced him? Had she been a temptress? She only had three dresses, and Sister Edith had given her two of them. How could they be immodest? Wasn't she modest? Even when the other kids went into the closet in the front room to fondle each other, she never went. What had she done? Deacon Jenkins did not follow her and she did not look back. Stunned and dazed, she walked to the door and left him where she had found him kneeling.

Lucy was standing in the hall. Her eyes bulging out, her mouth hanging loose as if her jaw had come unhinged from her head. Lucy had been staring into the window at them. Shaking her head, vigorous and confused, she seemed to be trying to shake something back into place.

Across what felt like a chasm, Ophelia and Lucy stood watching each other. Ophelia wanted to crumble into her friend's arms and cry. Her guts did somersaults. Deacon Jenkins' slobber was still on her neck. Yet something about Lucy gave her pause. Soon, Ophelia saw Lucy transform. She picked up her face, pursed her mouth precisely, and slipped back into her holiness.

"What did you do?"

"I didn't do anything."

"I saw you with Deacon Jenkins."

The Android for Jesus had returned, and Ophelia knew what she was thinking: shame, shame, shame.

"I didn't do anything . . ."

Her mouth felt attached to some other body's brain.

"You tempted him. You Judas! You fornicator!"

Ophelia could read on Lucy's face the movie that was playing in her thoughts: it featured Ophelia, the Whore of Babylon, the Great Deceiver, the Liar, the corrupting tramp. Lucy was the hero who had uncovered this serpent in their church garden. That summer she had spent hours listening to Lucy's impromptu sermons, Ophelia felt that she could read her intentions. What she read in them in that moment was Lucy's revenge.

Lucy approached Ophelia. Face serene with gloating. When they were nose to nose she crooned without pity, "If you don't want me to tell everyone what a whore you are, then leave here and don't ever come back."

And Ophelia turned, with her cumbersome heart, as if she carried the weight of the entire sky and left.

When she pushed open the front doors of the church, they felt heavy as a sack of hammers crushing her shoulders. They pushed back against her, and at first they did not move. Was she too weak? Were they too heavy? Were they perfectly matched, like Jacob wrestling the angel? Ophelia wondered if, like Jacob, she should dig her heels in and tell those doors, *I will not let you go until you bless me.* But soon the doors gave way and she entered into the stabbing glare of daylight.

Her breath and her sense of smell returned. With a tissue from her purse she wiped away the trail of drool Deacon Jenkins had left on her neck and armpit. Her neck and back unclenched in the fresh air. Her senses scrambled. Her body moved as if it belonged to someone else. *What did I do?* she heard her brain ask, but everything felt jumbled when she tried to think of what had happened.

Shame. Shame. Shame.

At the foot of the church steps were two bizarre teenagers smoking cigarettes and shoulder-punching each other. Maybe it was because she had the image of Jacob wrestling angels already in her imagination, but her first thought was, *They're angels.*

They appeared surreal. Their long limbs splashed in light. Their pitch-black faces were lengthy as their limbs. Equine, long, horse faces. Tranquil. Unbothered. They wore worn black leather jackets and black jeans and faded black T-shirts with no design on them. Everything about them had no precedent in Ophelia's life. Their posture, their polish, the picture of their dark twin symmetry gave them a foreignness she couldn't recognize.

From the bottom of the stairs, the boy twin looked up and said, "What the fuck are you looking at?" The girl twin gave him a reproachful look and waved to invite Ophelia over. The girl's mouth offered a welcoming smile. *We don't bite*, she seemed to say. Yet Ophelia had her doubts. Encounters with angels in the Bible could go either way: blessed messages, timely warnings or avenging scourges, plagues, and afflictions. But what did she have left to lose? She descended towards them.

"You go to church here?" The boy's voice was rough as gravel.

"Yeah?"

"You sure you go to church here?" the girl asked.

"Yeah, I'm sure . . . You . . . you shouldn't be here . . ."

"Whatever," the boy said. "We need you to settle a bet for us."

"Okay."

"Which one is longer? The Old Testament or the New Testament?" the girl asked.

"What?"

"She don't know," he said, but the girl retorted, "Give her a second. She knows. Which one is longer?"

And they both stared at her, taking deep draws from their cigarettes, their spooky eyes waiting.

"The Old Testament . . . it's a lot longer."

"Yes!" the girl erupted. "YES."

The boy watched her and mouthed but didn't say *Fuck you*, then reached into his pocket and started to count out bills. The girl yelled, "Better have my money, bitches!" and took the cash while laughing in his face.

Just then a car honked and startled the three of them. It was a gleaming black Lincoln, shiny like a beetle's shell, and Ophelia didn't need to read the license plate to know that it said "Pastor Hamilton."

As his car approached, somewhere inside, her imagination sprung to life. He would see her for the gentle lamb she was, and without her saying it, he would know that she'd been treated unfairly by Deacon Jenkins, by Lucy, by the Front Room, by Sister Marshala, and by everyone that laughed at Shevaun. If anyone could redeem her it was Pastor Ronelle Hamilton.

His driver pulled up and the back window rolled down slowly. The pastor held them in a cold stare for a long moment. Ophelia waited for him to recognize her and lift her up from where she had fallen. But when he spoke, he did so as if he had never seen her before.

"Get off this property, you trash. You can't be gambling in front of the Lord's House."

This flattened Ophelia. Worse than Lucy or Deacon Jenkins. This was Pastor Hamilton. The man who anointed her. His words fell like judgment. He spat them out of his mouth like something sour. His rigid eyes followed the twins as they walked off. Rooted to the ground, Ophelia held out hope that the pastor might still save her. But he never did.

His eyebrows raised at her as if to say, *What are you waiting for?* Then, with her head hung low, she walked past his car sullen and defeated. And as she passed, she heard the whir of the Lincoln's window slowly closing. The car drove off even slower. And Ophelia never returned to Ebenezer Baptist Church.

PART THREE

2004

Chapter Twenty-Eight

After ten years of not hearing a word from Shango Trouthands, a letter arrived at apartment 66.

> *Ophelia,*
>   *I've been away, but I want you to know that I am always closer than it seems. I think about you constantly. Take this letter to your Aunt Belle. It's late, but she'll enroll you at Northeastern. A Queen has come!*
>   *Shango*

Her auntie had handed it to Ophelia, who read it five times before she tried to hand it back. But Aiyanna refused. "It's your name on the envelope, not mine." Yet Ophelia's aunt couldn't hide her disappointment. "That school will make you boring just like Belle, you watch."

The letter had arrived the day before the first day of school, August 17, 2004—Ophelia's senior year. Everything that year was about Usher. Her walls were covered in posters of his slight waist, his imp's smile, that seductive strip of white teeth behind plump chocolate lips, and his rippled abs holding power poses. Ophelia knew his croons, his moves, his lyrics well enough to mouth whole albums. Frequently she daydreamed that his songs were about her. The sight of her boy's smile in the vague semi-light of her room steadied her breathing. It was her room now. The one the Brothers K had left now that they lived with their father. The bunk bed was gone, and instead a low futon mattress and a dresser with a chest of drawers loomed. It was painted lemon yellow, but Usher's torso obscured most of this. Her father's letter obscured even Usher that night. She fell asleep repeating its words while the rainfall beat a steady rhythm on the car roofs in the parking lot outside.

In the bathroom the next morning, Ophelia splashed her face in cold water and evaluated what she saw. She'd grown taller. Not quite the height of Shango or Aiyanna, but a head taller than Grandma Blue. Her curls were thick and lustrous and in their full August glory. But that day she would straighten them. The first day at a new school meant that she would have to walk a treacherous line: too cute and she might be labeled a slut, not cute enough and she might be ignored completely. Not least of all by her own aunt.

Before she started her makeup she lit a dried tobacco leaf in the ashtray by the sink. As the milky smoke streamed out of the bathroom, she wafted it over her head and said:

"Great Spirit—
Thank you for waking us.
For the land that feeds us.
For the people who keep us.
And thank you for the river, our Mother.
We will mind the river.
Amen."

Grandma Blue's prayer was one of the ways she tried to claim back her heritage. Another was the tattoo of a spiral of butterflies winding from her left hip bone up her rib cage and into her armpit. "Kamama" is what the internet said the Cherokee word was for butterfly. It meant freedom and rebirth. *Dream on,* she thought when she got the tattoo. Ophelia wished that she felt more connected with being Cherokee. But in the years since, she'd become more like Aiyanna than Grandma Blue. Memories of her childhood by the river seemed like a faded Polaroid. She'd accepted that it would always make her feel different, but never allow her to feel at home.

After she had contoured her lips and added a slight suggestion of gold to her eyelids, she stared at the young woman that peered back at her. All her worry showed on her face: trepidation bit at the corners of her lips and kept her heart beating unevenly. She wanted a new school, a new start—Stone River High— the Black high school—had not been fun since Durell moved to San Diego. Yet she hadn't prepared for the nail-biting reality of switching schools on day one of her final year. And to not just any school. Northeastern was the wealthy white high school where she knew no one. Except for Auntie Belle, who she was sure despised her because of all the money she'd paid Aiyanna to raise her. Staring down her anxiety, she said to her reflection, "There's a girl named Ophelia Blue Rivers, and this is her face."

Aiyanna had done what most believed was impossible: she'd gotten a job. She had lost the money the father of her sons gave her to raise them, and when Ophelia turned eighteen that year, she'd lose that money as well. Her appetite to party was watered down by her need to get up for her shifts at the Ford auto plant. Although she took every opportunity to devise new curses to fling at her ex and her younger, more accomplished sister, Aiyanna enjoyed the change. Getting that check with her own name, having her own money and knowing that she'd shown up on time, punched her time card, and swallowed her line manager's shit for another fortnight to earn it, puffed her up with pride. Did she miss her boys? "A mother's love can never be replaced," she'd say in a rehearsed show of maternal mourning. But secretly, not having to make their lunches, wash a mountain of their raunchy underwear, T-shirts, and jeans—or at least feel guilty while Ophelia did it—suited her just fine. And her factory job was like a dating service. Aiyanna walked the line for her boys: Yung in Welding, who was a bit too old for her; Tiny in Inspection, who was a giant; and Biggie in the Assembly Shop, who was almost a midget but had a large man's cock. Yes, she had lost her boys, but she had gained so much.

Ophelia thought that less booze and more physical labor looked good on her. At the door as she made to leave, Aiyanna teased Ophelia, "If you come back to this apartment talking French, we gonna fight, you heard me?"

Aiyanna rolled her lips, indicating that Ophelia should do the same to her lipstick. They both knew that their sisterly comradery suited the older woman fine. Aiyanna had always been a reluctant parent. And that day, as it seemed that their life together was about to irrevocably change, Ophelia appreciated that she'd tried her best. Aiyanna held her by the shoulders.

"Come here, let me see this game face."

They flared their nostrils and eyeballs and stuck out their canines like fangs. This was their game face. It never failed to turn down the drama. Their laughter relaxed Ophelia. "Don't let Belle push you around, alright?"

"To tell you the truth, it's not Auntie Belle that I'm worried about. It's all the white people."

Chapter Twenty-Nine

By the time Ophelia left at eight a.m., the rain had died down enough that she wasn't worried about getting her hair wet. She set out on Kaevon's old BMX bike across town to Northeastern High School to do what her daddy had told her to do: go see her Aunt Belle to enroll in the richest, whitest high school in Stone River.

To get to Pendleton she had to cross the bridge over the interstate, which always made her nervous. It was a neighborhood she didn't ever go to. The streets got suddenly wider, the lawns trimmer, and the grass greener. The double-story-high verandas took giant steps back from the road. She knew she wasn't in Stone River anymore. The subdivision bordered but was not fully part of Stone River. Its residents voted for partial separation from the rest of the city to control their own zoning, zip code, and high school.

While she zigged and zagged through Pendleton's streets the stares started. A George Clooney look-alike in his housecoat was watering his lawn and chewing absentmindedly on a half a cigar. He straightened up and mouthed, "What the . . ." and the cigar fell from between his lips. "Are you lost, little girl?" some Becky said as Ophelia whizzed by her and her twinzie in their Southern moo-moo chic. Ophelia wasn't stopping for nobody. Her daddy had sent her. That was all the gas her legs needed. It didn't matter if people thought she didn't belong; she had been told: *Take this letter to your Aunt Belle . . . she'll enroll you at Northeastern.*

In front of Northeastern High, kids slouched on their bikes or hopped out of suburban mom-mobiles in a roundabout that led to a wide sweep of steps, atop which were the main doors. Along these steps kids clumped, chatting. Their style was a smorgasbord of what kids at Stone River High—the Black high school—would ridicule a person for: printed pattern dress shirts, Abercrombie & Fitch, spiky moussed-up rock hair, blond highlights on everyone, iPods, skateboards, and Linkin Park rap-rock T-shirts. There was the thong-showing-at-the-back gang, the Juicy-tracksuit gang, the cutie-short-dress-we-love-Britney gang, the chubby boy we-dress-like-our-dad gang, the Justin-Timberlake-wannabe-b-boy gang. It made her wonder where the nerdy, all-mixed-up-Black-girl gang was.

Ophelia climbed the steps sucking on her bottom lip, chewing it like tough liver, her head on a swivel. A loudspeaker crackled out an indecipherable announcement. A furious bell sounded. The whole yard started urgently moving. The stares became dismissive teenaged eye rolls. Then against the flow of the crowd rushing into the school emerged two faces she could never forget. It was the twins. The same bizarre pair of teenagers from her last day at Ebenezer Baptist Church.

They were so Black they felt redacted. The shower of blackness began with their prune-colored skin. Then black leather jackets, T-shirts, sneakers, tapered skinny black jeans. Slim hips. Sprinter builds. A two-person Kenyan track team dressed by a punk band.

The Running Ramones. Their faces were long as horses'—thin jaws, high foreheads, bright eyes. They were exactly as Ophelia remembered them, and they were the last people she expected to bump into at Northeastern High School.

"Hello, Old Testament," the boy said. His voice had kept its nasty bite.

"We never introduced ourselves," the girl butted in, hers a jazz singer's whisper. Wooden wrist bangles *clank clank*ed. They were black—of course.

"I'm Keyinde, and this asshole is Taiwo."

"Key and Tai, baby," the boy said.

"You go to school here?" Ophelia was intimidated.

They glanced at each other knowingly.

"You're Ophelia, right?" she said, sweet as molasses.

"Ophelia Blue Rivers," he said, and his voice was as hard as stone grinding stone. "You still love the Lord?" he asked her. Smile cynical. Nothing came out of her mouth. The twins gave each other another knowing glance, raised their brows, then shook their heads.

"You're here to see Madame Belle?" Key asked. Without waiting for her answer, they about-faced and strode down the long main hallway. Ophelia rushed to keep up.

A long hallway and three flights of stairs later she was ushered into an office that didn't look like any high school teacher's office she'd ever seen. For one thing it was painted mauve and had a crystal chandelier lamp in the corner.

"Regarde ce vilain petit canard," hissed Madame Belle.

"What shall I do with this ugly duckling?" she translated herself, as if annoyed that she had to. Ophelia felt her chest tighten. Belle made everything tense. The slender slip of a woman stood in a scaly sequin pantsuit, blowing smoke out an open window. Her perfumed cigarette dangled from her manicure as if it was a part of her hand. She slinked over to Ophelia and examined her. Belle clipped her jawline in a bony talon and held Ophelia's eyes in her emerald gaze.

Whatever language she spoke, Madame Belle's aura said "no nonsense." Which was very Grandma Blue. But everything else about Belle made the idea of her being related to Grandma Blue seem ludicrous. Caught in the uncomfortable gaze of those reptile eyes, Ophelia couldn't help but wonder: *What happened to her?*

"Ecoutez," she said, "don't ask me anything about him—your father, my sister, or that bitch by the river. They sent you here, so I'll take you, but you better be as smart as they say you are. Comprenez-vous?"

Ophelia nodded compliance. She should have expected this she decided: her family hated each other, and no one ever wanted to talk about it. They held their hearts in a ruthless grip. They all inherited this from Grandma Blue.

"Travailler? Are you here to put in work, little duckling? Comprendre?"

Some part of Ophelia must've understood, because she mumbled something thin and weak.

"Speak up, petit canard," Belle barked, and exhaled more heady smoke.

"Don't work, don't eat," Ophelia repeated Grandma Blue's mantra.

Belle's amphibian eyes widened in recognition.

"Exactement." And she peeled back her lips where a discreet gold cap on her molar tooth shone with tiny diamonds. A snake smile.

"Turn," Belle commanded. Taking Ophelia's hand, she held it over her head and used it to spin her slowly around. "Turn, turn, turn, let me see you." Her scaly green eyes picked Ophelia apart as if she were weighing beans on a scale. Then she shrugged and slithered away to a canary-colored chair at the center of the room.

"You're still a green banana, a slight disposable thing. You will listen, you will learn, you will always be on time, n'est-ce pas?"

"Yes ... oui."

Belle's eyes narrowed with surprise. "Oui, madame. Not *madum*. Mah. Dam. Comprendre?"

"Oui, madame."

"Never call me 'Auntie' or 'Auntie Belle' or 'Belle' or anything familiar. From now on, you will live with my sister, but your ass is mine. Oui?"

"Oui, madame ..."

"Ahhaaa ..." she said. Ophelia would learn that this meant *we'll see.*

"Do you have any idea what we are doing here?"

"Going to school ... going to school, madame."

Belle fake-laughed until she coughed; her small eagle bones felt like they might break under the strain. Then she was suddenly serious again.

"Non, we are not 'going to school.' We are taking up space. We are modeling excellence. We are win-ning."

"I don't understand ..."

"Beauregard. Do you know Councilman Jack Beauregard? Of the Stone River Beauregards? Owner of most of the farmland and factories that employ this town? The man that contaminated that little stream we grew up next to? Do you know him?"

"I saw him once in Etsi when I was a kid, but no, I don't know him."

"Your grandmother is fighting him in the bush, and we are fighting him here."

Belle sighed at the confusion exploding out of Ophelia's face.

"Let me tell you the stakes we are playing for. There was a debate at the city council about whether Black children suffered from a lack of resources or a lack of ability. Beauregard argued that Black kids struggled because they were simply not smart enough. I dared him to prove it. The result is this . . . experiment. La belle école, the beautiful school—a school within a school. Oui? We are here to show that Black students, if given a chance, will beat them every time. Comprendre?"

"I think so." Ophelia had watched her speech closely, the way she smiled with her mouth but never with her scaly eyes, the way her sequins danced along her rib cage. Her voice never rising above a honeyed hiss.

"Bon! Because I will have none of this Aiyanna Trouthands lazy bacchanalia. Don't make me remind you. Above all you must win. WIN. You hear me? You'll be present at 7:45 every morning for our class. An hour before the rest of your Northeastern classes begin, you will be in mine, oui? I will review all your tests, essays, and presentations to ensure standards, oui?"

"Oui, madame."

"And remember, if you think you will get by on special treatment, vous vous trompez! Do you know what this means?"

"That I'm . . . not . . . gonna get by . . . ?"

"Exactement . . ."

Belle shook her chin in disdain, but underneath her cold-blooded glare there was something kind in her roughness, a quick squint of playfulness that Ophelia hoped would stay but was gone before she could verify that it existed. It was the second thing about Belle that reminded her of Grandma Blue.

"Bienvenue a La Belle École," she said, and sucked a huge draw of her lean cigarette, letting go a waft of jasmine smoke. Her wiry lips pursed as she kissed her teeth with a sucking sound.

"Doudou," she called out. "Doudou, come give this ugly duckling le grand tour. Check her in at the office and make sure she gets a locker in our hall."

Keyinde—the girl twin—came into the room. Ophelia was beginning to tell them apart. Key smelled like rose hips. Tai smelled like oiled metal. Like a gun.

"Oui, madame . . . and thank you."

Ophelia exhaled her relief.

"Thank you for giving me this opportunity. I won't let you down."

"Ahhaaa . . ." Belle said, as if to say, *We'll see.*

Chapter Thirty

There was no regret in Madame Belle. No shadow on her choices. Etsi's Cherokee arm was never long enough to reach her.

At thirteen she had won a mail-in writing contest in *Youth Magazine* and a scholarship to spend the summer with "gifted" children in Charleston. "The girl has talent," Mister Westlake, the man who mentored her, had insisted, suggesting to Grandma Blue that her child was too good for her. "You can give her a chance she'll never get if she stays here. A bright, sparkling future."

Belle was determined to go. Twice weekly she walked to Moytoy's store to get the magazine with the pictures of Paris, clipping out photos of the delicious red pumps, the geometric mustard-colored jackets, and the lips painted in fluorescence. She wanted it all. Belle read. Belle dreamed. Belle blamed her shabby life on her mother.

At fourteen she was offered a much more prestigious scholarship to Paris, France. It was then that Grandma Blue gave up. Her mother could understand the juvenile delinquency of Shango and the dumb, drunk, attention-seeking of Aiyanna, but the prodigy of her youngest baffled her. Belle was never hers. Hated to cook. Refused to garden. Told her frankly, "I'd rather take a whipping than pick up that sock." And her favorite saying when she wanted to twist the knife: "I was born in Etsi, but I'll never belong in Etsi."

After flirting with the runway, graduating from the Sorbonne, and an engagement with Klaus Innsbruck III—a Swiss banker from a famous family who could not stomach an American, no matter how clever—she cut ties, pawned the ring, and returned home. It filled her with loathing to be back. But she had to admit that it beat waiting in haute couture drawing rooms for the judgment of the gentry. France was a constant reminder that she would never escape her birth. To nobodies. In America class was not a birthright; it was a commodity she could buy.

After one too many interviews with the nouveau riche of Atlanta, she decided to believe her own motto: *I don't meet standards, I make standards.* She determined that she would build a life in Stone River. No skimping to spare the local blushes. Skinny lavender cigarettes, pumps, and all the palaver. Let them choke on their misgivings. After all, *wherever I am, je suis vraiment Parisienne.*

Two years before Ophelia showed up at Northeastern, there was a vote at Stone River City Council to force Pendleton's hand. The vote was to create a program to let a small group of gifted Black Stone River High students into Northeastern High. Madame Belle wanted to prove that if given the same teachers, the same support, the same opportunity, gifted Black students like her could outperform white students. Not "do just as well," but consistently beat them. This became her crusade. Jack Beauregard opposed the motion. "Why upset what's worked for decades? Indeed centuries?" he'd asked. "Worked for whom?" she'd asked back, and she won. *Et voila! La Belle École, the beautiful school—a school within a school. Oui?*

Belle became a teacher because—as she'd told herself—she wanted to give what had been given to her to other children: a bright, sparkling future. But her secret reason was that she hated having bosses. A classroom was a queendom where she could reign supervision-free. But what pampered slugs children could be. Never on her watch.

Then Shango's letter arrived. Family, she thought, you only hear from them when you're useful. Belle's instinct was to say no. Hadn't she contributed enough to clean up Shango's little cinnamon-skinned mess? But, of course, he got his mother to do his dirty work. And that curmudgeon knew which buttons to press. "Child, I know you won't pick her. To spite me you won't. But maybe you're worried that you're not the smartest kid from Etsi anymore?" That did the trick. Belle took her niece to prove her mother wrong. Not that Ophelia was smarter than her—that was Grandma Blue's petty fantasy—but to prove that she was above using Ophelia to spite Grandma Blue.

That first week, Ophelia was so tired from peddling all the way from apartment 66 to Pendleton and back that she didn't do Friday's reading—*The Stranger* by Albert Camus. Madame Belle spent twenty-two minutes telling her about herself. "Albert," which she pronounced *Al-Bear*, "Camus ate dates for dinner. His familie was so poor they couldn't afford food, and yet he won Le Prix Nobel. You cannot even read his book to better yourself? What will become of you? Huh? You will marry riche? You will sleep yourself into a chateau? Merde!"

And on and on she went like the Etsi River itself until Ophelia swore to her that she'd never go to bed without reading again.

Belle was hard but fair. On Monday morning, and most mornings after, unless she let Ophelia know the day before, she showed up at apartment 66 at seven a.m. sharp in her orchid-colored convertible coupe, a silk scarf headwrap, blackout sunglasses, and those reeking cigarettes.

"You ride with me from now on, ça va?"

"Oui, madame."

Yet only a week later Ophelia violated another of Madame Belle's pet peeves—talking in class.

"Why is she always so flashy though? Everybody is already looking at us." She thought she was speaking quietly.

"'Cause she needs to remind them that she's better than them," Key answered out the side of her mouth.

"Better at what?"

"Everything."

Belle wondered why they thought she couldn't hear them.

"Doudou et Ophelia, do you want me to shed your blood?" They snapped to attention in unison.

"No, madame."

Madame Belle's nails were doing a clicking dance, opening and shutting her fingers as she spoke. She took pride in them knowing that testing her would lead to catastrophe. "Discipline doesn't come free," she would say. "It's the price you pay for your success."

"Get up!" she screeched. "Se lever! Get up!"

She started out of the classroom, and without any motion from her, they all knew they were supposed to follow. It was Ophelia; the twins; Natasha, a thick Black girl who had been adopted as a baby by white parents; and Roger and Kevin, two Black brothers from the football team who acted dumb but were the smartest people in the class and had scholarship offers to Auburn and Georgia State. There was also Jewelle, a tall whip-clever girl from Martinique, and Charles Large, who was thirteen but a senior—he should have been in ninth grade but had skipped four grades. They all followed her down the stairs and onto the oval track surrounding the football field.

"Run," she said. "What are you waiting for? Run! Vite!"

They were half-asleep. Too sluggish to catch her meaning.

"You are too drowsy to pay attention ce matin, you will run."

The twins dashed off. Competition was their love language. They galloped out of the gate Kentucky Derby–style. Belle overheard the one-hundred-dollar bet they made as they darted.

"Run! Rapide!"

Ophelia wore dress shoes—her church shoes, which still fit. She started to run. Roger and Kevin blasted off past her and Jewelle was next, though her thick bifocal glasses and dorky laugh hid the fact that she could gallop. Natasha was in the middle in her low-rise jeans, and Charles Large and Ophelia—the two smallest—ran just behind her. Belle noted their camaraderie with a pang of pleasure; Charles and Ophelia had straggled behind Natasha because they didn't want her to feel singled out.

"Rapide!" Belle egged them on as they rounded the first bend.

Halfway around the track Ophelia started running with a limp. A cheer started up from the second-floor windows of Northeastern. They had an audience. It was eight a.m. Most of the school wouldn't get here for another thirty minutes, but those who were there loved what they saw: those uppity Black kids who thought they were better than everyone were getting their comeuppance. Belle didn't mind. This was good for the team spirit of La Belle École.

Around the third bend Belle noticed that her niece was struggling. *Oui, petit canard, let's see if you have any guts.* Charles Large and Natasha fell behind. Madame Belle puffed and watched and waited for Ophelia to give up. She refused to quit. Stubbornly she hobbled around the track, her fists pumped, her dress shoes chaffed at her heels.

By the time she collapsed on the ground after completing her full lap of the track, the twins had lit a cigarette and were passing it back and forth. Unlike the rest of them, they were unbothered by the sprint or the embarrassment.

Belle turned on her heels and asked without a care to hear anyone's reply, "Do I have your attention now?"

Chapter Thirty-One

Northeastern would be a fresh start, Ophelia hoped. A new beginning. Yet, if she felt that this meant fitting in, she was mistaken.

Early on, her classmates had decided that not only was she Black and a charity case they were being forced to go to school with, but she was also ugly and a geek: a perfect convergence of teenaged outcast.

Ryan welcomed her to her first class. He was a basketball player. So tall that his bony knees stuck out in front of his desk. His freckles gave him a mischievous *MAD* magazine prankster look.

Soon after, he accused her of stealing his pencil case. "It was right here, Mrs. Cranbrook, and after she passed it was gone." He threw up his hands and exclaimed, "I don't know what happened."

Mrs. Cranbrook took Ophelia into the hall. "Ophelia, I don't know how it was at Stone River High, but here we respect each other's things. Where is the pencil case?"

"I don't know, Mrs. Cranbrook, I wouldn't—"

"Are you sure you didn't mistake it for yours?"

"No, Mrs. Cranbrook, I didn't."

Her heart was in her mouth. All she could picture was Madame Belle kicking her out of La Belle École and Northeastern. Then the whole classroom erupted in laughter behind the door. Ryan had "found" his pencil case. When Ophelia sat back down at her desk there was a note waiting for her, *Welcome to Northeastern, Jemima.*

Mrs. Cranbrook wore big dumpy dresses and had eyebrows so white that they disappeared. Red lipstick exclusively was how she rolled. She usually wore slabs of foundation, an expression of fake rosiness, and a pearl chain for her reading glasses. Kids whispered that "her second divorce isn't going so well . . ."

She was Ophelia's first class in the mornings. It was math, Ophelia's favorite subject, the one that left her brain cells humming. Math had been a source of pride for her since the days of adding figures and making change in Grandma Blue's yard. Math was the subject that made Tejah start calling her "Nerdphelia."

Her white classmates took one and a half days to decide that she wasn't worth talking to. She'd been there before at Stone River High—the Black high school—and she knew the signs well: the giggles after she walked past, avoiding being in her group, but at Northeastern the worst part were the questions.

"Did you grow up in a ghetto?"

"No, I grew up in Stone River."

"You're good at math; were you a genius at Stone River High?"

"I was one of the kids who was good at math."

"Can I touch your hair?"

"No, and why would you ask me that?"

"Class, take a good look at this parabola," Mrs. Cranbrook

said. "To solve the problem, you first need to know what a derivative is . . . anyone?"

Ophelia's hand shot up instantly. Parabolas were easy. She wanted to move on to the complicated problems. Mrs. Cranbrook repeated, "Can anyone tell me what a derivative is?"

Mrs. Cranbrook, she started to notice, had a talent for not seeing her hand when she raised it. Ophelia kept repeating the answer in her head: *a derivative is the rate of change of a function with respect to a variable.* Mrs. Cranbrook looked left to right and front to back and did not appear to see her hand raised. Tiredness eventually forced Ophelia to lower her hand.

"Fine, if no one knows, please look it up in your textbooks."

There rose a chorus of textbook pages flipping. Her heart sank. She knew the answer; why was she letting all these people who didn't do their homework answer? Jane, whose dad owned the local fairgrounds, was pale as milk, with dirty-blond hair and a mouth in a permanent pout, answered, "A derivative is the rate of change of a function with respect to a variable."

"Well done, Jane."

Ophelia's blood boiled. Good in school was her thing. It didn't matter how much Tejah and her crew bullied her, or how cheap or secondhand her clothes were, or how much the kids in the cafeteria called her a dork. In class, if she did her homework, the teacher would let her answer. This was her revenge. Against everything she hated about herself. Doing the same at Northeastern was a given—she'd assumed. Mrs. Cranbrook stole this from her by making her invisible.

"Looking at this parabola, if you wanted to find the average rate of change between point x and point y, how would you do it?" Ophelia's hand shot up.

"How do we find the average rate of change between two

points of a function?" But this time, after having her hand up for only a few seconds, Ophelia decided not to wait. She loudly called out the answer. "Find the slope of the secant, where the change in x approaches zero."

Mrs. Cranbrook's pale eyebrows tried to jump off her forehead but couldn't quite make it, so they froze just under her hairline. It took her a full five seconds to acknowledge what had happened. And those five seconds opened like a chasm underneath Ophelia's desk. She had said the answer so loud that the whole class stopped, turned, stared, and held their breath. Five seconds, or was it five days, later, Mrs. Cranbrook steadied her glasses on her nose, smoothed her dress—it was peaches and giraffes that day—and cleared her throat with a false smile before she spoke. Ophelia knew it was a false smile because her lips moved, but the rest of her face remained statue still.

"Ophelia, I don't know what happens in your classrooms at Stone River High, but at Northeastern, you don't answer until the teacher calls on you. We call this 'manners.'"

After that, Ophelia decided to only put her hand up for every second question she knew the answer to.

In early October, not yet two months into the school year, Madame Belle called Ophelia by her real name.

"Ophelia."

The sound of her name in Belle's mouth made her wonder what she had done wrong.

"Oui, madame?"

Belle approached her with her slither walk; those bright green eyes weighed her on their scales.

"Have you decided what college you will apply to and for what?"

Ophelia exhaled.

"No, madame," and added quickly, "but I like calculus and history."

"Mrs. Cranbrook says that you are very good at math, but I haven't heard from your Mr. Holland in history. Do you have a favorite?"

"Mrs. Cranbrook said that? I thought she didn't like me. She pretends I don't exist. You teachers are good at making students vanish."

Somehow she knew that Belle had smiled at her comment, but to look at her face, nothing had changed. Ophelia had learned that if you cowered she would crush you, but if you showed some fight she'd be nicer.

Belle motioned at a chair. "Sit down . . . s'asseoir . . ." She moved behind Ophelia, out of her sight.

"C'est differente, isn't it? Being here instead of being around Black children?"

From behind, Belle dusted Ophelia's shoulders off with two swift flicks of her palm. Her perfume was distracting. Vanilla, jasmine, and lily of the valley. Ophelia savored its luscious cloud.

Belle's head appeared next to Ophelia's cheek. Her snake whisper got softer but somehow tougher.

"When you are around white children and their teachers, you will notice that they are sure that you are not their equal. No one will ever say it in words. They might not even know that they are doing it. But they will say it to you in many other ways."

Walking in front of Ophelia, she brought her face so close that their noses almost touched. All the creases of her eyes, the smoothness of her neck, the subtle mascara, those all-seeing green eyes came into focus. This is what she did when she wanted you to remember something important.

"You must never believe them." Belle's gaze gripped Ophelia. "If you do, your entire life will be lost, comprendre?"

"Oui, madame."

When Ophelia walked into Mrs. Cranbrook's math class that same morning, everyone was discussing a brochure they'd found on their desks. The writing on the board said, *Senior Trip—Washington, DC.*

"Isn't Abe a babe?" asked Cindy, who was a gray-eyed, dimple-faced, freckle-spined beauty. The kind some people called a "Southern belle." She didn't stoop to speak to Ophelia except for once when she needed help with her vectors, which no one else had understood.

"Abe is totally a babe," said Laurie, who was her wing girl and always agreed with what Cindy said. They were looking at a brochure of the Lincoln Memorial.

"I could take him. He don't look so tough." Ryan chuckled.

"Now, class, because this is your homeroom, your packages for your senior trip to Washington, DC, have come in and I've left them on your desks. I realize that you're full of anticipation, but please put them away to discuss with your parents. Today we have a lot of parabolas to cover. Yes, Ophelia?"

"I didn't get mine."

"Let's chat after class, okay?"

After class, Mrs. Cranbrook informed her, "The Northeastern senior trip is a tradition. We'd love it if all our seniors could attend, but it's quite expensive. You're very good at calculus, but I don't believe you Belle École students are the right fit for this."

In Etsi's one-room school at Riverwalk Elementary and at Stone River High, she'd always shut up and taken whatever people had dished out. But what Mrs. Cranbrook said had made all that bile she'd swallowed her whole childhood swell up and burst the banks of her brain. But not in a hot-blooded way, it was her calculating wolf that interrupted her.

"Can a high school teacher afford it? Can you afford it?"

"Well." Mrs. Cranbrook blushed. "I don't have any children, Ophelia, so that's beside the point. But yes, a teacher could afford such a trip."

"Charles Large's parents are both professors at Baxter College. Do they make more than a high school teacher?"

Mrs. Cranbrook's mouth opened into a circle of mortification.

"It's not polite to discuss—"

Ophelia interrupted her again.

"The twins' parents buy companies on Wall Street. Is that more money than a high school teacher makes?"

Mrs. Cranbrook's mouth closed. She forced her lips together as if she were struggling not to barf. Her head started to tremble unconsciously.

"Natasha's dad runs the Ford plant in Hope Valley. Is that more than a teacher makes?"

Mrs. Cranbrook walked through her indignation to the drawer behind her desk and came back with a brochure package for the senior trip.

They both knew she couldn't afford the trip. But for the first time at Northeastern, Ophelia walked out of class with a swagger in her step.

Chapter Thirty-Two

The boy's name was Chris, and at first, Ophelia avoided him as if he had a contagious infection.

It hadn't started that way. Early in the year, when she didn't know who he was, he approached her in an empty high school hallway. Ophelia had a long time to look as if she wasn't looking. Framed like a ballplayer, his stride had that easy kind of poise; he wore a Polo sweater, but there was a sag and a bounce to the way he walked, milky-pale skin, hair brown but speckled with blond, sad blue eyes like pieces of stolen sky. As he passed he said, "Hi, Ophelia."

"Hi," she said, and had no idea why she blushed.

How does he know my name? she wondered. She felt exposed. She needed to ask about him. So she slipped her crush into a container at the back of her mind until she could find out who he was.

"Christopher? Like Columbus?" she repeated after Key told her that his name was Christopher Beauregard. In the time it took to say his name, that boulder she kept in the pit of her stomach flattened her crush for him.

Key and Tai's favorite place was soon Ophelia's favorite place. It was a swampy field where a rotted airplane lay half-submerged in moss and water and weeds. They nicknamed it "The Orphanage." Though the twins weren't orphans, their parents lived on Long Island, New York, and had exiled them to South Carolina for bad behavior.

"We're trust-fund orphans, baby!" Tai said between push-ups.

"But with a condo and a coupe for consolation," Key finished, then asked, "What's your beef with Christopher Beauregard anyways?"

"That boy?" Ophelia then told them the tale of the soggy-looking boy with those sad eyes from that day in Etsi. The kid whose family had poisoned her river. She told the twins, "His daddy trotted him out like a show pony to trick us into not suing." He was on the other team.

"It probably wasn't his fault. But still. This whole never-ending lawsuit—that's ruining my Grandma Blue's health—is for a farm he's gonna own one day."

"You want us to fuck him up?" asked Tai, always ready to choose violence. "Hey Key, I bet you couldn't box him solo."

"I'd own that milk dud," Key dismissed this idea sweetly.

"Nah, c'mon chill. I don't want to beat him up; I just can't figure out how he knows my name."

"I know," Tai said, and then they finished in unison, "'Cause he tryna get his ass beat."

They high-fived to his joke, and Tai flexed his neck and bulged his eyes into a game face like Aiyanna and Ophelia would do. Ophelia laughed.

"Look, you two felons, lemme at least see who wins the lawsuit first?"

"Then we'll beat his ass?" Tai asked, looking at his sister, who confirmed lovingly, "Then we'll beat his ass." Ophelia had no idea whether they were serious or not, but she appreciated that they had her back.

Ophelia recalled how haggard her grandmother had looked in June when she'd visited. A tremor in her hands, brown spots on her eyeballs, she was a deflated sack of skin over bones. Grandma Blue, indomitable no more. The confusion of seeing her frail and mortal returned to Ophelia when she heard the name: Christopher Beauregard. Buck Cronkite had been true to his word to her grandmother: Etsi had won the suit, but Jack Beauregard had tied it up for years in appeals court and in their state supreme court. Meanwhile the Beauregard offers to settle were getting as thin as Grandma Blue's once burly forearms.

To Ophelia, Christopher Beauregard was the cause. Etsi was a distant memory. But this boy she could hate. With his two-hundred-dollar Jordans, his Polo fleece, his Mercedes, and his certainty. Ophelia had never scorned a stranger. Once she had figured out who he was, he was hard to avoid. Tall, rich, and poised. He was the boy all the girls wanted but couldn't get. And yet he never passed her in the halls or at the football game without saying, "Hi, Ophelia," in that same casual way, as if it weren't nothing but might be everything.

"It's annoying," she told Key and Tai, but they didn't believe her because of how she snickered when she said it. After a while she waited for him to say it. Found herself in places where he might show up and say it. This drove her crazy with shame. *Grandma Blue out there dying to protect our people and this is who I'm trying to crush on?*

"Why you always got some BIG feelings, O?" said Taiwo. "The Big e-m-O. Emo to the death!"

"Tai, let that girl get her Capulet and Montague on, aight?" his sister said, pretending to defend Ophelia while still teasing her.

"I'm not feeling him," she declared all angry. "Richy Rich, the fucking glamour boy? Forget that noise."

Key and Tai got silent but gave her knowing grins. Feeling like she had to prove something to them, she mocked him with her own words: "Christopher? Like Columbus? No way."

Chapter Thirty-Three

Ophelia turned eighteen on December 12, 2004. That January, the twins planned to take her to Charlotte to celebrate. Tai said, "It's Get Yur Freak On Fridays." Key grabbed her by the face and hollered, "We going dancing, family!"

When Friday came and she pulled up at their swanky parent-funded condominium, the twins were not feeling Ophelia's outfit at all.

"What's wrong with what I'm wearing?"

She had bought the sweater just for the occasion. In her defense it did have a sporty, midriff-out vibe. But it was a turtle-neck. With shoulder pads.

"What's wrong? You look like Cameo's backup dancer?"

"Who?"

They both yelled louder as if that would make her know who it was. "Cameo!"

"I thought you'd like this outfit."

"Shoulder pads, O? Come on," Key said, disgusted. "You ain't going to Charlotte looking like that."

She had missed the dress code for her own birthday party.

It was the worst start to the night. From the twenty-fifth floor, the view of the lights from downtown Stone River that usually thrilled her only made her despair. Before she could feel truly awful, Taiwo shut off the music, while Key appeared from the kitchen and presented her with two shopping bags.

"Good thing we got you this."

Her head felt like it would pop like a pimple when Key handed her the bag. They both gathered round and watched as Ophelia tentatively pulled out the pretty stuffing and unwrapped the fancy box. It was a dress. A shiny, tiny black sequined dress. She knew this dress. Weeks before, as if she needed advice, Key had asked her which one of three dresses she'd wear. Ophelia was flattered. Key never asked for fashion tips. But all along, it was a gift for her. Ophelia's face burst like a dam at this realization. She started to tremble and weep.

"Thank you."

The twins stood with their thin horseheads astounded. Key mock clapped and shook her head. "You sure is a precious snow-flake, aren't you?"

Tai dropped to his knees, rolled over on his back, and kicked his feet in the air, laughing at her.

"This why I fuck wid you, O. You're a real one. You and dem big-assed feelings!"

"Fuck wid" is how he said *this is why I like you*. Even amid her tears she noticed that this was the first time either of them had said why they were her friend.

Key said, "Why don't you try it on."

Ophelia went to the bathroom to change. It was a pretty, scaly thing. The back was open, and the front gripped her chest tight as a bear hug. The sheer lacy fabric on the inside felt soft against her stomach. When she checked out the back in the mirror, the dress barely covered her butt. She fluffed her curls and hoped that they would like it.

"CHEA BITCH! CHEA BITCH! CHEEEEEA BITCH!" With Tai a "chea bitch" was the highest praise. "You look el fuego, mami!" said Key, with her dirty, up-to-something sneer.

"You don't think it's too short?"

"Guuuurl, your slim-thick bootie is poppin' just like it should. Now let's do something about them lips."

When they left the condo, Ophelia's lips were blacked out to match Taiwo's and Keyinde's. They were kitted out in all-black everything. Key in tights and flats, a skintight, mid-thigh, long-sleeved dress on, silver and black wooden bracelets orbiting her tiny wrist bones like electrons around an atom. Tai with little square silver buckles on his heels, long-sleeve shirt tucked into jet-black, airtight jeans. The skin of their faces glowed like black hole suns. God help whatever got in their way.

"Ya'll we look like comic book superheroes. You know that?"

The black lipstick gang made Ophelia feel more beautiful than any time she could remember. It occurred to her that she had picked the sequin dress because of Madame Belle. This thought made her glow a bit. She didn't know what else could happen in this wild new world, where "beautiful" was a thing that she could be, but whatever it was, some of Madame Belle's slithering snake energy felt like exactly what she needed.

They parked the twins' Audi on a downtown Charlotte side street, ducked down an alley that reeked of piss and rotten collard greens, and got let in at a back door after two minutes of knocking. They were all still underage, but Key and Tai had finessed their access.

Inside, the bass pounded and shook the walls as if they were in a giant womb. It wasn't the first club they had snuck her into, but Ophelia could tell by the way they talked about Bup Daddy's that it was their favorite. This was their element. The bump and grind. The sweat and sweetness. The fights. The pheromones. The raw, feral animal unleashed by booze and horniness. This drew the twins like bees to nectar. As soon as they got into the main room, Key and Tai scattered in opposite directions and left her to fend for herself. This was also how they rolled, birthday or no. But this time their abandonment suited her. Ophelia felt like being around people. She wanted to do her own thing and see just what kind of sexy she was.

There was a white boy owning the dance floor with a gang of dudes. This got Ophelia hot right off. *Why are they always all up in our business? As soon as my people get something popping—ta-da!— white people jump in like they own it.* Ophelia knew that she was a hater. She couldn't help it. After having her own Blackness questioned, she hated how some white guys and girls could just stroll into a Black club and be accepted. They could do the moves, wear the clothes, talk the talk, sing the song, but when it was all said and done, they got to change clothes and become something else. She couldn't change her skin. Her fight for acceptance was permanent. This is why she was a hater. Still she thought, *Damn, that white boy can move though.*

Ophelia found herself adjusting to take in the scene around him. He bopped seamlessly to "Get Ur Freak On," that Missy Elliott song, and when the DJ pulled it, he switched up his flow to Ciara's "1, 2 Step" without missing a beat. Enamored with that sweaty dance floor man smell, she circled the crowd, trying to find an angle where she could keep watching him do his thing.

Bass from the speakers mingled with cologne and spilled vodka. That recipe was pulling her in. And in the center of it was this white boy with his baby-blue bucket hat. Tall, ballplayer-ripped shoulders—*them shoulders though*—and the baby-blue Larry Johnson #2 Charlotte Hornets jersey with the pants sagging just so, 23s on his feet, and his hat pulled low so all she could see were his lips mouthing the words to every song.

Unconsciously she dipped into the middle of the crowded pack of bodies bouncing but kept track of where he was. Kept moving in his direction. Circling him like a planet does its sun. When she got near the middle of the floor, Lil Jon dropped. "Called it!" she yelled, and the validation put the batteries in her back: She punched her hand up, pointed at the roof, and started to shake.

TO DA WINDOOOOOW. TO DA WALL!

Mezcal was her drink for the birthday turnup. Feeling herself, she tilted her head back and let her hips bang to the beat. Her mouth tasted fiery and delicious. The strapped-up heels—that she had borrowed from Key—tapped out the beat. Her whole body started to lean and tingle.

Out the corner of her eyes, there he was again. What she could see of his face glowed alabaster bright under the lights. A slight gap in his teeth left his face with the residue of a rascal. And he knew all the steps. Hitting the turns. Popping. Locking. Floor game tight too. Came out of a split mouthing Yeah! Yeah! like he was auditioning for the Usher video shoot. *Damn, that boy could move though. See? They shoulda never given Justin Timberlake money. Elvis, Rick Astley, none-a-dem.*

Suddenly three things happened. First, the DJ dropped "Pony," which was HER SONG. As in, she owned it. Ginuwine might have sung it, but it was her song. Then, the white boy suddenly butterflies, knees bent slightly opening and closing like wings flapping in slow motion. *Butterfly!* But then his hat flipped up and his exposed eyes lasered into hers. It was Christopher. The lights lit up those sad baby blues. Electricity shot through her spine. Again she remembered the sad boy-fox and the way his eyes had haunted her in Etsi—so long ago. Finally, just as he reached her, he spun away and walked off.

Who he think he is? her mind spoke to her in Beyoncé, and just as her breath was about to catch up to her pulse, he spun back, and with a gap-toothed mouth full of mischief he said the first words of the song: "I'm just a bachelor."

Stunned into stillness, Ophelia stopped moving completely. Grandma Blue's image popped into her head along with a pang of reproach. "Those old people already had their turn . . ." Aiyanna had said. But Grandma Blue's face wouldn't let her go so easily. She felt the old woman's judgment as if she were sitting at the bar watching her play herself. *Hmpff,* Ophelia imagined her saying, which meant *mind the river. You hear me? Mind it good.*

Suddenly, Christopher rushed back into her space. Gun fingers rotating. His peach-sliced lips mouthed the song's words. Heat from his chest caught her nostrils and they drank hungrily. The way he moved—so sure, so confident—inebriated her. Ophelia chose to keep dancing.

They grooved to four songs in a row after that: "Yeah!" by her boy Usher and Lil Jon, and she felt as though she was in a music video that she and Christopher were starring in. She gave him the dirtiest smile she knew how to and started to go lower and lower and lower, and get him as low as she could to the ground for the next song, "Drop It Like It's Hot." He was ballplayer tall, and she was little, but he went just as low as her, which made the whole place cheer. She was vaguely aware that she was biting the corner of her lower lip when Beyoncé came on. They just circled each other, and he egged her on as if she was Bey herself. He threw up his hands and made a fan over her and kept waving energy toward her, and somewhere she heard the crowd chanting, "Heeey . . . hoooo . . . heeey . . . hoooo . . ."

It was like a dream where she was a rock star, featured and special, and he was that hot boy, that popular boy, serving fools with flyness. As he was dusting off her shoulder, she noticed that his fingernails were painted black, just like her lips. *We must look so good right now.* Ophelia didn't know why she felt like she had to impress him, but she was sure that she needed him to like her. Not seeing his eyes anymore added to the mystery. Then she spun out and turned so he could get a good long look at the almost-there hem of her dress. She grinned, assuming that he was gazing at her goodies. So, she walked away to let her hips talk. Imagining him drooling.

But when she turned around, he was gone.

"Why you so distracted, O?" Key teased her on the drive home. "Somebody stole your ice cream?"

"I'm cool."

"If you gon' throw up, don't do it in the whip," Tai said from shotgun.

"Nah, I'm straight."

"Then why you acting all suss?"

"Did you see WHO I was dancing with? Ya'll didn't, did you?" If they hadn't recognized Christopher, she wasn't about to tell them. Something about that dance floor made her want to keep it to herself.

"HAAAAAWWWW!" said Tai, "Pay up, Key. You owe me fifty dollars."

Key looked at him and shook her head. Then watched Ophelia in the rearview. "You got yourself some love on the dance floor, huh? From a white boy?"

"Did you bet Tai that I wouldn't?"

"I bet him that you'd get attention from the boys. He bet me that you'd get caught up."

"HAAAAAAAAAW!"

"I'm not caught up."

"Girl to girl, you look caught up."

"HAAAAAAAAAW!"

"Taiwo, behave. It's her first time. Manners much?"

"HAAAAW! The big e-m-O strikes again!"

"Don't listen to him, O. Tell me about this white boy."

"He was alright. He was a good dancer. That's all."

But then she went missing from the car and floated back to the club and the dance floor and those moves, the way he knew exactly where to be, how to send her one way and go the next, how to put some slight pressure on her hip to tell her where to be and how fast she needed to be there, it was like they were talking the whole time but there weren't any words being said. *Heeey . . . hoooo . . . heeey . . . hoooo . . .*

When Ophelia's spirit came back to her body, Key's eyes were drinking in the sight of her through the rearview mirror. She'd seen the secret reminiscing smile, and that she was still biting the corner of her bottom lip. There was no hiding it; Ophelia was caught up.

Chapter Thirty-Four

Key and Tai were gone that Monday. Their texts were unsentimental. Typed with a shrug. Just as everything they did.

> Key: "We got summoned back to Long Island to kiss Papa's pinky ring."

> Tai: "They claim they want us to be 'a family again,' but they'll get sick of us. Just watch."

> Key: "Sorry we couldn't say goodbye."

> Tai: "You is good peoples O. That's why we fuck wid you."

Ophelia was in school when she got their messages. There was suddenly no oxygen left in the air. Her lungs collapsed and her knees buckled, and before she could understand how, she was on the ground, legs splayed out. She grasped at the door of her locker but was unable to get ahold of anything.

When she had put herself back together, she found Madame Belle and demanded, "Did you know about this?"

Belle was sitting in her office by the chandelier lamp, her claws clamped onto a skinny cigarette, her reptile eyes staring out at nothing.

"Did you know about this?" she repeated louder.

"Imbecile! You will not talk to me with this tone."

"Did you know?"

"Will you make me repeat myself?"

"You knew, didn't you?"

"I am sorry, Ophelia. Je suis désolé. Their mother called me on the weekend and asked me to get them on the plane. They started their new high school in Westbury, New York, this morning."

"All I got were texts."

"They were on a private jet to LaGuardia by ten o'clock Sunday morning. You were still sleeping. Do you know who their parents are? These are not people you want to make wait."

"You helped them leave?"

"You will taste the back of my hand if you speak to me in this tone again."

"Nobody cares."

"Of course nobody cares. C'est la vie. People come, people go. This is life."

"This is my life. They were my friends. The only real friends I ever had. The only friends . . ."

It felt as though some crucial part of Ophelia had fallen and smashed on the high school floor. Shango's ghost haunted her. She thought of him more often than she knew she did, and would admit to doing so even less. Yet in moments when she felt distraught, his absence would come roaring into her to feed her frustration, and she would pity herself. She screamed, "Why do people always abandon me?!"

But when she arrived back at her locker, there was a tall, blue-eyed Polo-wearing boy leaning on it. Through her grief she couldn't help but notice how different Christopher was to Friday night when he'd disappeared from the Bup Daddy's dance floor. Bucket hat gone. Hornets jersey gone. Ballplayer swag gone. He had transformed into something else: a preppy rich kid. Only his black fingernails were left to reveal his other self.

"Sorry I vanished," he said. "I knew I'd see you again . . ."

Ophelia, still full of angst, didn't want to deal with all those dimples and shoulders. Romance wasn't a mood she had any energy for. That vacancy the news about the twins created made it easier for her to shut Christopher down.

"We can't be doing this . . ." she said.

"What are we doing?"

"Playing Romeo and Juliet? The club was fun, but your family and my family aren't cool."

Almost imperceptibly, he closed the distance between them, and his soft sandalwood scent distracted her.

"Isn't that exactly how Romeo and Juliet goes?"

Ophelia grinned. She didn't know why.

"That's not what I mean. My grandmother is the plaintiff in the lawsuit against your farm. You infected our water."

"Your grandmother? For real?"

He sighed and raked his hair with his fingers until the specks of blond reshuffled themselves. The mournfulness of his eyes worked against her. There was something vulnerable there that made Ophelia melt.

"Did you know that my great-great-great-grandmother Rebecca Latimer Beauregard incorporated the town of Stone River? She was a feminist; she campaigned for women to vote and own property. But she wasn't no leftie. She campaigned to hang random Black men 'for the sexual purity of the white race.'"

"So your family is a pack of racists. I'm shocked."

He sighed and pretended not to notice her sarcasm.

"What I mean to say is"—he sighed again—"I'm not my family, Ophelia. I'm not like them. I'm different. Don't you have things about your family you don't want to inherit?"

His logic and his freckles were irrefutable.

"I guess I do."

Sensing her soften, he took his chance. "You know where the sunken plane is? In the marsh?"

"Yeah." A pang of remembrance of Key and Tai washed over her.

"If you walk past there, there's a field, then a hill of magnolias. Meet me there after school on Friday?"

She hesitated.

"C'mon, girl. Gimme a chance?"

The hole in her life that the twins had left kept her dazed all that week. She dragged herself through her days, there in body but not in spirit. Her face felt numb. Her stomach ached. Languid and distracted, she drifted between class and home. Ophelia drifted through the week, cut off from her senses, like a bug trapped in amber and separated from the air. On Friday Madame Belle said, "This weight will not get lighter, petit canard. You must get stronger to lift it."

Ophelia was top of her classes and Belle had been encouraging her to apply to Baxter University. Belle believed she might get a scholarship. Ophelia dismissed the idea. *Me? Is that even realistic? Everybody I know from Riverwalk Elementary is already working at the Ford plant, flipping burgers, selling dope on Beauregard Avenue, or gone away to Charlotte or Atlanta. College? Me? People like me don't go to college.*

"Besides, what if I don't get a scholarship?"

This last question she asked Madame Belle in her office that Friday morning before class. Belle hissed her contempt in serpent-speak. "So, you will not run the race because you're afraid you might lose?"

"What business does somebody like me have going to college?"

Ophelia's depression had made her brave.

"You want to go back to the cabin in the bush with grand-mère? Is that it?"

"What's wrong with that? I learned a lot in that cabin in the bush."

"Like what?"

"Like how to cook. The twins said they were going to open a restaurant with me."

"Merde! Petit idiot. Be serious."

"I am being serious. Just because you're too ashamed to admit you were born there—"

Belle crossed the space between them so rapidly that Ophelia's jaw was in her claws before she could turn away. Belle's left hand hovered ominously. A thunderclap waiting to fall.

"Do it. I'm tired of being afraid. Nobody cares about me anyways. Why should they? If my own mother and father left me, then why should anybody else care?"

The hand fell back down to Belle's side.

"Get out of here, petit canard, before I murder you."

Ophelia left Belle's office and went up the main hallway and out of Northeastern High. She rode her bike out past the long rows of abandoned factories, retracing the route she and the twins would often take. Up the dirt path and under the barbed wire where the sign read NO TRESPASSING, next to a drawing of a pump-action shotgun, but in one corner, on a sticker, she noticed that it read BEAUREGARD FARMS. It was starting to make sense why Christopher had asked her to meet him there.

The wind blew from the south and she pulled her hoodie close around her. As she walked her bike up the dirt path, across the field, and towards the next hill, she could smell magnolias in the distance. And she could see their blossoms in flight. Her life felt like an inconsequential thing. As if the breeze could just lift her off the ground and toss her towards the trees, drag her across the hillsides and plop her down into some distant river's rush. She felt like Stone Dress, wandering the wilderness, looking for something to devour.

Ophelia drifted into a clearing where the sun cut through the branches and caught her in its flow. Being surrounded by trees and the breeze took her back to that time when butterflies covered her and lifted her off her feet. There was a part of her that knew she had imagined flying, but that didn't stop her from longing for it. As she walked into that clearing, she wished for butterflies to surround her, lift her up and fly her away.

"It's so childish," she said, "to want something so silly."

Ophelia went to the center of the field, closed her eyes, spread her arms wide, and waited for little butterfly legs to touch her face. When she opened her eyes, a wall of colors squashed her breath and made her eyes water at the edges. Breeze, birdsong, and the bright heat became one voice. It painted her vision in a cascading curtain of colors. It covered everything she could see. It swirled warm and restless. Her skin bristled against the onslaught of the wind, and as it subsided, she heard a boy's voice calling.

"Helloooo . . . Helloooo . . ."

At first she was pissed off to be suddenly pulled out of her miracle.

Christopher teased her, "You're one of those Pretty School people, right?"

It was preppy Christopher. There were no 23s on his feet, no baggy pants, no b-boy lean in his stance, no idea that he might be a ballplayer or the best dancer she had ever seen. Just golf shorts and a Georgia State sweater vest, and yet it was the same boy. Those shoulders. She'd recognize them anywhere. Ophelia said, "Beautiful School. Belle École. It means 'Beautiful School.'"

"Why does your teacher call it that?"

"Why do you care why she called it that?" Her brain asked her face, *Why are you smirking?*

"Well . . . I'm here . . . here's your chance . . ."

Without the bucket hat, his mouth had lost all its mystery but none of its charm. He had that slightly gap-toothed, pearly-white smile full of mischief, and a spray of freckles down the side of his face.

Ophelia got her back up.

"Why can't it be the Beautiful School? I can't be pretty? That's what you saying?"

Sad, sad eyes. They peered into the space that surrounded her.

"Nah. Come on now. I didn't say that."

A fox. That's what she thought right then. He reminded her of a fox. He moved light on his feet and had those penetrating melancholy eyes—like a sky full of rain, but no clouds. He had that build too: lithe, lean, nimble as he moved. She noticed the knots of muscles where his shoulders imprinted under his shirt. A fox.

"You damn pretty." He smiled that gap-toothed smile.

Pretty. He said it so easy too, so sure, as if he was saying *the sky is blue* or *warm bread is delicious.*

All tension left her body. The hollowness in her guts from losing Key and Tai, the tangle of stress in her neck, the vice that locked her temples into pain, all of this released and fell, in slow motion, to the ground in the span of one breath. She locked into his eyes, which were distant and unhappy. And the wind whipped their clothes and blew wisps of dandelions into their faces. It felt as though they too could be lifted away and carried on a gust to somewhere where they could dance and he would not run away, and she wouldn't despise his family. It made her feel relaxed, refreshed, and completely his.

It was all too much for her.

Like a rabbit might scamper across a field at the sight of a hunting fox, Ophelia turned away from Christopher and ran. She dashed, hopped on her bike, and didn't stop peddling until she got to apartment 66.

Chapter Thirty-Five

That night when she got home, she tried to think of anything but Christopher. But her head kept lighting up with his moves from the dance floor that night at Bup Daddy's, how it felt when he put his hands on her waist and spun her strong but gently, how he made a fan with his arms and kept beaming energy at her, how the whole floor was howling: *Heeey . . . hoooo . . . heeey . . . hoooo . . .*

She needed to think about anything but the boy-fox right then, or how mysterious he was, with that black nail polish, or how he mouthed the words to the songs while he was looking at her like he could see something nobody else could, or how everything he said about her was said so easy breezy, as if it'd be foolish for anyone to think she was anything but special.

It was late when Auntie Aiyanna came back. But Ophelia barely noticed. She washed her face and stared down her little hickory nose and eyes and wondered what that boy saw in her. To distract herself, she laid in bed and her Discman played Marvin Gaye's "Distant Lover"—Shango's song from that day he brought her to apartment 66. Letting the squeal of the ladies in the crowd wash over her, she imagined that she was there again: his old man muscle car, that oily sweet smell, the wheel slipping through his rough hands, his voice humming: *Distant Lovaaaaaaaaah*. And her whole body felt weightless. Levitating through the roof, and into the stars, she fell asleep in the darkness behind them.

"You came back," Christopher said to her the next day when she found him again at the hill of magnolias. He said it simple as apple pie, as if he had been waiting there since she'd left.

"Why you think I'm pretty?" she asked.

He smiled, and his dimples came out like the summer constellations over Etsi.

"Ah tell you if you win."

She thanked the Lord that her skin hid her blushes.

"Win what?"

"The race."

"Boy, say what you mean." She thought she was annoyed, but her voice came out all giggly.

"Race you to the magnolias." He flashed a gap-toothed grin and took off before she could ask which direction that was. So she chased him. Ophelia wasn't gonna let him punk her, but she didn't want him to be gone so soon either.

He burst into a circle of magnolias right before she did, and the tart, citrusy smell soaked her senses. She closed her eyes and took a long, deep pull of the magnolia fragrance until he tapped her on her shoulder and startled her back to reality.

"Boy, if you don't stop sneaking up on me . . ."

She was annoyed, but still it came out giggly.

"Pretty cool, huh?" he said, and ran his hands through his

hair. His hair was cut shortish and rolled down his face a little bit above his eyes.

"So, tell me why," she said, still catching her breath, but he was gone again. He'd run off towards a big-trunked elm not twenty feet away. At the foot of the massive tree, he started climbing. She dashed after him and saw slats of wood nailed into the tree to form a stepladder. She could see from the bottom looking up that there was a tree house hidden in the branches.

"Ya'll put a house up there?"

"C'mon!" he called, and she started to climb the ladder.

Is this thing gonna fall out from under my feet? she thought as she took the first step and reached up to grab the one above her head. But the slats were drilled through in that smooth, consistent way machines did. A real carpenter made those stairs.

As Ophelia climbed up, a forest of magnolias rose on her left, and above her the tree house came into view. It was made of weathered wood and looked like it had been made to be a real house you could live in except that it was small. When she got to the top, the wooden door slid open sideways. Inside it had a solid floor, a couch, a sink, a mini fridge, and a small cot with pillows and an ugly *Star Wars* blanket.

"You made this?" she asked in wonder at his little domain in the trees, but before he could answer she asked, "Wait. Is this where you live? Are you homeless?"

"You think so, huh?" he said, eyes wild, daring her to call him homeless again. "Do I look like I live in a tree?"

There was something playful about how he asked her, as if she had taken the dare and he was upping the stakes.

"I guess not. Hobos don't wear brand-new Air Jordans and dance at clubs either."

"It's my family's. I used to come here a lot more when I was a kid."

"So your family owns this forest?"

"A lot of it, yeah," he said, as if to own an apartment in a tree was the same as a backpack or a pair of sneakers.

More magnolia blossoms came blowing through the huge window. Ophelia could see that they were in acres of those magnolia trees. She'd only ever seen two or three of them at most in one place. White and fuchsia flowers leapt into the wind and drifted up. Their perfume filled the horizon.

He came up beside her and they watched the blossoms float.

"Can I tell you why you're pretty now?" His dimple parade was banging its drum. "Because all the other Black girls make their hair straight and white-looking, but you keep yours natural. Because when I asked about you, they say you always have the answers in calculus class and because you're not afraid to come running after preppy white boys in tree houses."

Ophelia had spent all day wondering what his answer to that would be, and it wasn't even what he said but how he said it. Same way as everything he said, as if the truth of it was a foregone conclusion, as if he was calling grass green or water wet. His mischievous mouth twinkled at her.

"And you an alright dancer too . . ."

"Alright? Just alright?" She punched his arm playfully. "You not bad yourself."

His smile took her back to that dance floor and the way he moved, the gentleness, the certainty, the perfection of everyone looking at them and knowing that they were magic, him and her, they were a team and they had them spellbound for those five songs at Bup Daddy's. In her head, he was eternally in that baby-blue bucket hat, gap tooth singing the words to every song while nailing the swag like a Beyoncé backup dancer. He was the prettiest thing she'd ever seen.

They spent what felt like years talking about Madame Belle; hating Stone River; their favorite nineties movies—hers was *Poetic Justice*, his was *Boyz n the Hood*; if he could cook and what his best recipes were (Kraft Mac & Cheese). "Eew!" she screamed. And lasagna. Best three muscle cars—Camaro, Trans Am, Cutlass, they agreed. All-time best and worst dance moves, which is when he got up and did what Ophelia called "a white lady grandma dance" called the Charleston. She tried to show him the Chicken Head dance, but he already knew how it went.

"Is that the move from *You Got Served*? From Elgin in the opening scene? How did you learn that?"

"Around . . ." Another gap-toothed grin. His fox eyes were still sad, still distant, but for a second twinkled.

"Around where?"

"Just around."

"Oh, you get around do you?"

"I like to dance. You gotta go where the good music is."

"You mean where the Black music is, huh?"

"Hey, I'm a fan."

"Boy, you know all the moves and all the songs. You Blacker than me!"

"Nah, not even close," he said, and he leaned at the hip, watched her cold in her eyes, and as he hinged up he rotated his shoulder blades in time to some beat only he could hear. The fox moved so light and so precise that she thought he might be a puppet on imaginary strings. It made her giggle to watch him move. *Damn, those shoulders though.*

"Not even close," he said again, and again it was as sure as if he had just added two and two and said it was four.

They dialed in his little radio and Billy Graham was preaching. "Neeeext," they both yelled in unison. Which made them erupt into cackles. Finally, she got TLC's "Baby-Baby-Baby" on, and he knew the words and so they sang it to each other. Then they were up and dancing, and she didn't even wonder about if the tree house might fall, 'cause it felt so solid under her feet. And suddenly without the bucket hat or the 23s or the sagging pants, they were back at Bup Daddy's. Except he was so sunny and innocent and playful and bit his lower lip the whole time and bounced with her without any turns or pops or locks, just swayed his chest and shoulders while he held on to her waist, and she needed that song to last forever because being close to him felt like there was nothing else occurring anywhere in the universe.

When the song ended, he came close enough that she could smell his cologne—that sandalwood scent again—and see the small gold-studded earrings he wore and the pores of his cheek and the pink peachiness of his long slip of a mouth that seemed permanently up to something. It was all dangerously close.

Her heart thump-thumped in her ear and her neck.

The sun was tumbling in the west and made the world the color of cognac.

"I have to go," he said softly.

"I do too," she said desperately.

It happened suddenly, like they were falling downhill. His hands grazed her face, fingertips on her earlobes, cuddled her cheek and pulled her in close, and he took a deep breath that warmed the impossible blue of his eyes.

"Do you want a kiss?" he said, and she nodded, her mouth

already half-open. She had not had much practice kissing boys, so she hoped that he knew what he was doing. But she knew that she wanted it.

Ophelia inhaled as he closed in and shut her eyes and her whole head got hazy off the taste of his tongue and the sugary, lemony flavor of magnolia flowers in the air. She leaned her neck back slowly and tiptoed to meet his mouth, and when their lips touched, he tasted like vanilla and pie, and everything became the warm softness of his mouth, and she felt as though she too was caught up in a strong spring breeze. His kiss lifted her up-up-up and out of her body and into the air and over the trees and over the cloudless sky and into forever.

Has anyone ever gotten kissed so deep that it snatched their soul right out of them? Has anyone ever felt a trembling that made their toes curl till they cramped? Their spine twist like a Twizzler? Their nipples shoot sparks like Fourth of July fireworks? Has anyone ever felt every hair on their spine raise up and salute their neck so they think they might have been electrocuted? And some sound come out their mouth like a moan that's a groan, that's a plea for help, 'cause it felt so good they weren't sure they'd survive?

Has anybody ever died from a kiss?

Chapter Thirty-Six

Christopher had always been his parents' battleground. He couldn't remember a time when they had a group hug, but he had a Hall of Fame for fights they'd had. It was full of shattered crystal, terrified servants, and furniture brandished in violence. Jack had married Cornelia because she, like him, was the scion of a great Southern edifice. Her branch of the Hollingsworths had squandered their wealth, and as the third daughter of six siblings, she was expected to "find old money and marry it."

Cornelia wasn't clever and was a hemophiliac but—lucky for her—her icy-blue eyes, delicate nose, and pale, opaque skin made her a great beauty in society. Among her siblings there was a claws-out competition for everything: the cars, privacy, her dresses— which her jealous sisters loved to "borrow," and never return. Her sisters despised her for her show-stealing looks, and her brothers despised her for her habit of seducing their classmates. Cornelia, being the second youngest and least witty, always lost. But be-sides beauty, she considered her stamina her greatest weapon: she would wait them out, until she left or they died, or Georgia sank into the sea. When she was sixteen she discovered Sazerac: rye whiskey, simple syrup, and bitters—Peychaud's preferably—and together Cornelia and Sazerac charmed their tipsy way into her twenties. It was at a Charleston garden party, after berating the hostess for her bartender's catastrophic inability to mix a good Sazerac, that she met Jack Beauregard.

Jack in those days was beyond debonair. Muscular, cultivated, and always three steps ahead of the room. His only failing was his inability to switch off. Jack, unlike many society boys, liked to roll up his sleeves. He cut an officer's figure in a sailing jacket, he was a Vanderbilt man, and he was curious about everything to do with making money. He expanded the family real estate holdings in Atlanta and Charleston, became a corporate landlord with a business park in Orlando, and convinced his ailing father to close the dying Beauregard tool and dye factories to fund all this expansion.

But undoubtedly Jack's finest moment came in the late eighties when drinking with his older hoary chum, the Charleston lawyer Don Smithers. Don had hatched a long shot scheme to talk the Etsi Cherokee into privatizing their reserve. Smithers cooed, "Now, Jack, I know you're from out that way, do you know how much land along that river those Cherokee own?"

Jack, too shrewd to let on, played dumb.

"Now, Don, isn't all that Cherokee land federally protected?"

"Bless your heart. Jack-My-Boy, it sure is. But I bet you didn't know that Etsi isn't a federally mandated reserve."

Don had a cousin in Canada and had managed to bring in a pair of Cohiba, Numero Dos, which he claimed were Fidel Castro's favorite cigars. He turned the end of one slowly on the tip of his lighter's orange flame and sucked it alight before he continued.

"No, sir. They bought that land themselves and had it recognized in 1866, after the War of Northern Aggression. With a bill promulgated by President Andrew Johnson, Lincoln's successor himself."

"Now, Don, I'm no historian, but why would Johnson, a Democrat and a friend of the South, give federal protection to the only band of Cherokee left in the Carolinas?"

The older man's two caterpillar eyebrows raised shrewdly.

"An astute question, Mister Beauregard. The answer is: a sizable bribe and a promise to leave the land under federal regulation for one hundred years."

"This seems a bit far-fetched, Don." Jack pretended that he didn't know the story well. The white Southerner who brokered the deal had been adopted by the Cherokee as a boy. When Johnson found out that he had been tricked, a compromise was struck. The Cherokee of Etsi became a federally recognized band and got to keep their land. Don's new discovery of an expired hundred-year clause had, to Jack, the smell of profit all over it.

"Now, guess who has a copy of said statute?"

Don watched with wickedness over his bushy brows. Jack played along.

"I wouldn't be standing smoking some of Cuba's finest with him, would I?"

A high-pitched hee hee hee hee scratched out of Don's throat, and his guts shook with glee. Jack raised his glass in a toast to Don's genius plan, even as he made mental notes on how to undermine it.

Jack knew exactly how valuable that Cherokee land was. He had worked managing the family farm ten miles downstream from Etsi and knew that the land was prime for grazing, and it being right on the river made it easy to manage the runoff.

The instant Don's scheme worked, and the land was privatized, Jack stealthily bought up the lots one by one. By spring 1991 he had modernized the old farm with electric fences, climate-controlled sheds, security cameras, automated feeders and portable water tanks, and took the family's herd of Black Angus cattle from fifty-two to four hundred and forty. Etsi's land had helped turn Beauregard Farms into South Carolina's biggest industrial livestock concern.

By this time, Cornelia's affection for rye whiskey had shriveled her skin and bloated her self-pity. In the mid-eighties Jack had hoped that a child would satisfy her boredom, but when the child was born, she had no desire to even hold it. Cornelia was not the motherly type. Christopher's wet nurse Adelia, a Black woman raised in Stone River, became his only source of affection.

"I'll take the brat and leave this god-forsaken estate if you don't start seeing about me," Cornelia threatened Jack before Christopher was even five months old. Jack calculated correctly that this was an empty threat, and his caged bird had no choice but to sip away her days on the veranda, abuse the help, and entertain herself with lowborn lovers.

Jack enjoyed his work. And the privileges it afforded him. No mayor had ever won an election in Stone River without the Beauregard blessing. His power was such that when the wealthy barons of the town complained about integrating its two high schools, he proposed Pendleton: a specially zoned neighborhood they could control. He kept a series of prostitutes—limber Spanish twenty-somethings were his type—in an apartment off Sturgis Avenue, but Jack rarely visited. Only money aroused him. And the Beauregard stranglehold on the county was how he ensured that the trough stayed full. That and the tutelage of his son Christopher.

Christopher, as an heir, showed troubling signs: truancy at

school, a slow head for numbers, no ambition except to play basketball and dance to Negro music. This fault Jack laid fully at the feet of his over-imbibed wife. "Well, what do you expect, Cornelia? You let a nigger woman raise him and now he wants to be a nigger."

Chris had learned early that his mom's interest in him would be fleeting and his father's interests would be his money, so he medicated himself with Black culture. Adelia's sons Ray and Dion fed it to him, and he slurped it up because it fed a place inside him that his parents could not touch. It was something all his own. Christopher longed desperately to escape the legacy of a two-hundred-year-old name, a half dozen estates, diversified holdings, family trusts, the Miami beach condo, and all the expectations that came with being the Prince of Stone River. He found this in dancing the 1, 2 Step and the Cha Cha Slide and heard it in Shawty Lo, Lil Jon, Ying Yang Twins, sagging jeans, 808 pops, fresh Jordans, diamond studs, icy chains, and being "the white boy that could." It gave him an identity that wasn't sterile, cut off, or ancient. It was now. It was fresh. It stunk. It sweated. It surged in his blood. It was alive.

And along with this insatiable appetite for Black culture, Christopher discovered his equally unfillable appetite for Black girls.

Chapter Thirty-Seven

"I'm one kiss away from falling in love," Ophelia told herself on her way home. Which meant that she was already in love.

Back at apartment 66, Ophelia noticed that the clock said 9:01 p.m. when she started to think about the "L" word again. Why? What reason did she have to believe that she was in love? She didn't know anything about love. She'd never seen parents' tender moments in the kitchen or being gross like her friends said parents could be or catch them when they stole a smooch on their way out of the house. What did she know about what men and women did? She'd seen Auntie Aiyanna kissing men and heard the bed creak and the yelling from the room next door. But she knew enough to know that that wasn't love. What did she know about love?

She listened to Lauryn Hill's *Miseducation* album where the kids in the classroom said what they thought love meant. Did she love Christopher because he wore fancy Adidas? Well . . . he preferred Nikes, but did she love him for superficial reasons? Because he was a pretty, Caucasian Usher without the singing but with the abs and the moves and the shoulders?

"Look at you, acting like a Ninny." She said one of her persistent Grandma Blue-isms to herself in the mirror at 9:15. Her eyes felt big as plates, her head felt like one of those giant balloon heads that float over the Stone River Fish Fry, her face filled with a smirk that started in one earlobe and split her face open all the way over to the other earlobe. It was a circus clown grin. She was all teeth and she wanted it to stop, but she couldn't make it stop. *There's a girl in the mirror named Ophelia Blue Rivers, and she's acting like a dummy*, but for once she was feeling herself, drinking her own Kool-Aid.

9:43 is what the clock said when she realized that her heart was beating irregularly, like throwing pots down the stairs, *clangclangalang-clang*, and she wondered if she was dying.

The clock said 9:53 when Auntie Aiyanna came home and started talking to her. She was remembering his tree house and that perfume—those facefuls of magnolia—and how his lips felt like slender slips of something velvet. How they left their warmth on hers, and before the imprint could fade, she needed to kiss him again to discover that soft warmness all over again.

10:35 was what the clock said when she realized that she had been talking to Aiyanna for a while and had no idea what Aiyanna had said.

Auntie Aiyanna had stopped talking to eye Ophelia suspiciously. Her googly eyeballs seemed to bobble, and her gold-capped mouth twinkled at her, and her heavy fingers tapped the table, but she didn't say anything. Aiyanna watched her as if she'd caught her lying and said, "Arright, Miss Ophelia, you think you're smart?"

12:42 is what the clock said the last time she looked at it, when she was falling asleep trying to memorize the five songs they had danced to, in the order they had danced to them: Ginuwine. Usher. Snoop. 'Yoncé. Jay Z. Pony. Yeah. Drop it. Naughty. Shoulder. This led to her memory of Christopher's eyes. Recalling the light catching them in the club, the times she had put herself in his path at school, the first moment she had seen them in Etsi, and they had thrust their sadness into her consciousness. They seduced her into drowsiness. Sky blue, sky blue.

Loving the coziness of his tree house couch, they talked gently on it the next day. It was feathery and sank down slowly while his little radio played "I Wanna Be Down" by Brandy. Christopher kissed her collarbones, neck, and behind her ears, and she felt as though sparkles had popped off in the room. When they were both naked, she could feel the whole bonfire of his skin pressed up against hers, belly to belly, nose to nose, and his shoulders thick with ripples—their skin dissolved into each other. The whole world seemed to pulse with the fragrance of magnolia flowers, the radio's staticky bounce, the midnight of her closed eyelids and the hot soup of his mouth.

Yet after that first encounter, there was nothing sweet about the two weeks that followed.

There was no cute sneaking ups or *tell me why I'm beautiful*. On day three she barely noticed the magnolias. It was a sprint, a rush downhill, up the tree ladder, lips suctioned, bra around stomach, panties around ankles. *How did he get his whole polo outfit off so fast?* His arms, the heat of his skin, her head in his palms, kisses to her eyelids, those lips like slices of fruit pressed to her face, a cascade of hairs lifting and falling with the voltage that flooded her backbone, her nipples tasted with his hungry tongue, how they stood at attention, so painfully hard, so much aching hardness. His mouth traced the path from her engorged nipples, down the trail of tattooed butterflies, to rest on her navel, tickled her belly button, a brief eternity on her pubic hair, until its flame flickered inside her. A mass of brownish blond between her, beneath her, surrounding her, worshipping her.

He turned her every which way. He rearranged her cells. He put his spoon in her soup and whipped her up into a thick, sweaty lather. His hands were soft but hungry. They moved steadily and surely. She felt like her body was the land and she was the Etsi River melting into the pools of rushing, sopping fluid. When she closed her eyes, it felt as if the top of her head glittered like a star cluster and her sockets were two moons, her stomach was the fields, the bush, and the river. It was as if she was as big as a continent. Limitless and expanding.

After week two of meeting every day, talking became a thing again.

"Did your friends say anything?" She was holding his head on her abs. It was a trip being so close to anyone. Seeing all this naked boy still startled her.

"They asked why I canceled our plans three times last week."

His tone never seemed to change from cool and calm, whether he was talking about muscle cars or her anxious questions. Her pulse went up.

"What did you say, Chris?"

This was the big test. Getting a bad reputation at school was one thing, but Madame Belle finding out that she did something without her approval? Catastrophe.

"I told them nothing's going on," he said.

"What else?" She didn't want him to think she believed him.

"And to mind their business."

"You didn't brag about bagging a Black girl? I know how you boys are."

He raised his head to look her in her eye, and his dejected, crystal-blue eyes caught the light.

"You think I'd do that?"

His sincerity knocked her back.

"Ophelia, I'm not like that. Why would I do that when my Queen's come?"

Suddenly she was ripped out of the tree house and back into her memories of Shango and his car and his singing. That oily scent. That growl of the engine. That steering wheel slipping between his sturdy, gentle hands. Shango's voice singing: *Distant Lovaaaaaaaah.*

"What did you say?"

"I said I wouldn't do that."

"No. Not that. What did you call me?"

"Ummm ... you mean ... my Queen?" He shrugged, and she felt as though she were stuck half in her memories and half in the tree house there with him.

"Is that wrong?" he asked. "I swear to you, Ophelia, I'll never talk our business. I want you all to myself. I don't need to brag."

It was just him and her there. Washed with the aroma of those flowers, a blanket on the floor, their sex juice stinking. Her senses felt alert and buzzing. Ophelia realized that she was grinning like something feral. How long had they been there? Hours? Days? Decades? What on earth was happening to her? She couldn't remember a time that felt so delicious, so filling, so right.

Chapter Thirty-Eight

Auntie Aiyanna knew right away that Ophelia was pregnant.

She always got up with the sun—Grandma Blue time. So, on the third morning of her sleeping in and throwing up like that girl in *The Exorcist*—like a demon had possessed her—Aiyanna stopped her from leaving the bathroom and interrogated her. She held Ophelia's head in her thick hands, and with knowing in those googly eyes, she asked flatly, "Who is the father?" Before Ophelia could answer, she added, "You better hope he got some money." Ophelia tried to step around her but Aiyanna would not let her leave. She continued her inquisition with an uncommon grit in her voice: "Since when did you start to spread your legs?"

Ophelia stood mumbled-mouthed.

"Since when?" her aunt demanded, sterner.

"We started doing it about two months ago."

"Two months!?"

"Yes, in March."

"Is he a white boy?"

Ophelia could feel Auntie Aiyanna's voice getting more severe.

"Yes . . . a white boy . . ."

"What's his name?"

"Chris. Christopher."

"Does he have money?"

"I didn't ask to see his bank account."

Aiyanna blocked the bathroom doorway when she attempted escape.

"You didn't stop to ask much, did you?"

"His family has money."

"You have his number?"

"Yes."

"Good. Don't tell him anything yet. You need to decide fast. Two months are already gone. You need to decide."

"Decide? What do I need to decide?"

"Girl, don't be dumb. You need to decide if you're going to get an abortion."

Ophelia's head pounded. The floor had opened into a black hole that had no bottom and no top and no chill in pulling her under. *Pregnant?* Her guts turned and rolled like a washing machine. She was hyperventilating. A great, ugly cloud loomed in the distance, and her body squirmed every way it could to somehow avoid the truth.

How was this possible? They had been careful. She was sure. But then when she thought about the entire month of April and Christopher and that tree house, she realized that so much of it was a hazy headful of sensations. Maybe they hadn't been so careful.

"Girl, pee on this. Let's find out for certain."

Auntie Aiyanna handed her a plastic package with a white stick inside. In pink it read: CLEAR RESPONSE. Double lines meant that she was pregnant, while a single line meant that she was not. Ophelia felt numb. A ghost watching their former self pee on a stick. Quicker than she expected, the test revealed double lines. Pregnant.

Without knowing why, she cradled her belly protectively. It was only two minutes since she had peed, but her belly suddenly felt as if it was made of the thinnest, most brittle treasure. It felt warmer, rounder, and heavier too.

Aiyanna hovered by the bathroom door with a second test. "Again."

Once again it came back: ||. Ophelia laid both sticks out on the edge of the bathroom sink and, in dabs and sniffles, she cried. A cry of confusion, her body's response to her brain's bewilderment. Auntie Aiyanna wrapped her up in her flabby arms and all her considerable flesh, and it felt as if she would fold into her, that her aunt's size would protect her. Aiyanna stroked her head and said over and over, "Girl, don't worry. We'll figure this out."

But the more they talked about it, the more Ophelia felt that there was no easy way out of the baby in her belly. The massive weight of all that shame. And the worst thought: She had proven them all right. Everyone that had ever doubted her. The people at Etsi who called her a "Pretendian," as well as Lucy, Sister Marshala, Tejah, Mrs. Cranbrook—anyone who had ever thought she was nothing now had proof. She thought that she might throw up.

Abortion. That word. It stuck in her like a sharp paring knife when she slipped deboning chicken. It hammered home her new reality. And all she wanted to do was call Christopher to meet her at the tree house so she could bury herself in his chest and grip those shoulders and hear his voice tell her that everything would be okay. And in her imagination he said it how he said everything: with certainty.

Ophelia got her wish later that day. When she told Christopher, he stayed so calm that it stunned her. He didn't even flinch. He faced her at the steps up the tree house, and her gaze tracked his hand as it made tender circles on her tummy. "Don't worry," he said, his voice confident as ever. "We're in this together." His lips grazed her forehead right between her eyes. Tears erupted from Ophelia's chest. Tears of relief. A relief that she hadn't even realized she was waiting for.

"Boy, I don't know who raised you, but they sure did it right."

He held her and held together her crumbling parts and the terrifying anxiety that threatened to leak out of her. His heat dissolved it into nothing. She felt like maybe, just maybe—a great big maybe—everything was going to be alright. A candle of hope had been lit.

By the following day her candle of hope became a glorious blazing bonfire; she was going to be a mother. She was going to have a family of her own.

Rarely did Ophelia think of her mother. The mother who had her but whom she never had. The mother who was probably terrified when she got pregnant, just like Ophelia had been before Christopher's hug. The mother whom—she wanted to believe—had died so that she could live. Ophelia imagined that if her mother had been there, her life would've been different. A childhood of hugs and birthday parties, Christmas presents and kisses goodnight would have been hers. She would've grown up in the safety of knowing that wherever her mother was, was where she belonged. All this longing she finally allowed herself to feel. Nothing in her life ever made more sense before this: she was going to be the mother that her mother could never be for her. And her child would know where they came from. And not only would they know their daddy, but they'd know of their daddy's daddy's daddy—going back to forever.

Except that, when she came back to meet Christopher the next day as they had planned—Christopher never showed up. Christopher didn't answer her calls, didn't show up for school, didn't show up at the tree house. Not that day, or the next, or the next. It took five days in a row of her leaving him messages, going to the tree house hoping to see him, and leaving there with an even bigger hole in her heart for Ophelia to believe the truth: Christopher wasn't coming back.

After seven days more of crying her face raw, vomiting daily before sunrise, and laying about apartment 66 like an unwashed zombie, Madame Belle knocked on their door.

"Tu petit imbecile."

She insulted Ophelia because insults were the dialect she spoke, but her voice was pillow-soft and full of worry. "You little fool," she repeated in English, and for some reason, the most in-control woman she knew wiped a tear from the corner of her eye.

Auntie Aiyanna brought some tissues, because she too had gotten weepy. She said, "I'm sorry, Ophelia. I know I'm not a very good auntie to you. But we are going to deal with this."

Madame Belle got her composure back first. "How long has this been going on?" Turning to Ophelia and then to Aiyanna, she got no response.

"You and your loose morals did this," she accused Aiyanna. "Your parties and your men and your rum. This is what happens when a girl grows up in a frat house."

"Don't blame me for this. You and your fancy school did this. She didn't meet no horny white boy in here!"

"What white boy?" she hissed, emerald serpent's eyes narrowed to slits.

"Christopher ..."

"Christopher who?"

"Beauregard."

"Christopher Beauregard?"

The name fell into apartment 66 like a stone. Drops from the loose faucet chimed in the empty sink. *Ping. Ping. Ping.* They fell into a vast hush and echoed out between the three women. It vibrated, called out, summoned them to some uneasy fate. Aiyanna stared at the floor; some spirit had snatched her tongue. Ophelia began to cry in dabs all over again. Belle crossed and uncrossed her legs in a heated quarrel with herself. Though Ophelia's lips moved, no words could be heard.

At last, Belle smoothed her pantsuit and commanded, "Get up!"

Ophelia, woozy and full of despair, sat up.

"You're not keeping this baby. I won't let them take your future."

There was a rush of blood to the veins in Ophelia's neck. Again she protectively clutched her stomach without realizing what she was doing.

Belle repeated this with even more conviction, daring Ophelia and Aiyanna and all of creation to challenge her: "You're not keeping this baby."

Then she left the room. From inside they could hear her on the balcony hissing into her phone. Then she paused. Then she spoke brisk and clipped, and then she waited. Finally, she said, "Lunch. At noon. We will be there."

Auntie Aiyanna sat at the kitchen table with conflicted eyes, and every now and then she glanced a mournful look at Ophelia.

Madame Belle snaked her way back over, pulled a chair so that she was eyeball to eyeball with Ophelia, weighing her up as she liked to do.

"Of all the boys you could've fucked."

"What do you mean?"

"You think you're the first duckling he's plucked?"

She waited for Ophelia to do the calculus.

"He's gotten other girls pregnant?"

"Merde! Don't be naïve. He is the scion of the Beauregard family. Beauregard Farms? Beauregard Avenue? Beauregard Estates? He is Stone River royalty, and by my count you are the third little Black girl he's gotten pregnant."

Ophelia refused to believe it.

Chris . . . Chris where are you? she thought, and she longed for a bit of his sureness. Her sad-eyed boy-fox who knew who his daddy's daddy's daddy was? That little boy couldn't be—she fumbled for the words: *A Player? A Slut? A Liar?*

Belle watched Ophelia like something disgusting she was about to swallow.

"See? This is why we must always be better."

Belle lit a skinny cigarette, and the well-worn wrinkle lines around her mouth revealed themselves. She watched her niece coldly. "Ecoutez, I know you were just being what you are: a child. But we don't get to be children in this world."

Ophelia shrunk from her scorn. "Has he really done this to two other girls?"

Madame Belle answered but was too disgusted to look at her, "Oui, bien sur, he has done this before, and his papa has bailed him out every time. This is how the world works, petit canard. It's full of the bastards of rich men's sons."

And then Belle glanced towards Ophelia with pity in her cold-blooded eyes. Aiyanna took another swallow of rum and slumped against the living room wall like a deflated balloon. Belle watched her with disdain, lit lavender cigarette in hand, about to head back to the balcony.

Timidly, Ophelia asked, "What do we do now, madame?"

"Get ready by the time I finish this smoke. We are expected for lunch."

Chapter Thirty-Nine

Madame Belle squealed her convertible's tires leaving apartment 66's parking lot.

Five miles into the countryside they stopped at a giant metal gate between two august pillars. For miles a high fence ran in either direction. A great angel oak, thick with moss, had draped itself majestically over the fence. There was a little black box. Madame Belle pulled up to it and pushed the button. They waited. She pushed it again and waited. After a few minutes the intercom crackled with a man's voice.

"Good morning, welcome to Beauregard Estates."

"Madame Belle and Ophelia Blue Rivers. We have an appointment with Mr. Beauregard."

"And would that be senior or junior?"

"Both."

Ophelia bolted upright as she heard what was happening. She'd spent the drive distracted. Longing to see Christopher. So when she heard who they were having lunch with, her head surged into overdrive. *So this is where he lives?* It also occurred to her that although she had seen Christopher's dad speak when she was a child, and Stone River was awash with his legend, she had never met him. That was about to change. She was about to meet her baby's grandfather. But most importantly, she was about to see her man again. A cold sweat dripped down her back. A strong wind kicked up in the trees. Her elation and her trepidation boiled over. Reaching down, she cuddled her stomach.

Belle pulled a skinny cigarette from her silver case, then snapped it shut.

"You will be quiet, petit canard. I will do the talking, comprendre?"

"But what are we doing here?"

"Saving your life."

To which Ophelia had no response.

Hope swelled inside of her. This idea grew on her: They would simply sit down and work things out. Christopher couldn't be the person that Belle described. Not her Christopher—the sweet, sensitive boy with the black nail polish and the sad eyes. Everyone makes mistakes. But the person Belle described? That wasn't who she knew. Who kissed her within an inch of her life? Who spoke so certainly about why she was pretty? Who danced so fly that she felt like a pop star? So special. No one knew him the way she did.

After a few minutes of listening to the wind, the gate slowly rolled open. The Beauregard driveway was lined with angel oaks, just like Grandma Blue's walkway, except the Beauregards' driveway was a mile and a half long. It ended in a cobblestone cul-de-sac in front of a massive three-story house. It was the biggest house Ophelia had ever seen. Tall pillars stood across the front, as did several verandas. It gleamed like a monument in stark, chalky white. Their home was surrounded by bursts of colorful flowers and tall, well-trimmed trees of all varieties. Wafting across the property, Ophelia discerned the scent of magnolia. The familiar fragrance made her breath settle. Something approaching calm descended.

Madame Belle was not fazed. She strode out of the car and stamped her heels at how slowly the servants were moving. Eventually they were ushered into a grand foyer. It was as tall as the building and collected a dizzying set of staircases and hallways. Before Ophelia could process the spectacle, they were led down a hall and into a bright sun-speckled room with cushy purple chairs.

Sitting there was an old white man with a mouth like a beak, sickly spots under his thinning hair, and an eagle cane in his hands. Standing next to him was a middle-aged man who looked just like Christopher, but uglier, older, fatter—the build and the nose and the peachy long mouth was the giveaway to Ophelia that this was his father. At the far end of the room lounged a woman who must have been very pretty once, but now all Ophelia saw were deep ridges of lines fanning down from her eyes and a sour set to her mouth. She wore a doll's pleated, bubblegum-colored dress and was the only one who did not get up to greet them as they entered. The opulence was jarring.

What movie have I wandered into? Ophelia wondered.

A great wave of inadequacy swept over her. What made her think she could bargain with all of this? In her Walmart hoodie, with her swampy armpits, and spot-bleeding between her legs. These facts told her that she was not good enough to be in a room so rich. And that she was woefully unprepared for what she had just walked into. Her breath lost all its calm.

When she saw Christopher, her chest leapt into her throat. Seated to the right of the door, he was the last one she noticed. Abercrombie & Fitch T-shirt and shorts. A preppy disguise.

There was no sign of her baller boy. But the sight of him only reminded her that—unlike everyone else in that room—she knew who he really was. This thought settled her nerves. Wherever he was, she belonged. Rooms like this she had never seen, but he had. She remembered that he was her passport to fitting in. And their baby would never have to wonder where they belonged.

Watching from across the room, she observed Christopher as he shook Madame Belle's hand and politely asked, "How you all doing?" He didn't look at Ophelia, but just being near his calm made her feel that maybe everything would be alright.

Jack Beauregard in his navy blazer, white dress shirt, and navy-blue cravat started, "Belle, it is lovely to see you. I see that you are as chic as ever."

"Bonjour, Jack, this is my niece Ophelia."

"How do you do, young lady? Belle, this is my son Christopher, who you may have met at school—though he rarely puts in an appearance. This is the family's lawyer Buck Cronkite."

He motioned towards the old man, who offered his best smile. "Charmed, Belle. I've heard so very much about you."

Glancing at the two men, Ophelia tried to reconcile them with the two men who had walked into Chief's. It was them, but the difference of years and the lavishness of the drawing room made Chief's seem like it was another continent, not twenty miles away. *Was that the same eagle-headed cane he'd banged on the floor while everybody booed his boss? Was this the same Jack Beauregard Grandma Blue was fighting? He doesn't smell like rotten eggs.*

Jack then raised his hand towards the still seated Mrs. Beauregard. "And this is my wife Cornelia." Stone-faced and barely moving her lips she asked, "So, this is her? Let me see this one."

Unlike the men, Christopher's mother Cornelia did not rise when she spoke. The whole room stopped talking and cleared the way so that she could get a good look at her. Ophelia's palms began to bead with sweat under Cornelia's scrutiny. When she found the courage to look up, she saw that his mother had the botched blood vessels of someone who had been drinking too much for too long. This made Ophelia brave enough to run her eyes up and down Cornelia's varicose veins, but she avoided her firm, frigid eyes.

"Christopher darling, I know you love your Negro whores, but this scrawny thing?"

Madame Belle stiffened. That hiss she had perfected at La Belle École came soft and dangerous. "You will watch your tone with my niece, or I will claw your eyes out. Oui?" Something about this exchange made Ophelia realize that the men in the room were not the ones who would decide what happened that day.

Jack jumped in nervously. "Now, Belle, you and I have had our disagreements, but I like to think of us as practical people. I am sure that you didn't call on us today to bicker."

Madame Belle turned her back to Cornelia and set herself up on the chaise lounge. Only when she had crossed her legs and composed herself did she answer, "Oui, we are here to offer you a chance to fix this."

Buck Cronkite spoke up in his reedy voice, "Oh-Feel-Ya, I've had the honor of many a pleasant congress with your grandmother. She speaks very highly of you."

"We didn't come here for pleasantries," Belle interrupted.

"I can see that you and your mother have a lot in common," Buck said to her, adjusting his bow tie. "Down to business, then."

Everyone sat. Buck Cronkite and Jack across from Belle and Ophelia, Cornelia to their right, and Christopher across from his mother, but so far that he seemed an outside observer rather than a participant in the conversation. Ophelia kept trying to make eye contact with him. Just one glimpse of those sky-blue eyes, she thought, and all this drama would go away. Yet his refusal to look at her fueled her growing fear that nothing would ever be the same.

Buck continued, "Belle, if what you say is true, what would fix this for you?"

Cornelia scoffed. "Let's stop playing games. How do we know that this ugly half-breed Indian nigger is even pregnant?"

Ophelia gasped. Belle remained glacial. "If you didn't already know that she's pregnant, we wouldn't be here, would we?"

"Cornelia, honey," Jack intervened. "We know you're upset, but please let us handle this, okay? You're not helping."

Ophelia watched Christopher squirm his way deeper and deeper into the lushness of his chair. He refused to look anywhere but at his feet. *Why won't he look at me?* She too felt as though she was sinking deeper and deeper into something.

Jack continued, "We are not admitting to anything. We're just having a hypothetical conversation as concerned citizens for Christopher's schoolmate. Now, at this point I'll let Buck quarterback this situation."

Buck cleared his throat and leaned forward on his cane—the bronze eagle seemed to peer out at Ophelia—and said, "Now, if—and that's a big 'if'—this young lady should happen to be pregnant, not saying by whom, but if she should so happen to be with child of unstated origin, as concerned citizens, interested and compassionate about the well-being of one of their son's classmates, the Beauregard family would be willing to use their influence on the Board of Baxter University to gain Miss Ophelia admittance to any four-year program of her choice, with tuition and room and board to be fully paid for by the Beauregard Charity Trust, if—and I say this as the one and only absolute condition—if Miss Rivers would be willing to verifiably terminate this pregnancy."

He used so many words that Ophelia had to play it back in her head to decipher what he'd said. They wanted her to have an abortion in exchange for an education. She was almost hyperventilating. The more Christopher avoided her, the more it dawned on her that she might not know him as well as she thought she did. And the more this thought grew, the more foolish she felt sitting there. The more alone. A tear passed down her cheek.

Madame Belle said, "Oui, and what if she doesn't take your deal?"

"Doesn't take our deal?" Christopher's dad asked, but Buck answered, "Well, Belle, if you're not aware what you're up against, you can ask your mother. We both know that you do not have the finances to fight us. You will never get a paternity test, and we have the wherewithal to tie you up in court until this young girl of . . . eighteen, is it? Until she is 118 and that thing growing inside her is ready to follow her to the grave."

Pining for Christopher to step in and make all of this abortion talk go away, Ophelia heard herself sniffle. In her head, as she listened, she concentrated on using her willpower to force him to raise his head.

Buck rephrased his answer, "That's all you're gonna get."

Cornelia spiced the offer with her spite: "And if you have to leave here to think about it, the whole thing is off the table."

Inside Ophelia's head, the world started to tilt left to right. Nausea came with this rocking. Her hand reached out and she steadied herself on the arm of the chaise lounge. *Why won't you look at me!* It wasn't a question anymore; it was a wailing in her mind.

Jack continued, "Belle, you're a practical woman. If this girl is half as smart as they say she is—yes, we inquired about her marks—then this is a godsend. Think of all the wasted potential if she's a single mother—no prospects, no education. We both know how that story ends. On the other hand, all you got to do is say yes, tell us what she wants to study, and she walks out of here with a full ride into a fantastic future."

Barely audible, Belle spoke so that only Ophelia could hear, "A bright, sparkling future."

"Chris . . . Christopher? Christopher?" Ophelia heard herself say. Tears spouted quietly down her face. Madame Belle squeezed her shoulder. It penetrated her sorrow and, for a few seconds, the nausea lifted and she recalled Madame Belle's words: *You must never believe them. If you do, your entire life will be lost.*

"Christopher, please . . ." she pleaded.

"Don't speak to my son, you ugly little bitch."

Before Cornelia could finish, Belle was moving in her direction. Jack jumped between them. Buck tried but couldn't get up. The yelling and commotion barely registered with Ophelia.

Her gaze had not left Christopher, and his had not left his fancy Adidas. And in an instant, clarity came. A truth dawned that no one had bothered to tell her: Christopher would go places she would never see. He would be things she could never be. They would welcome him in places where she'd be refused entry. Christopher and she inhabited the same town, attended the same school, and for a time they shared the same breath, but they inhabited different universes. Just like he'd done to those other girls, he'd stabbed her in the back. And that certainty of his—that she adored so much—was the knife that stabbed her. The sad boy-fox was not coming to save her.

"No," she heard herself say, and all the bile that was building inside her spilled out with it.

She howled, "Nooo!"

The room got very quiet. They turned on her. All tilting stopped. In the pit of her stomach, she felt herself solidify, and Grandma Blue's words rippled to the surface. *Sometimes the way is hard and all you can do is be harder.*

"Ophelia, what are you saying?" asked a stunned Belle.

She whispered the rest.

"No. I will not abort my child. I won't abandon them like my parents did to me. No. I don't need your stinking money. And no, I don't want to see you people ever again."

Her world muted. All luxury drained from the purple chairs. That room became drab and used-up. Stale now, next to the clarity in Ophelia's gut: abortion was their idea. The child growing in her belly was the only person she could rely on. Her family. And she had to protect her family.

It was also clear who she had to protect it from. From face to face she gave each of them a cold glare. Jack. Buck. Cornelia. Belle. And before anyone's shock could wear off, Ophelia got to her feet, forced herself not to look at Christopher, and walked out of the room.

Back in the car, Madame Belle appeared about to pop off about lost opportunities. A look at Ophelia's face shut her mouth. Instead she lit a lavender cigarette and peeled off down the oak-lined driveway, out the metal gate, and back into the real world.

The sun was still high in the day; there were miles to go before it would set. Ophelia refused to cry on the ride back. She cradled her belly. Held on to her future. Held in her heartbreak. These two things, she knew now, were all she had left. Her forehead pressed against the car's window. The trees rushed by like a stream around a boulder. She felt angry yet sad, empty yet full, bleached of all her daydreams.

And she thought, *This is what life does to girls like me, isn't it? It turns us into stone. It takes our dreams, takes our pride, takes what we care for most. It strips us naked and shatters us. And when our pieces are together again, we're strong, but we're untouchable. We're partying to forget, like Auntie Aiyanna. We're winning so we can feel like Madame Belle. We're holding in our wounds like Grandma Blue. Life turns all mixed-up girls into Stone Dress. And sends us out to eat or be eaten.*

But not me. And not my child.

Something hard was born in Ophelia that day, and she was certain it would do whatever needed to be done.

PART FOUR

2005

Chapter Forty

In Ophelia's third trimester, Grandma Blue called a family re-union.

As her pregnancy progressed, Ophelia lost her enthusiasm. She was ever nauseous, had to stop three times to catch her breath just to go to the veranda, and hadn't shit for four days. Sitting in the rocking chair on the veranda, she addressed her stomach sarcastically, and said, "You'd better be cute. All this trouble you're causing me."

Grandma Blue disturbed their moment. "Open your mouth and take some more of this soup. It'll give you some get-up-and-go."

It was midmorning. Though the sun was high there was still some shade on that side of the cabin, and a light breeze kissed the tops of the beech trees. Grandma Blue sat down on the chair next to her and fed her split pea soup with little chunks of bacon in it. Tired of her fussing about it being too hot, Grandma Blue blew on each spoonful. It was the most coddling Ophelia had ever gotten from the old woman.

When she decided to have her child, Ophelia ate for two,

ANTONIO MICHAEL DOWNING

breathed for two, set the table of her fiercest heart for two. But as the baby grew and turned and moved and made its presence felt, Ophelia hated her life. Above not seeing her feet and the constant ache in her flanks, her mind settled into a thickening gloom. *Should I have taken the Beauregards' deal? How can I bring a child into this world with no money?*

Shoulders slumped, she rocked in the rocking chair and stared blankly toward the road. Soft groans emanated from her chest as she fell deeper into her dreary thoughts. *How can I bring a baby into this world to suffer?*

Grandma Blue looked over at her pregnant grandchild. Since her stroke that summer the old woman's face sagged down to one side like melted plastic. Like a doll's face held too long and too close to a flame. The stroke happened in the middle of a phone call with the Etsi lawyer Rip Smithers. It felt as though a fist of fingers had grasped her heart and was squeezing without mercy. Luckily for her, Sequoia was also on the line and called an ambulance. Sometimes her stubborn tongue still refused to form her words. Yet she could get about the cabin—with a tiny hitch in her step—and dig in the garden and chop her own vegetables for her pots. And that was all Grandma Blue needed.

Suddenly, Grandma Blue stood up straight and leaned her good ear towards the road, then she grinned her dead-dog grin when she recognized who was coming. It was Shango, her first child, coming down the oak-lined lane. He was home.

He sat low in a wheelchair and was pushed by a stranger in nurse's scrubs. Sunlight glanced off the chair's metal wheels. When he'd gotten ten feet in, Ophelia made out his face, and his new denim jacket, which was just like his old denim jacket. *But what was he doing in a wheelchair?*

Ophelia was up and out of the rocking chair far too quickly—her head wobbled as she rose, her belly almost tilted her over as she waddled down the stairs. Even at a distance it felt as though he looked at her but through her all at once. His chair bumped and jerked over the uneven ground, and as he came closer and closer his face became more tangible: his broad nose; his grand, epic mouth; those perfect little white teeth. Ophelia's head started to sing, *Distant Lovaaaaaaaah* . . .

"Osiyo," Shango said when he reached the landing.

He looked Grandma Blue up and down and asked, "How's the Chief's wife?"

The old lady answered with a scramble down the steps to where he sat, and she tried but failed to pick him up into her arms as if he were a toddler.

"What have they done to you, boy?"

"Nothing I didn't deserve, Mama."

Shango wept. Not for himself but for her. His mother stood back and stared at him in his chair and shook her head as if she were trying to shake his crippled condition out of her memories.

Seeing his face charged Ophelia's nerves raw. Before she knew what she was doing, she raised her right hand and brought it down square across his face.

SMACK!

Grandma Blue said to him straight-faced, "Can't say you didn't have that coming."

Shango's arrival reminded Grandma Blue that she had preparations to make. Aiyanna and Belle were due to arrive any second now. Her pace wasn't her pace from older days, but she started to dig a square hole with her hand shovel for her firepit.

To Shango and Ophelia, she nodded at the big brown basket beside them. It was filled with corn.

"Get shucking, you two."

"Where the fuck ..." Ophelia said to her father, biting into the *f* with all the poison she could muster, "have you been?"

"I know you mad, Ophelia. You have a right to be ..."

"I'm not mad; I'm happy to see you."

"Are ya?"

He leaned in to hug her and she punched his hand away.

"I was in jail," he said. "I was in jail. That's where I got this ..."

He tapped the wheelchair as if it were his loving pet dog.

"Where?"

"Next county over. Like I said in my letter: 'I am always closer than it seems.'"

"What were you in jail for?"

"What difference does it make?"

The baby in her belly rolled and kicked as if she wanted to join the conversation. Shango reached into the brown basket, dropped some corn into his lap, and concentrated on shucking. Ophelia realized that she did not know him. All he had ever been to her was a ghost. An apparition from the Spirit World. He appeared. He vanished. He left her only a headful of shifting sensations. Vapors drifting through her childhood. To Ophelia, he had never been something tangible.

"You got a name for it yet?"

"She. And yes, I do."

There was an unspoken *and it's none of your business.*

"Did you miss me?"

Her pot of emotions churned but knew no words.

"Look. Ophelia. I know I haven't been around, but I want to be. This is my only grandchild. Gimme a chance to be in her life?"

"I'm tired of men asking me for chances," she started. "You had eighteen years. Eighteen years of chances, and you weren't here." She paused for air and patted her stomach, her brow creased with resignation. "How can I miss something I never had?"

No answers—just shucked corn falling into the basket, filling the space between them.

"Isn't there anything I can do for you?"

"Yeah," Ophelia said hopefully. "There is one thing . . ."

Shango saw his opening. "Whatever you want."

"Can you tell me more about my mother?"

That afternoon, Sequoia brought sensational news to Grandma Blue.

She arrived in her dancing dress, whipping wisps of fabric as she strode in ahead of Nola, Moytoy, and a dozen others from Etsi. They came in a gust of noise and jubilation.

"We won," Sequoia said. "Jack Beauregard, that jackrabbit, has run out of running to run."

As if she had been shot, Grandma Blue collapsed in her living room chair. Ophelia waddled in from the back patch just in time to catch her awkwardly as her legs gave out. Since the stroke, Sequoia had taken over the legwork for the lawsuit. But she never thought of it as anything but finishing the old woman's work. She continued, relishing Grandma Blue's astonishment.

"I got the call from Rip Smithers today. They're going to pay the judgment in full: $100,000 per acre of riverfront and $5 million to be split between every man, woman, and child in Etsi."

There's some burdens you don't know you carry until you put them down. Grandma Blue carried the weight of Etsi's future—and its pride—for so long that she forgot when she picked it up.

Sequoia cackled with so much abandon that Aiyanna and Belle came rushing in from the yard to see what had happened.

The baby had ended their feud. Ophelia's stubborn clinging to its life had shown them that there was still something to fight for in Etsi. Ophelia had even caught them sharing a joke, guffaws tumbling, clinging to each other for dear life. They were an odd pair: Aiyanna a giant, Belle a slender slip. And for the first time, Ophelia saw them behave like sisters.

When they heard the cause of the commotion in the cabin, they smothered their mother in kisses and hugs. Piling on, Ophelia joined in. Damn the old lady's reservations. Grandma Blue sobbed with joy.

Then all of Etsi came to Grandma Blue.

They came with Jim Silverfish and Kevin Ganega's drums and voices. They brought hominy, sochan, hogs' feet, cornbread, and whatever they could quickly prepare. For hours they came in a steady stream of honking cars by road and makeshift boats by river to raise up the old woman's name. Jim Silverfish—the scar across his cheek smoother and less angry—backed his pickup truck onto the lawn and hitched his huge bin speakers to the cab and blasted new country music. Walela Trouthands showed up to celebrate and gossip about what everyone did with their money. Auntie Kay, who had never left Etsi, arrived in a dress of petunias and pink bangles gangling and hugged Ophelia's pregnant belly.

Waya and Wes Ganega found their way there eventually.

Wes, who had spit at Grandma Blue on Moytoy's store's floor, never left Etsi. He came with his shy wife and his two young boys.

"Grandma Blue, these are my little ones. I'd be honored if you'd give them your blessing."

She did not flinch or speak but kissed each of his perky, pudgy-faced kids on their foreheads and then let them run free to play.

Waya Ganega approached, eating a plate of succotash. "Yours and my family have never gotten along. We all know that you didn't have to take on this fight. But you signed your name and showed up, for the good of the people, and you showed me what it means to be a real Cherokee Elder. Wado, Grandma Blue. Thank you."

Rip Smithers came to Grandma Blue's that day and was welcomed with a chant of "Rip! Rip! Rip!" When he first came to Etsi, it was to carry on his father's legacy of making money off the Cherokee there. When his father Don admitted that he had been the one to tip Jack Beauregard off about privatizing Etsi's land, Rip drove around Charleston for hours in a blind rage. Growing close to the people of Etsi meant that their cause had become his cause. So, that day, in Grandma Blue's front yard, he celebrated two wins: the lawsuit and becoming his own man.

Until the afternoon had slipped into a rapturous evening, Ophelia drifted in and out of the party. The whole of Etsi crowded into Grandma Blue's yard and showed no signs of ever leaving. Eventually she retreated to a corner of the deck and rocked in Grandma Blue's rocking chair with a plate of succotash.

Birth fluid had leaked between her legs, which told her she should get up and change, but her hazy brain disagreed. While she considered these options, an ironic cheer went up—whistles, hooting, and merriness was aimed at someone who had just walked in from the road. When she looked she saw that it was Christopher. He was back in his baller boy gear: gray sweats, white Air Jordans, hair longer than Ophelia had ever seen it. But unlike his last visit to Etsi, there was no Buck Cronkite to hammer his eagle cane and quiet everyone down. With scornful cheers and ironic clapping, they welcomed him. Etsi was ecstatic to have a Beauregard there to laugh at.

"Why are you here?" she scowled.

"How is . . . how is . . . the baby?"

"She. Is fine."

"So this is where you grew up? This river's what all the fuss is about?"

He shrugged, unimpressed. The nighthawks came out. The crickets began their evening cantata, but the boom of Jim Silverfish's pickup had made their song a backdrop.

"Why did you come here?" Ophelia asked again, and those distant, ice-blue eyes that could not look at her the last time they met rested fully on her face.

"I'm not like my family."

To her, Christopher felt on the edge of a brewing rebellion. As if he was contemplating some reckless gesture to prove to her that he was different. But Ophelia was not having it. Sucking her teeth at him, she swallowed her longing.

There seemed to be no one left in the world but them. Not a blade of grass shook. No breeze. No music. No pickup truck tailgate party. Etsi went nowhere, and yet—for those two—it faded into the background.

He said, "I'm sorry. Okay? Give me a chance?"

This reminder of her talk with Shango riled her up.

"To do what?"

"To make it up to you? Look, I'm not asking you to forgive me. I'm not asking you to take me back. I'm not even asking you to let me see her. I'm just asking you to let me help. Even if it's just money. Let me help."

Ophelia eyed him suspiciously. All his b-boy swag was gone. His certainty was gone. What remained was just a lost fox searching for a home. But Ophelia had turned to stone.

"Thanks for coming by, but I can't let my girl grow up like I did, with a dad she can't count on. I'm the only person she needs."

Christopher fidgeted towards her, arms wide.

"Can I at least give you a hug?"

"Fine ..."

But she turned her back to hide her tears. From behind, his arms wrapped her up. Tenderly his hands slipped down her stomach. She stiffened like alabaster to fight off the warmth, the sanctuary of his chest. She wrenched her shoulders free from him. He backed away.

"You're right. How's a messed-up kid like me gonna be a good father? Don't give me a chance. Give her a chance. Can't you see? Your people, my people, all we've ever done is hurt each other. She's our chance to do better. Can't you see?"

And it felt, all at once, as though she could see where the river had come from. All the way back to Ophelia Blue Rivers. The first Black baby born free in Etsi. She could see all the days, all the summers since before Grandma Blue was a girl. The Beauregards. The Trouthands. The Ganegas. The Blue Rivers. All the crops. All the hate. All the Cherokee, Blacks, and whites. Cooked up in a single pot like succotash.

Leisurely, her baby kicked and rolled over.

Chapter Forty-One

Six months later, Ophelia awoke in the calm of the cabin.

Drunk with oblivion, her limbs hung heavy on her body and her head slumped comfortably, deciding between this world and the next. When her eyes caught up to the dimness between realities, she started to notice her family: Grandma Blue slept on her side by the night-light on the sofa bed. Her back was to Belle and Aiyanna, who rested in a contented cuddle. Ophelia had never seen them like this: nestled together like toddlers. Shango slept on the mattress they had pulled out for him, the silver of his wheelchair gleamed in the shadows next to his head.

She heard her daughter roll over and she reached toward the crib. *Kamama* was her name. It meant *butterfly*. She had Grandma Blue's deep, coffee-bean eyes. Stretching suddenly, she opened those sleep-laden eyes and stared at her mother before closing them again.

Some air is what Ophelia needed, so she wrapped Kamama snug against her chest. It was close to dawn, which was why she found the tobacco, matches, three eagle feathers, and tucked them into the baby's sling. That warm solidness radiating from the child made her feel grounded, and she stepped gingerly to not disturb her slumber.

She walked onto the back deck facing the river. Night poured over her like a jar of molasses, then got clearer, breath by breath, with the coming dawn. A single owl hooted from across the river, and a chorus of chickadees began to chirp their concerto. The court-mandated cleanup of the Etsi River had been a success; it no longer stunk of eggs. It rushed off, indifferent, to the schemes of the people by its banks.

At the edge of the water, she lit up the tobacco, wafted its smoke over her and her child, and she prayed. It was then that the first tiny pair of butterfly legs landed on her forehead. She thought nothing of it at first. Then all at once, a dozen more landed on her face and on Kamama's untucked ear.

Whiffs of tobacco smoke surrounded them. Oak and birch branches waved goodbye to the disappearing shadows. Night frogs quieted their chorus. And the river babbled on. It swept past her toes and vanished into a future she could not see.

Acknowledgments

What becomes of a society that excludes rightful members unjustly? It creates a wound, a rupture in the fabric of that society. A hurt that can only be healed by truth-telling and the restoration of lost memory. *Black Cherokee* began as my attempt to understand a particular girl growing up in a particular stream of history. It became my attempt to understand family, childhood, adolescence, America, memory, and time itself.

I have had the benefit of the vision and courage of three great editors. Yahdon Israel, thank you for challenging me to pull up a chair at the table of our heroes. Janie Yoon, thank you for always championing Ophelia's heart. Brittany Lavery, thank you for being engaged and driven to uplift this work. I'm full of gratitude for my agents at Westwood Creative Artists—John Pearce and Chris Casuccio. This book is a testament to your belief in me as a person and an artist. Thanks to Heather Debling, whose care and editorial skill was my constant guide.

I'm greatly indebted to the careful reading and guidance of fellow novelists katherena vermette and Michael Harris.

To my readers aka co-conspirators aka patient friends Cris-

ACKNOWLEDGMENTS

tian "Chachi" Snyder, Eva Schubert, Max Wallace, and Stefana Karadjimirli. To Natalie Ricard, who I saw grow up Black and Indigenous. To Auntie Joan and Miss Excelly, who never let me forget that the past is never over, and the future is always now. To Coach and Elaine, who adopted me into their hearts and their family.

The list of scholars, homies, and strangers on whose shoulders and research this work stands is great, but I must single out Tiya Miles, Terry L. Norton, Theda Purdue, William Loren Katz, the Cherokee Nation Language Department, and the descendants of Freedmen of the Five Civilized Tribes Association. *Wado igohida* to the proud and still fighting Black Freedmen of the Cherokee, Creek, Seminole, Choctaw, and Chickasaw Nations.